To Biddy —

with all my love,

Aunt Anne

Christmas, 1950

GUARDIAN HEART

Other books by ELIZABETH YATES:

>>>>>>>>>>>>>><<<<<<<<<<<<<<<

BELOVED BONDAGE

NEARBY

WIND OF SPRING

MOUNTAIN BORN

UNDER THE LITTLE FIR

ONCE IN THE YEAR

ELIZABETH YATES

>>>>>>>>>>>>>>>>>>>>>>>>><<<<<<<<<<<<<<<<<<<<<<<<<<

GUARDIAN HEART

>>>>>>>>>>>>>>>>>>>>>>>>><<<<<<<<<<<<<<<<<<<<<<<<<<

Coward-McCann, Inc.   New York

". . . if the root be holy, so are the branches. And if some of the branches be broken off, and thou, being a wild olive tree, wert graffed in among them, and with them partakest of the root and fatness of the olive tree; boast not against the branches."

ROMANS II:16-18

GUARDIAN HEART

I.

FREELY was eighteen years old when her grandfather preached his last sermon in the Simonton Meetinghouse. There was only a handful of people to listen to it, but Freely and her grandmother sat in the front pew as they had every Sunday all the years that Freely could remember, and each of them listened with eager attention to Benedict Simon's words.

It was the first Sunday in December and Freely had garlanded the windows of the Meetinghouse with ropes of ground pine which she had brought from the woods. The room was plain and bare with a score or so of straight-backed pews, an organ at one end, a raised platform at the other, and a chunk stove at one side, but the green garlands gave it a festive look.

Benedict had smiled at them. "They'll last longer than I will," he had said.

Freely laughed. "I'll take them down after the first of the year, the way we always do with the Christmas greens."

But Benedict knew better. His life was the life of his church and when it went from one it began to wane from the other. He died on Christmas Eve, quietly and without pain, little different from falling asleep, except that it was the deep sleep of a tired man. He had asked Freely to read to him, for her eyes were strong enough to see in the light of the room's single candle.

"What shall I read, Grandpa?" she had asked.

The Bible was beside him and from it Susannah had been reading during the evening; but it was a small book in a worn leather cover to which Benedict now gestured. Freely recognized it as one that had been their companion often during long summer days in the woods or on winter evenings by the fire. She smiled reassuringly. Perhaps Benedict was feeling better, she thought, since his desire had turned to poetry. She handed him the book and he turned the pages, knowing what he wanted to hear.

"This is the one," he said, pointing.

" *'Dominus, Illuminatio Mea,'* " she read the title. Latin was no stranger to her, but the poem was one she could not remember ever having seen before.

He moved his head in confirmation. "Read it, Freely. Read slowly. I want to hear every word."

She began in a clear voice:

> *"In the hour of death, after this life's whim,*
> *When the heart beats low, and the eyes grow dim,*
> *And pain has exhausted every limb—*
> *The lover of the Lord shall trust in Him."*

She looked up from the book. Benedict was watching her with his eyes, but no words came from his parted lips.

Susannah was standing beside the bed, her hand resting on the pillow near Benedict's head. "Go on," she said gently.

Fighting back the tears that were gathering in her eyes and the grief that was clutching at her throat like two hands trying to strangle her, Freely read:

4

"When the will has forgotten the lifelong aim,
And the mind can only disgrace its fame,
And a man is uncertain of his own name—
The power of the Lord shall fill this frame.

"When the last sigh is heaved, and the last tear shed,
And the coffin is waiting beside the bed,
And the widow and child forsake the dead—
The angel of the Lord shall lift this head.

"For even the purest delight may pall,
And power must fail, and the pride must fall,
And the love of the dearest friends grow small—
But the glory of the Lord is all in all."

Verse by verse, Freely fought her way through to say the words, refusing to look up, knowing that her eyes would flood and overflow if she removed her gaze from its fixation on the printed page. When she came to the end, she knew by the look on her grandmother's face and the change in that of her grandfather's that he had left them.

A sudden passion of fear overcame her, greater even than grief. She put the book down quickly and stood up beside her grandmother. "Don't you leave me—don't, don't, Grandma!"

Susannah put her arms around the girl and held her close to her. "I won't, Freely. I don't want to until you're grown."

"Not then, not then, not ever," Freely stormed through her weeping, stamping her foot on the ground in her insistence.

Susannah said no more. Sometimes her years rested heavily on her and tonight, at the moment when Benedict had gone, she had had a desperate longing to go with him, to stand beside him as she had for half a century. But at the sound of Freely's voice reading the lines Benedict had wanted to hear, choking out the words, stumbling over them, Susannah had set aside her longing, loosed her hold on her husband, and prayed inwardly for the girl.

When the wailing infant, only a few hours old, had been brought to her eighteen years ago, she had felt unable to care for it. It was hard for a woman nearing sixty to do what a young mother should do. But Susannah had taken it in her arms because it was a helpless thing and there was no one else to care for it, and because it was her own flesh and blood. Gradually the natural love within her welled up and brought back to her all she had once known of the care needed by a small child. She had prayed then that she might be spared long enough to mother the child and see her grow to maturity.

"I won't go, Freely, until you're grown," she said reassuringly. "Until you are married and have someone to care for you."

Freely shook her head, rebellious at the thought.

Susannah went on soothingly, "I think God would not want me until then."

"Why did He want Grandfather?"

"I don't know, child. Perhaps it was because Benedict's work in Simonton was finished and he—" but Susannah could not go on.

Seeing her grandmother quietly weeping into her hands filled Freely with indignation. "I think it's wrong for anyone to die at Christmastime," she said bitterly.

"No time is ever easy for those who are left," Susannah replied. "But for Grandfather this night may be the best of all possible times."

Freely did not want to think so. Releasing herself from her grandmother's arms, she ran out of the room. Soon she had gone out of the house and was crossing the small green from which the Meetinghouse rose up square and white and solid in the moonlight. Down the road for a space and over the stone wall into the graveyard she ran, past the slim gray slate headstones until she came to one where she stopped and flung herself down on the grass that covered the mound. The earth, with a month of frost in it, was hard and the night air was cold, but grief kept Freely warm.

She put her arms around the headstone, lying with her body in the grass. And the tears came. Tears of anger, of rebellion, tears that were in essence the anguish of her heart for one whom she loved dearly. Benedict had meant comfort and cheer and safety and wisdom to her all the days of her life; without him the world was a void and her life had become meaningless. She reached up to caress the headstone with her hand. Instinctively she traced its letters with her fingers, feeling in the grooves the chisel had made, along the angles of the F, down the deep curve of the S, then into the numerals of the years that, like strange bookends, held between them all that had been her mother's life.

FREELOVE SIMON

1864–1881

To her who loveth much, much shall be forgiven.

God's peace be hers, His joy, the quiet of His Kingdom.

Aet. 17

She had learned to read from the simple epitaph, for it had within it all but two of the letters of the alphabet. Sitting in the grass beside her grandfather, she had traced the letters, her small fingers following his upon the stone. Through them she had learned that she bore her mother's name and that it was a name to bear with honor. But there was no room in her heart tonight for anything but grief. Stretched flat on the ground with her toes pressed deep into a tangle of dried grass and one arm around the headstone, Freely wept. Her tears were the warmest rain the earth had known for a long time.

In the house, Susannah performed the duties she had done for so many others in her lifetime but never for one of her own. Tomorrow, she thought, she would send Freely down the hill to the river village with a note for Dr. Vernon. There would be need for many things. A coffin would have to be made. A grave dug. A burial service read. But for the while she had done what was needful. She lit a fresh candle, for the one that had been burning all evening was almost gone, and she drew up a chair to the bedside. She sat down and folded her hands in her lap. Grief had gone in the activity of the past hour. In its place was a dull aching, the knowledge of loss which would be with her always.

She looked at the clock ticking away as it had on the mantelpiece since she had come to Simonton to live. Life-death, death-life, it seemed to say until the words merged and had no separate meaning. She wished Freely were with her, but she felt no anxiety for her. The girl was always safe. She bore some kinship with the world of nature that guided her through the dark of woods or night. Wherever she was, it was not far and she would come back when she had spent her sorrow.

The moon moved on across the sky, leaving the Simonton women alone with their dead.

2.

SIMONTON was a hamlet on a hilltop. Its founder had foreseen it to be a city but it did not become one.

When Mark Simon, journeying with his family in 1775, drew near to his land grant, he discovered that the hundred acres allotted him consisted mainly of a vast hill; but there were stout trees standing on it, more than one brook coursing down it, and the soil was good though it had its share of rocks as all New England had. Mark Simon was a powerful man; his three sons—Gideon, Godfrey, and Benedict—were grown enough to wield axes; and his team of oxen was a pair of strong beasts. He left his wife and the wagon with all their possessions in the cleared lowland near the cabin of one of the settlers, and with his three sons went up the rough trail to inspect his grant. When they reached level land, Mark Simon stopped. Looking around him and seeing that the ground rose no higher, he said:

"Here shall stand a city that is set on an hill."

It did not seem like a city to Benedict, youngest of the three sons, for when he looked around him he saw only trees reaching heaven high and the wide ranges of forest land. But his father had spoken, and Benedict had learned to respect his father's words.

They searched for water and found near some rocks a slow seepage that might denote a spring. Gideon and Godfrey knelt down and scooped earth and fallen leaves away until they had a fair-sized hole into which the water came flowing. Leaning back, they watched the water fill the hole and the sediment they had roused gradually subside. Then they waited for their father to have the first drink. Mark Simon dropped to one knee and leaned over the spring. Then he drank, not as one who had come far through the woods on a hot day but rather as one who was putting his lips to a chalice. He cupped up a handful of water and, rising, tossed it into the air.

"This place I christen Simonton and here shall someday stand a city that will do honor to the Lord."

Then the boys drank in turn.

Before they went down the trail again, each one had felled a tree so the beginning of a clearing had been made, and Mark Simon had blazed a giant oak beside which he said he would build his house.

And so Mark Simon and his sons hewed their trees and built their first home—a stout log cabin. Gradually, as the clearings increased, they made fields with the help of the oxen, dragging stones to form boundary walls and pulling out stumps where they could or leaving them to rot. They were joined by other families who made clearings and soon the rising land to the hilltop boasted only those trees that had been spared for their shade, and wherever the eye ranged it saw open fields with sheep grazing in them or tillage land where crops were growing.

By the turn of the century Simonton had a dozen or more houses, for the rude log cabins had soon been replaced by white frame dwellings. Center of them all was a stalwart meetinghouse, square built as were the barns but with a small tower. It could be seen and its bell could be heard for miles around. By then, Gideon and Godfrey had houses of their own with growing families in them. Awaiting the time when Simonton might have a minister, they took turns reading from the Scriptures on Sundays. By 1810, Simonton had its own minister, the Reverend Timothy Collett.

One of Mr. Collett's first official duties was to read Mark Simon's burial service when he died at the age of ninety—still able to swing an ax and handle an ox team, still confident that Simonton would sometime be a city. One of Mr. Collett's next duties was to marry his daughter Mary to Benedict who past forty and unwed was a rarity in a New England community. Benedict's children were not the only ones that the Reverend Timothy Collett christened, for the families sprung from the hill were large with children, but Benedict's youngest and only son, Benedict, was the last child but one to be christened in the Simonton Meetinghouse and that child would not be christened for almost forty years.

Benedict, intent on studying for the church, went to Harvard College. While still a student, he met Susannah Wentworth, daughter of a clipper-ship captain who had spent most of her childhood on her father's vessel and already sailed twice around the world. She was strong bodied and stouthearted, a good match for the sensitive, dreamy Benedict, and she gave him twin boys and a third son in the first three years of their marriage. Benedict, by then, had the care of a small church near Boston, but when the Reverend Timothy Collett died the people of Simonton wanted none other than the grandson of their founder to come and be their minister. So Benedict and Susannah, with their three small sons, returned to Simonton in 1849 to live in Mark Simon's homestead.

They were both twenty-five years old and they loved each other with a love that was to know no wavering, a completely natural giving of each to the other as if such had been ordained before the morning stars sang together. Susannah, who had delighted in the sound of waves against the wooden walls of a ship and the far horizons of the sea, now delighted in the

11

sound of wind through a great oak by her dooryard and the near horizons of the hills. And she, whose early days had been marked by adventure, now gave herself to a round of domesticity and the rearing of her children. She had thought that there would be more children, but it was not until 1864 that the fourth and last child was born, a girl.

The finely chiseled granite stone that had served as a christening basin had to be scrubbed and scoured before it was ready, so long had it been unused. When Benedict christened his daughter he gave her the old name Freelove, borne by many of the Simon women.

"May she give her love freely as you have given yours," he said to Susannah as they carried the child across the small space of green between the Meetinghouse and their home. Roger, Roland, and young Mark walked behind them, awed by the intrusion of this small and vocal girl into the more masculine household which had been theirs. Some of the neighbors followed; others had gone ahead to prepare the dinner.

Susannah looked down at the bundle in her arms. It was strange to have a girl child when her life for so many years had been keyed to men and boys. She felt a sense of responsibility she had not felt when the others were born, but she had been so young then; she was nearing forty now and she had become more familiar with life.

"To give herself freely in love," Susannah murmured, turning her eyes to the rim of hills, to the new growth of forest around them. There was so much to love—beauty in the world, wisdom in books, and then as if to bring both together, one's own kind. That was life: no less a man's than a woman's. "Freelove," she said, looking down at the child, calling her daughter for the first time by her name.

The Simons' three tall sons were the only young people at the christening party and after they had had their fill of good things to eat they slipped away. They went down the hill to the village, which had grown up by the river and where they could find their friends.

Something had been happening to Simonton for the past twenty years and several factors had contributed to it. The established families did not admit it at first, did not even see it as happening, but by 1864 it was something to be reckoned with. After the land had been cleared it had been worked hard for two generations and the soil, thin to begin with, became so exhausted that it had little fertility. Soon the plows began to turn up more rocks than anything else and, one by one, the fields that had been cleared with such prodigious labor of men and oxen were abandoned. Nature, after a space of time, began to do her own sowing with a crop she knew would do well. Alder and juniper, hardhack and blueberry bushes began to appear, while in and among them the gray birch rooted itself. At last the seedling white pine came, taking over the fields and the pastures, marching up the hill.

The growth was almost unnoticed at first. One year a man would say to himself, "I'll clear out that pasture next summer when the boy is big enough to help me." Then time would slide along and by the time the boy was big enough to help he had gone down the hill to get work in the river village, and the trees had become too big for a man to handle alone. So he let them take over the land, selling off some of his cows and using a smaller pasture, for there were not so many people needing milk as once there had been. Many a man witnessed, in his own lifetime, cleared fields become forests of pine and hemlock, for as the village moved down the hill the forest moved up.

The growth of the river village had been as gradual. It had started first with a saw mill where men brought their lumber to be finished, and a tannery where they brought their hides to be dressed, but it had grown to include a general store, a schoolhouse, and a church. A doctor came there to establish his practice. A textile factory was built that could utilize water power and wool from the sheep on the farms. The Simonton people journeyed down the hill with wool to sell, or to see the doctor, or to purchase supplies. The children went to school there.

As the younger men forsook farming for work in the factory, whole families began to move down the hill, not just with their possessions but with their houses too—putting them on skids drawn by oxen and leaving behind a pile of bricks where a chimney had stood. One thing the river village did not possess yet was a burying ground, so the people who left Simonton to seek their fortunes returned to it to be laid to rest in ground sanctified by their ancestors.

In 1864, when Freelove Simon was born, there were still a dozen houses clustered around the church, and there were still hard-working families getting their living from the land. Flocks of sheep grazed the rough pastures, and every household had a cow or two, horses, some chickens, and a few pigs; but there were no children. Life in Simonton was a hard struggle, the soil was poor, the wind blew relentlessly around the hilltop, and youth was realistic. When the young people married, they moved down to the town where they had gone to school, establishing their homes and families where there was opportunity and a future. Even those who still had farming bred in them could farm more profitably in the acres along the river where the soil was deeper than on the stony hilltop.

But now that a child had been born again in Simonton, there were some who felt that the tide had been turned, that life would come back to the hamlet. Yet, at the dinner that followed the christening, a question that was often asked with foreboding was asked in simple inquiry.

"Benedict, how long do you plan to stay on in Simonton?"

"As long as there is a church here," he answered without hesitation. "And as long as the church will have me as its pastor."

"I'm getting too old to work the farm without any help," John Dexter replied. "And Martha's been poorly for a while. We're thinking of moving down to the river village for the winter. If we like it there and if I can get some work we may move the house down in the late spring."

Susannah, standing beside Benedict, felt a catch in her throat. The Dexters had been one of the first settlers in Simonton and their house was one of the oldest. If they went, that would mean only ten other houses beside their own in the township.

"What work do you expect to do, John?" Benedict asked.

"I'm not particular. Anything that will help me make a living. Carpentering comes as easy to my hand as farming and there should be a need for carpenters, the town is growing so. Now that the railroad has come through they say it won't be long before it will be a city."

Benedict thought of his grandfather and of the city he had visioned. Yet, only two miles from where Mark Simon had put his stake in the ground, the city was coming into being. "Your sons like it since they've moved down there, don't they, John?"

"The older one does. He's set up his law office and isn't likely to move as long as he's doing well, but the younger boy went off to California when he heard new mines were opening up." John Dexter hesitated, then he went on in a quieter voice, "We haven't heard from him for six months. I hope he's all right."

Again Susannah felt a flutter in her throat. She put her hand quickly to her heart as if something were trying to catch at it.

Benedict saw the gesture. "Are you all right, my dear?"

She nodded. There was nothing to say. They would have smiled if she had told them that whenever California was mentioned it stirred her oddly, not with desire but in fear. For the West, in those expanding days of the nation, was drawing people like a magnet. Many of the young men were not content with the river village any longer, they were pushing off to the rich farm land in the Ohio country, and farther than that to the mining lodes in the mountains. It was a long journey and a dangerous one, and once they left New England they were not apt to return.

After the neighbors had gone back to their homes, Susannah looked at Benedict, her eyes full of impatient curiosity. "Why didn't you urge John Dexter to stay on in Simonton?" she asked.

"Because, my dear, when one sees the handwriting on the wall there is little another can do," Benedict replied. "And, John Dexter feels that he has seen it."

"And you have not?"

"No," he said briefly, "not for myself, not for ourselves."

She put her hand in his. Whatever Benedict chose to do, Susannah knew that her life was with him.

The baby was crying so Susannah went to the cradle that had sheltered all the Simons that had been born in that house and picked her up. She sat down in a low chair by the hearth, rocking the child in her arms.

Benedict, watching her, said reverently, " 'Behold, this child is set for the fall and rising again of many in Israel.' "

Susannah smiled up at him. "You think that life may come back to Simonton, don't you, Benedict?" She asked eagerly.

"I do," he answered stoutly.

"So do I," Susannah said, looking at the child that was a symbol of the new life.

When Benedict went back to the Meetinghouse to set it

to rights after the christening, Susannah tucked the baby into her cradle. While Benedict was out, the boys returned, trooping into the house noisily, ready to eat up all the food the neighbors had left and to tell their mother of all they had been doing.

"We heard there was a ship in at Boston wharf ready to take people to California," Roger began.

"And to give free passage for those who could work on her," Roland added eagerly.

Susannah looked at them. It was hard to believe that they were eighteen, those two tall sons of hers, and ready to make their way in the world. She put her hands quickly to her heart. She had thought the days of ships were far behind her, but she could hear now as clearly as when she was a girl of fifteen the dashing of the waves against the prow and the thrumming of wind in the sails.

"There isn't any use going to school any more when there's gold to be found," young Mark said complacently.

They talked for an hour beside the fire, then Benedict returned and the boys told him their plan.

"What does your mother say?" he asked.

"She says—" all three boys began and then stopped.

Susannah could not face Benedict. She looked away into the undemanding coals of the fire. "I said they ought to go—if they wanted to so much."

Late that night, after the eager voices of the boys had at last given to silence in the room above them, Benedict said to Susannah, "Why didn't you try to get them to stay?"

"Because," she answered quietly, "I know now that when one sees the handwriting on the wall there is little another can do."

3.

BENEDICT prevailed upon the two older boys to stay through the harvest, but when the barn was stocked for the winter, the potatoes dug, the squashes and onions stored, the apples picked, there was nothing that could restrain Roger and Roland any longer. They had missed their ship, and there was not apt to be another one that time of year at the Boston wharf, so they prepared to go overland. Benedict was firm about Mark, refusing to give him permission to go until he had finished his last year at school. In his heart, Benedict hoped that by then the Western lure would have diminished for he longed to have one of his sons go on to college and follow him in the ministry.

On a night in early November, Benedict and Susannah drove down the hill to the river village with the two boys. Mark had been left at home to care for his small sister and to keep the fires going as the first thrust of winter had been felt over the land. The boys talked jovially all the way down of the money they would make and of how they would come back in a few years time and do fine things for their parents with it.

"We'll put a new roof on the church, Father, if you can make that old one last another year or two."

"And we'll get a Western horse for Freelove—they say

there are no better ones bred anywhere. Then she can ride all over the hills."

"What will you do for me?" Susannah asked with a gaiety she did not feel.

"We'll have a necklace of the purest gold, worth a king's ransom, made for you."

"And earrings!"

"And a bracelet!"

"Oh, boys, stop," she laughed. "What would I do with so much finery living in Simonton?"

"But we won't let you live in Simonton," Roger said. "We want to build you a handsome house."

"In the river village?" she asked, smiling.

"No, not *there*," Roland said scornfully. "In a big city like Boston or New York, where grand people live and you can be like a real lady and give parties, and Freelove can go to a big school, and Father—" Roland stopped, for Benedict was gazing ahead of him into the night, the horse's reins loose in his hands and a look on his face that told his sons he was taking no part in any of their plans.

Susannah saw the look, one she knew well, and she was aware of the sudden cessation in Roland's aircastling. She spoke quickly. "How long have you been making these plans?" she asked, still gaily as if she were bantering with suitors instead of spending a last hour with her sons.

"Oh, for years and years," Roger explained. "Ever since we knew there was a world outside Simonton."

Driving slowly down the long hill they went on with their chatter, into all of which Susannah entered as glibly and gleefully as if she were their contemporary but Benedict maintained his silence and his attitude was as if the clopping of the horse's hoofs and the turning of the wagon wheels were the only sounds in the night for him. Benedict knew he should have many things to say to his sons on this eve of their adventure into the world, yet what was in his heart he could not utter and what was in his mind they were in no mood to heed.

They stood in the dark on the station platform and waited for the train. The boys were making small talk with their father and Susannah held her eyes on the name printed on a board in strong white letters and fastened to a post beside the tracks. Millville. That was where they had gone to school, she told herself. Simonton—that was where they had been born and where they had grown up; but Millville and Simonton they were leaving and where they were going had no name as yet. It was only a direction.

"Five minutes more and then they'll be gone," Susannah said to herself. "Four minutes more." She turned to the boys and smiled at them, reminding them to wear their rubbers and remember their manners, laughing as she spoke.

"Three minutes more," she said to herself, and then she told them to take care of themselves and write as often as they could.

"Two minutes more." The train could be heard in the distance. Susannah's heart beat faster than the approaching wheels and far louder. "Hurry, hurry," something within her was saying. Now that the time was near she wanted it to be over with quickly. She wanted the boys to remember her as their gay comrade; whatever hold she had on them it would in that way best endure the stretch of a continent.

"Good-by, sons," Benedict was saying.

They shook hands with him solemnly.

"We'll be back before too long," Roger said.

"I know you will," Benedict smiled.

"Or perhaps you'll come and join us," Roland suggested.

"I doubt it," Benedict shook his head. "My life is in Simonton."

Susannah held each one close to her for a moment, then

she held them off at arm's length and looked deep into their eyes, the blue of Roger's, the gray of Roland's. "God is with you," she said simply. It was her benediction, her farewell.

The boys were in the carriage now, their young faces pressed close to a window. The train wheels were moving slowly. They were waving.

"Hurry, hurry—" something within Susannah was saying, as she longed for the moment when night and distance and gathering speed would take her sons from her and allow her the blessed relief of tears.

"They've gone," Benedict said, when the train was out of sight at last. "But I think they'll be back before too many years have passed."

"Yes," Susannah replied, conscious of her lie, for in her heart she knew they would never come back. But it was the look in Benedict's face that made her lie to him and made her steel herself against any show of feeling.

They went back to the wagon and got in. Benedict turned the horse and they started up the road to Simonton. Benedict was the one who talked during the journey, reliving the boys' early years, recalling their sayings, remembering that Roger always said he would be a sailor—he who had never seen the sea—and Roland had said he would be a farmer, until he found out what it meant to work the stony hilltop. "And now they've gone to try themselves," Benedict concluded, cheered by his reminiscing, "but they'll be back. Simonton is in their blood and it will draw them. What they've always had, what belongs to them, must be more in the end than this Western urge."

"Perhaps they'll be taking that—what they've always had, what belongs to them—to where they're going," Susannah suggested.

"They could take nothing better," Benedict said, proud of his heritage and his home.

It's a hard thing for a woman to lose her sons, Susannah thought to herself. But it's far harder for a man who has looked to them to carry on his name, his life. Aloud she said, "The spirit that founded this country is the spirit that is building it. Your sons are doing no different than Mark Simon did when he left the coastal farm of his father and pushed into the wilderness to found his city."

Benedict made no reply.

Susannah sat with her hands folded in her lap and never had the slow journey up the hill to Simonton seemed so long.

Mark was relieved to see them for Freelove had been coughing and he had not known what to do. Susannah took charge immediately and soothed the baby; then she rubbed her chest with grease and held her in her arms until the spasms ceased. Slowly the child, half sobbing, half choking, subsided into quiet.

Benedict was in bed by the time Susannah was ready to go to bed. It was still and dark. The menfolk were asleep, the baby peaceful and on the edge of slumber. Susannah felt she could give way to her grief now, to the feelings that had torn her heart and ached behind her eyes; but when she lay down in bed she found no grief in her heart to give vent to, only a quiet acceptance of what was inevitable.

Mark went daily to school in the river village, trudging up and down the long hill, missing his brothers more than he could make his parents realize and little comforted by the presence of his baby sister. On Christmas Eve he told Benedict and Susannah that he wanted to enlist in the war between the states.

"Everyone thinks I'm eighteen," he said eagerly, "and they're needing soldiers so that they'll take me. I know they will."

"Why don't you want to stay in Simonton?" Benedict asked.

Mark drew his toe stubbornly across the hearth bricks. "Because," he said after a long clumsy pause, "there isn't any life here."

"Life isn't always what you find. It's what you make," Benedict reminded him.

"Mark," Susannah said quickly, "go to the barn and see if you can find some more eggs for me."

The boy looked surprised. "I brought you in a whole hatful before supper, Mother. There aren't likely to be any more until tomorrow."

"Go and see, Mark. I've a deal of cooking to do over Christmas and I'll need every egg there is."

Mark went noisily out of the room. Susannah turned to Benedict and spoke in quick low tones. "Benedict, we must be willing to let him go. It's the only way we can hold his heart. Oppose him and we'll lose everything."

Benedict sighed. "Why does he have to do this to us at Christmastime?"

"Youth never thinks of time and it is always impatient."

Benedict nodded.

Susannah put her hand on his. "Sometimes it seems to me that we're fighting a losing battle here in Simonton, Benedict. Perhaps we would make a better home for our children if we moved elsewhere."

Benedict looked at her as if she had spoken treason. "As long as there is a church in Simonton, it shall have a minister," he replied.

That was the first and the last time Susannah ever broached the idea of leaving the village on the hill. It was her husband's world and she realized that he could no more be dislodged from it than could one of the granite boulders that made the hilltop. Since it was his world it was hers too, and she could only hope to make it a right place for their remaining child to grow in.

Mark left Simonton before the new year on a day when the snow lay so deep that even a horse and sleigh could not make the journey to the river village. He said good-by to his parents on their doorstep.

"If I see Roger and Roland I'll give them the news," he said casually.

Benedict chided him on his geography. "They're in California and I'll be surprised if you get farther west than Tennessee."

Mark grinned. He kissed his mother, shook hands with his father, and plunged down the road through the snow, turning to wave one last time before the drop of the hill took him from their sight. He went off with a New Hampshire regiment and was soon in the midst of active fighting, but the more excitement there was the more he reveled in it and his letters home were ecstatic. Letters from the older boys arrived with fair regularity and Susannah read them first with Benedict, then again to herself, grateful that she had this much of her sons.

Mark was on hand when Lee surrendered at Appomattox and the account he wrote home of it was vivid and glowing, so much so that it almost took the sting away from the postscript he had scrawled at the bottom of his letter. "When I'm mustered out, I think I'll go on to California for a while and see how the boys are getting on."

So that had been his plan all along, Susannah thought, feeling suddenly hurt within herself that he had not spoken of it to her; but he evidently had not felt he could trust her not to dissuade him and it was imperative to him to follow his own leadings.

The years of Freelove's growing up were punctuated by the arrival of letters from her brothers, for a month did not pass without its letters telling of the hard work and the rugged life, the gradual assimilation of a new way of living, and the relinquishment of prospecting for the surer life of homesteading. Each bought land—to Benedict the acreage of which they talked so easily seemed as big as a township—and because farming had been bred into them it became the way of life for them. They married and in time the letters began to be full of the arrival of the children and their doings. Susannah kept the letters in a box, then in a series of boxes, and she read them over and over. It was hard for Freelove to grasp that the three who called themselves Roger, Roland, and Mark, whom she could not remember and who lived in the far West, were her brothers, but the letters they wrote were as good as any storybooks and she listened eagerly to her mother or father reading them. Then pridefully she related them to her friends in the river village.

The letters might punctuate the months but it was her father's sermons that punctuated the weeks. Freelove, sitting beside her mother in the front pew with its hard seat and straight back, listened to them attentively, for they were stories, too, in their way.

The families remaining in Simonton attended church regularly and on fine days or on festive occasions many people drove up the hill from the river village to have their service in the old Meetinghouse and a long line of surreys and wagons, buggies and carryalls, with horses standing patiently by the hitching posts, would be waiting outside. Some walked, for there were farms not far distant, but the children who walked would generally go barefoot, carrying their Sunday shoes in their hands and putting them on only when they got near the church.

It was the summer Sunday mornings that Freelove liked best of all the week. The Meetinghouse was scrubbed and shining, and there were always flowers from Susannah's garden. The people who had come from near and far sat quietly thinking their own thoughts or thinking about what their pastor had said to them. In the warm quietness, the little girl in the front pew felt aware of the fragrance of the flowers filling the room—elusive, pervasive, lying on the air then lifted and scattered by a breeze—but she was aware of another fragrance, equally pervasive, that came from thankful hearts. All things were praising, each in their own way, Freelove thought, for the whole world on a summer Sunday morning was filled with the fragrance of praise.

Sunday dinner was a communal affair, all the families going to one house. On particularly fine days tables would be spread on the grass outside the church. Freelove was happy, flitting about among the people, helping to serve, or sometimes standing with wide eyes and partly open mouth before someone who had a story to tell.

Susannah felt that the seas she had sailed as a girl must have left some impress which this child had captured, for Freelove bore no resemblance either to herself or to Benedict. There was a dreaminess in her eyes like the eyes of one who has seen great beauty and is forever after seeing it inwardly, but there was an impetuousness about her mouth. She could not wait for things to happen. She was eager to the point of restlessness, yet a mood of peace could descend on her in the midst of her impatience and she could become tranquility itself. She could not bear the sight of suffering, but it was her nature to run away from it rather than to try to alleviate it. Benedict did not pretend to understand her and Susannah spent hours endeavoring to explain the child to him, and as many hours endeavoring to excuse her curious ways.

Until the time Freelove was twelve she accepted Simonton without question or wondering. She went down the hill to school in the morning and she trudged up it again in the afternoon. She had no feeling for household chores, but Susannah insisted that she spend all of Saturday in domesticity.

Freelove rebelled, but Susannah could be firm when she had a mind to be.

There were times during the winter when Simonton would be snowbound and Freelove went for days without seeing any of her friends. These were lonely times for her since she could not share her father's world nor find in books the friends he had; her talent was one of listening. There were happy days in the summer when her friends from the river village would come to stay with her or when other householders in Simonton would be entertaining their grandchildren and the hilltop was alive with the sound of young voices. They had games to play but they had their tasks to do, and in the season they picked berries and trooped down to the river village to sell them so they might have money to buy their own shoes and stockings for winter schooldays. But work or play, Freelove was happy in it with boys and girls of her own age.

The older she grew the longer the time she seemed to want to spend away from the village on the hill. Susannah, looking at her closely and beginning to see in her what others might see, felt a strange, uneasy concern. For Freelove, at sixteen, was lovely to look at—dark and slender, with gentle eyes and lips that flashed eager smiles or shaped spirited words. Susannah tried to talk to Benedict about Freelove, feeling that the life on the hill was too cloistered for one so full of fire and adventure, but Benedict could not see it as anything but his home and therefore the place for his daughter until someone came to marry her, and when that happened he would build her a house on the hill and new life would come to Simonton with her children. It was his continuing sorrow that the place into which he had poured so much of his strength and his heart, as his father and his father's father had before him, could not hold his sons; but he was confident that it would hold his daughter.

The Simonton life was a good life; those who lived it enjoyed pleasures that were at hand or could be improvised, and whatever the pleasures were the people profited by them. There were singing schools held weekly in one or another of the hilltop homes, where all gathered to read music and learn to sing; but though Freelove went with her parents her voice was often the only young one in the group. There were writing schools, held at the various houses and to which everyone went equipped with writing materials and a small kerosene lamp. There were reading clubs, meeting on a set night each week to read the plays of Shakespeare and discuss them later over cider and fresh-made doughnuts. Freelove went obediently and sat quietly or took part shyly, but Susannah felt uneasy about her. There was a look to the girl that said to Susannah she was only biding her time.

To Benedict, Freelove was still a child and he treated her as such. To Susannah, Freelove had become something that could be desired and—what made Susannah apprehensive —Freelove was conscious of the fact that she wanted to be desired. Susannah became deeply concerned when Freelove, who had always been honest, refused to tell her why she was late home from school one afternoon. The sudden dropping of the girl's long lashes, the color rising in her cheeks, made such panic leap into Susannah's heart as she had not felt since the word "California" rang a knell in her household.

"Tell me, Freelove, tell me where you have been to be so late?"

But Freelove shook her head.

Then one day Susannah found a letter pinned to the girl's pillow and she knew Freelove would not be home that night, or any night. It was hard to break the news to Benedict, but curiously enough he seemed to blame only himself.

"I never understood her," he said, "and I was hard on her because of that."

She had gone away with the man she loved, the note said. She would write them and tell them where she was living. They must not try to follow her. She had a right to her own life in the world.

"But Simonton is in the world," Benedict said sorrowfully.

Susannah shook her head. "Not her world. Simonton is your world, Benedict. You forget how small it is, and growing smaller all the time. To a young person the world must grow larger or it becomes a prison."

They heard nothing more from Freelove for several months, though there was gossip in the river village and rumor even found its way to the families in the village on the hill; but Susannah and Benedict did not listen to it.

On a wind-tossed, rain-washed evening the following spring, a man knocked at their door. He was a rough-looking fellow, speaking broken English, and he handed Benedict a letter which he had taken from his pocket. The letter said "Please come. We need you." It was unsigned, but Freelove's handwriting was unmistakable.

"I take you," the man said, pointing to his horse and wagon outside. "No far. Ten mile. Hurry."

Susannah went to get her coat, but suddenly she who had been strong and nerveless all her days felt a constricting of her heart so sharp that she sat down in the nearest chair, frightened by the rebellion of her body.

"You go, Benedict, I—I can't," she said, breathing hard. "I'll be all right when you return," she assured him.

So Benedict went with the stranger, clattering down the long hill, through the river village and up into the woodland country that lay on the far side of the hills that could be seen from Simonton. No words passed between them until they reached a lumber camp, a group of rude cabins in one of which a light was burning.

"We here," the man said.

Benedict got out of the wagon and knocked on the cabin door, walking in before it was opened. A man and a woman were standing by the hearth and two children sat at a table near them. At one end of the room was a bed on which Benedict saw his daughter.

"Freelove," he cried quickly, crossing the room to her. But he knew before he reached her that her impetuous lips would not shape the answering word "Father."

He knelt by the bed, praying as he had by so many death-beds. Then he was aware of a stirring under the covers. Drawing them back, he saw an infant, not more than a few hours old, held in the crook Freelove had made with her arm.

"Oh, my darling," Benedict sobbed.

The man who had been standing by the hearth crossed the room to stand beside the bed. Aware of his presence, Benedict rose to his feet and faced him, but his heart was too full of anguish to speak.

"My wife, she does not want your daughter's baby so we sent for you."

"Your wife?" Benedict acknowledged the person by the hearth, then he looked at Freelove. "But my daughter?"

"She—my woman," the man said, and his lips that had been set in a hard line quivered.

Three hours later Benedict made the journey back to Simonton, holding on his lap the baby. Behind him in the cart, in an improvised coffin, was the body of his daughter.

The next day, in the old graveyard at Simonton, there was a burial service. No one attended but Parson Benedict, who had read so many services that he knew it by heart, and Susannah, lost in sorrow and overcome by a feeling of her years, and old Abner Wheelman who had dug the grave and was waiting solemnly to fill it up again.

A few days later, Benedict thought to christen the child, so he took her in his arms alone to the granite fount in the church where her mother had been the last child to be christened. He carried a jug of fresh spring water with him and he laid the child down on a bench in one of the front pews so he might pour the water into the fount. Some writing had been chalked on the granite and before he emptied the jug he bent closer to read it.

"No child of sin shall be christened at this holy fount," he read.

He drew back with the swift involuntary gesture of one resisting a blow; then he turned to pick up the child. Outside the church he emptied the water on the ground. Then he went to the spring at the side of his house, the spring with whose waters the first Mark Simon had christened the hilltop and from whose waters creatures and humans had quenched their thirst for nearly a hundred years.

"I christen thee Freelove Simon," he said, as he sprinkled a few drops of spring water on the small puckered face, "in the name of the Father, and of the Son, and of the Holy Ghost." Then he raised his head and in heartspoken words dedicated her to God.

4·

>>>>>>>>>>>>>>>>>>>>>>>><<<<<<<<<<<<<<<<<<<<<<<<<<

SUSANNAH found it difficult to care for the child
at first, but after a few days the old skill came back to her and
she was as competent with Freelove's baby as she had been with
any of her own. In her care for the child she eased the grief
she felt for her daughter. Benedict loved the child, regarding
it with a reverence he had not shown for his own. He had
felt so sure of his sons and when they had not lived up to his
dreams for them his heart had broken with disappointment;
he had been so unaware of his daughter's real nature that he
had failed to know her. Of this infant, dropped like a change-
ling on their doorstep, he expected nothing; he made no plans
for her future; he enjoyed her.

The villagers avoided Benedict and Susannah for a few
days after the arrival of the child at Simonton, and on the
first Sunday Benedict preached to a congregation that consisted only of Susannah sitting in the front pew in her best
merino gown with her hymn book held in her gloved hands.
Before another week had passed, curiosity coupled with na-
tive good will overcame the villagers and they began to call
on Susannah and ask to see the child.

Susannah pointed to the cradle standing near the stove in
the kitchen. So small a morsel of humanity as a week-old
infant could not call forth much admiration, though it did
elicit comment.

"Such a sad thing to lose your only daughter," Mrs Wheelman said sympathetically. "She must have had a hard time of it."

"The baby came early," Susannah said in explanation.

Mrs. Wheelman nodded. "Ah well, that can make it hard. I know."

"Too bad that the father can't make a home for her," said Mrs. Dexter, who had driven up from the river village to see the child that everyone was talking about.

"Her father is interested in lumbering and he has to be in too many different places to make a home for his daughter," Susannah replied.

"Is that so?" Mrs. Dexter commented. She had heard otherwise about the child's father, but Susannah should know if anyone did. Lumber men could tuck away sizable fortunes and someday the child might be better cared for than anyone in the river village said she would be.

"What is your granddaughter's name?" Mattie Emerson asked, who rarely listened long enough to hear the answers to her questions, but this time she did listen.

"Freelove Simon," Susannah answered.

"Just like her mother!" Mattie exclaimed. "How odd that your daughter should have married into the same name."

Susannah shook her head. "We gave the child our name," she explained. "Her father wished it so. His is a rather long French name and he thought it would be easier for Freelove to be a Simon in Simonton."

Mattie Emerson's eyebrows went up and she whispered something to Mrs. Dexter, who apparently did not hear her.

"Well, well," Mrs. Wheelman said, "aren't we going to have a chance to meet the little one's father sometime?"

"Oh, I'm sure you will," Susannah replied warmly. "He's in New York state now on a lumbering contract, but he should be back before too long."

"Is that so?" Mattie Emerson said, for she had heard differently in the river village.

Susannah, wearied by the questioning which no matter how kind in words was barbed in its intent, smiled at Mattie Emerson. She had little desire to prolong the conversation, knowing that Mattie undoubtedly knew far more than she did. Susannah's smile had warmth in it and finality.

"And now, if you will excuse me, I shall put the baby upstairs," she said. "She isn't too used to company yet and I wouldn't want her to disgrace us all by crying." Susannah picked the baby up and went out of the room. What her visitors said in her absence she would not know, nor did she care.

Freely was an easy baby to care for, quiet and content for hours at a time, and thriving well on cow's milk with its mixture of water and sugar, which Susannah prepared for her. A small object placed near her would hold her attention indefinitely, or even with nothing to amuse her she would gurgle happily to herself during her wakeful times. She cried only when actual pain or some urgent need made her vocal in her demand for attention. Born in the spring, she grew with the year and during the long warm days of summer and early autumn she was outside more than she was in. By Christmas she was taking her first experimental steps and her rambling language was beginning to adopt the shapes and sounds of words.

As soon as she could walk, she followed Benedict everywhere; and as soon as she could receive he began to teach her. Susannah did not always know what the two of them were up to when they went off together, but it made Benedict happy and it kept the child occupied, so she went on with her household duties. Except for the care that was incumbent on her, she let Benedict have full charge of the child. With his own sons Benedict had always been so busy—farm work

had demanded their time and always there was the constant
struggle to clear the brooks and pastures from encroaching
alder and juniper. Now, with the cleared land shrunken in
size, his parish diminished, and the hilltop that was Simonton
going back to forest, Benedict at sixty at last had the time
he had not had at any other period of his life.

One cow, a horse, and a small flock of hens did not require
much care. The spring season divided itself between the boiling down of the sap for their year's supply of maple syrup
and sugar, and days spent in the woodlot to work up cordwood for the next winter. At haying time his neighbors
helped him fill his barn as he helped them in turn, and during the summer months there was only a small vegetable
garden to tend, as their needs seemed to lessen with the years.
Life on the hilltop was not so self-sufficient as it once had
been for they were all becoming more dependent on supplies
from the river village. But Benedict did not resist the trend
of the times. He found there was much that made life
easier and gave him more time.

He had the care of the church, which he loved, and the
writing of his Sunday sermons; occasionally there would be
a funeral; sometimes grown children of former residents in
Simonton came back to be married in the old Meetinghouse.
But there were hours between, whole days and weeks, when
life pressed no demands and Benedict could give himself to
his books, to long quiet thinking which had always been his
delight, to walking in the woods, and to being with the child.

Freely did not go to school in the river village until she
was ten years old and when she did, so well had Benedict
schooled her, she was well up to the children of her own age
in reading and sums, and far ahead of them in practical knowledge. She wrote a clear hand and her geography, though it
stemmed from a hamlet, embraced a wider range than that
of her classmates. But Freely's world was the Simonton

hilltop, shrunken in size as it was; and Freely's companions were old people, though to her they were not old. They were peaceful, unhurried, undemanding people, and in the orbit of their presence she knew security. Freely's circle of friends did not stop with people. It included the birds who made their homes in the leafy branches and the creatures who dwelt in the thick woods. It could almost be said to include the flowers in Susannah's garden and the forest trees themselves, for Benedict had taught her respect for all growing things, for all that made up the universe.

Benedict had not shepherded his flock, small as it was, for the working years of his life without having acquired wisdom, and something more than wisdom, something so rooted and grounded that it was the essence of his life. In Freely he found not the patient listening he was accustomed to when in the pulpit or the emotional need when talking with someone in trouble or despair, but one eager and willing to receive his wisdom because it was good and life was good.

He taught her what it meant to do things for the love of God, freely, outgoingly; not for the approval of others or for their praise but because joy was in the doing. He taught her to look upon all creation as part of a plan that was unfolding, complete in the mind of God and appearing to men as they became more like God. He taught her to be true to herself, assuring her that if she kept that trust she would have power sufficient for any need. In his quiet voice that carried such compelling emphasis, he told her at all times to hold her head high but to keep her knees flexible.

Before she started school he took her to her mother's grave and told her about the daughter whom he had loved deeply but never understood. It was a familiar place to Freely. They had gone there often and she had first learned the shapes of letters and then the form of words from tracing those on the slate headstone. It was a warm September day when they sat in the grass by the curved mound. Freely stretched flat on the ground and, cupping her chin in her hands, looked earnestly at her grandfather as he told her about her mother.

"Love can narrow to a person or it can include the world," he said as he came to the end of the story. "You belong to yourself now, Freely, and to God, but someday when you are grown someone may come into your life to whom you will want to belong."

She looked at him seriously. "But my mother felt that way and it didn't make her happy."

"Perhaps she was happy, Freely, for a little while."

The child nodded thoughtfully and broke off a piece of grass which she put in her mouth, sucking it. "If I felt that way," she said deliberately, "how would I know that it was right?"

Benedict did not say anything for a long moment. Then his words came slowly, "I think you would know the rightness by the quietness in your heart."

Freely put her head down in the grass and Benedict looked off across her to the distant hills. The wind blowing over them was warm and sweet, still heavy with the feel of summer though it carried leaves on their downward course.

"Tell me, Grandpa," Freely gazed up at him, her eyes wide and appealing, "what that friend of yours said about the candle."

He looked surprised, reaching back in his mind for something she could recall that did not come readily to him. He smiled. "Do you mean my friend Thomas Traherne?"

She nodded vigorously.

Benedict repeated words familiar to them both, " 'Thy body was given thee to be a lantern only to the candle of love that shineth in thy soul.' "

"Thank you, Grandpa."

Freely's gaze became centered on an ant carrying a burden twice his size. Leaving Benedict she followed the ant halfway across the graveyard until he reached his hill safely. When she returned to sit beside her grandfather, she commented, "That ant had only five legs but he got to where he wanted to all right. I was going to help him but he didn't need it."

To Freely, a suffering animal needed no less care than a suffering person; a broken limb of a tree elicited the sympathy that she felt for the squirrel's nest found with it. But Benedict had taught her that sympathy as sorrow was of little value; as a means to enable one to set things right it was a fingerpost to usefulness. Of two things Freely was sure: there was God and there was herself. She could not think of one without thinking of the other. Watching her as she went about her play, or preaching to a drowsy congregation but conscious of one small serene face looking up at him, Benedict felt sure that a link had been forged which would endure whatever tests might come.

Freely did not want to go to school but she went to please Benedict and, as she reminded herself, for the love of God. Like a bird hatched out of the nest and later brought back to it, she could not bear to leave Simonton. The cheerful house, the white church, the silent woods, these offered all her nature might need or her spirit crave. Only the thought of being among them soon again could console her for having to part with them.

Before Freely left in the morning, Benedict would read from the Bible. It was a stimulant to his day and a source of pleasure for Susannah, but to Freely it was a solemn delight. The words lingered in her mind and wove themselves through the doings of the day. After the reading, Benedict and Susannah and the small granddaughter had a time of prayer sitting around the kitchen table. Benedict's prayers were always prayers of thanksgiving and Freely went forward into the day not with perplexity but with assurance of the good it held and for which they had already thanked God.

Freely stood on the doorstep and said good-by, turning her face first to Susannah and then to Benedict to deliver a kiss. The feel of her grandmother's lips on hers was all Freely asked for affection. Benedict never kissed her on her lips but on her forehead, and to Freely it was a salutation, a holy charge for the day. She wondered if David had felt like that when Samuel chose him above his brothers and anointed him with the holy oil. Sometimes she felt that her forehead must shine from the impress of Benedict's love and all that it meant. Then she started on her way.

Benedict and Susannah stood in the doorway and watched her.

"It seems a long way for those short legs to go," Susannah said.

"You never thought it seemed long for the boys," Benedict reminded her. "Or for Freelove."

"True," Susannah answered. "But Freely is different. She seems tenderer somehow, more deserving of special care." Then Susannah laughed at herself. "But perhaps that's because I'm getting old. I'm thinking of her as a little thing still and she's ten years old. Why, the boys at ten were strong as men, and Freelove—"

"Freely is different," Benedict agreed. "But I wouldn't call her tenderer. She's got more assurance than people twice her age. She's honest and she's fearless and that ought to be sufficient armor for her."

"I still think it's a long way for her to walk alone," Susannah commented.

"She isn't alone," Benedict said.

At that moment Freely reached the place where the road dipped to the hill and would take her from sight. She turned and waved. Benedict and Susannah waved back. Then she was gone, resolutely forward into a world she had no use for but was willing to temporize with for a while. She did not linger over her farewell—a fling of her hand into the air, a smile, then a quick turning and the bobbing of the pack on her back that told them she was running.

"She looks like an autumn leaf herself," Susannah said as a gust of wind tossed a cluster of leaves into the air.

"She does," Benedict agreed, for Freely had sandy hair and amber eyes and her skin was pale except during the summer when it became golden; but even in its pallor there was a glow beneath it and her eyes with their light lashes could shine like candles. She was a sturdy child and the New England nature with its compound of candor and common sense ran strong in her. Her legs were well built and her arms were muscular, but she had a curious grace about her—the grace of naturalness, like that of a wild thing in its own environment.

Freely was honest in her appraisal of school. It hardly seemed fair to compare it with her grandfather's teaching since it was so inferior, but she took his word for the fact that it was a necessity to be submitted to for a reasonable period of time. She filled her head with an assortment of knowledge which she recited gleefully to the trees as she walked home to Simonton, and she imagined that the trees bowed their heads and clapped their hands at what she said; but sometimes she preferred to recite to the gray impassivity of the stone walls bordering the road, for what she had to say did not seem important enough to get excited about.

She did not linger on her way home from school. She had had enough of the town and its ways and she was longing for the embrace of the old house on the hill. After she had seen Benedict and Susannah, and had a glass of milk and some cookies, there was the lovely secret silence of the woods waiting for her, and there she would go to play. It was the leave-taking in the morning and the home-coming in the afternoon that lightened the in-between hours at school.

As Freely grew older and the stocky body of the child began to take on the contours of the girl, Susannah asked Benedict more than once if they were giving her all she should have to prepare her for the world.

Benedict would nod slowly. "She has happiness. She walks without fear, and she has learned something of what it is to walk with God. I think Freely will find her own way through life."

"It's a lonely life up on this hill."

"But not for Freely."

"Oh, I know she has the woods and the wild creatures, and she cares more for them now than she does for boys and girls of her own age at school," Susannah said. "But is it right to keep her so sheltered? We can't live forever and when we're gone what equipment will she have to face the world?"

"Strength in her mind. Friendship with nature. Quietness within herself. What more could she have?"

"I don't know," Susannah murmured. "But something more practical."

It was only when Freely was at school that Susannah felt concerned, for when the girl was home there was such an air of contentment that it seemed to pervade the hilltop. About her household tasks or playing in the woods, Freely never seemed to be without someone to talk with, to listen to. Susannah used to wonder if the strange complacence the child had would keep her from loving, and she wanted her to know love —not as Freelove had but as any woman should in its fullness and richness, in its fine flowering. It puzzled Susannah, Freely's secret companionship, but it pleased Benedict for he knew what it was. Call it by whatever name one would—a guardian spirit, an angel guide, a beloved companion—such a

41

one was always with Freely. All men had such, though many did not discover it until late in years and many never developed the friendship; but Freely was one of the blessed ones who were born knowing it and born with the ability to converse and listen. An angel with her was not entertained unawares; it was a daily reality.

"Who is it that I talk to inside myself when I'm alone?" she asked Benedict one day.

And he told her that it was her angel, the part of her that was always in the presence of God.

Freely did not understand all that Benedict said to her; she knew only that she never felt alone. She never feared the long road home, or night if she woke suddenly and found herself surrounded by darkness, for she could turn within herself and find companionship. So she would hold her head high with the assurance this gave her and she would keep her knees flexible, as Benedict had said.

Benedict had told her that prayer could not be fixed within a time or to a place; that it was the reaching out of the heart to God any time, any place. But no matter what Benedict said, the white church was still the place of prayer that he loved, and any time during the day or night he might be seen going to or coming from it.

Freely had her place of prayer. It was a small dell, halfway down the hill, quite off the road and, as far as she knew, known only to herself. Even Benedict had never gone there with her. She had found it one spring day when searching for wild flowers. Tall trees towered overhead; boulders covered with moss and wide leaves of arbutus were there, and ferns were uncurling. There was a spring bubbling under a roof of flat stone and from which she drank, lying on the earth and reaching her head under the stone. There was a trail over which woods animals passed that led back up the hill and lost itself in the forest. Freely had called it God's Dell when she first discovered it because of its untouched beauty, and she had gone on calling it that—not because she could not find God anywhere but because it was a little easier to find Him there.

She told Benedict about it and he nodded understandingly, for he knew that the dell was to Freely what the Simonton church was to him, and he knew that every man must have such a harbor. But a harbor was not only a refuge from storms, it was a place of quiet between voyages from which one made ready to set sail.

5·

>>>>>>>>>>>>>>>>>>>>>>>><<<<<<<<<<<<<<<<<<<<<<<

SUSANNAH looked up at the clock. She was not anxious about the girl but she was eager for her presence. The house had not seemed so still in a long time—not since the spring night when Benedict had gone off with the stranger and she had been left alone, suddenly conscious after years of rugged health that her body had been able to impose a limitation on her. Now she was acutely conscious, after years of close companionship, that life could impose loneliness. She was aware of the ache within her, as she had been that other time, and both times it was her heart that had been the unruly member. But she would not have it otherwise tonight. Love had been her life, and when it was one had to be willing to pay the cost of sorrow as well as of joy.

She and Benedict had known that when they had first known each other and the feeling had grown with the years. Held between memory and faith she bore her sorrow, for the years with Benedict had been so many, the years without him could not possibly be long. Benedict was dead, yet love had made of herself and him a full circle; and, like the new moon holding its fullness within it, the circle still was complete though for a while she would be cognizant only of the crescent. It would be hard for Freely, she thought, who would have to carry on alone. And Freely was so young—eighteen this spring; yet it was not so young. Freely's mother had been

44

married before she was eighteen. Susannah caught herself. No, not married, she thought, except in the heart's intent.

Susannah was aware that the outer door was being opened and shut quietly. She heard familiar sounds as Freely took off her coat and hung it in the closet. Then the girl came into the room. She stood behind Susannah for a moment, reaching down and kissing the older woman's head. Susannah was conscious of something cold and clean, as if the sharp strength of the winter night had come into the room bringing vigor with it. Freely crossed the room and stood on the hearth. She looked into the fire, holding her hands to the blaze; then she turned and faced Susannah. Her eyes were shining. Her cheeks were glowing from the night air. Her sandy hair had been tossed by the wind. There was a radiance about her that brought light into the room that had known since twilight only the gleaming of a candle.

"Are you cold, dear?"

"Not very. I've been running up the hill and that made me warm."

"Where have you been?" Needless question, Susannah realized, for at such a time as tonight there was only one place where Freely would have gone.

"At the dell."

"Wasn't it—" and then Susannah checked herself. No need to ask Freely if it was cold there, for Freely exulted in weather and if it had been cold she would have enjoyed it. "Was it lovely there?"

"Oh yes," Freely breathed deeply. "It was quiet and filled with moonlight. There was not even the sound of water for ice has formed over the spring. There was just the whisper of it running far down in the earth." She paused, remembering the rapture, reliving it; for she had left her sorrow behind her in the graveyard and in the dell she had known peace. "It was so quiet. It made me feel quiet inside myself." Freely closed her eyes, seeing the secret beauty of the dell, feeling its welcoming embrace. It was her cloister and at the place where she entered it from the road a white birch stood like a slim tall sentinel.

"The birch was so white in the moonlight!" Freely exclaimed. Then, realizing that her grandmother had had no dell, no shining winter night, but only the hours of sitting quietly by the sheeted figure of one long loved, Freely crossed the room quickly and knelt on the floor in front of Susannah; reassuringly she put her strong young arms around the older woman. "He can't be very far from us ever," Freely said.

Susannah smoothed the girl's tumbled hair, thinking what comfort there was in the mere sound of words.

They looked into each other's eyes and smiled, knowing then that loving the same person as they had, they had each loosed him and let him go. Susannah had her memories to find Benedict in and Freely had the wisdom he had given her, and they had each other.

Freely picked up the book Susannah had been reading, which had fallen to the floor. She recognized it as one of Benedict's good companions—William Penn's *Fruits of Solitude*.

"Read to me," Susannah said. "Read where my marker is."

Freely opened to the page and read, " 'They that love beyond the world cannot be separated by it. Death cannot kill what never dies. Nor can spirits ever be divided, that love and live in the same principle; the root and record of their friendship. If absence be not death, neither is theirs. Death is but the crossing the world, as friends do the seas; they live in one another still. For they must needs be present, that love and live in that which is omnipresent. In this divine glass they see face to face; and their converse is free. . . .' " Freely looked up at Susannah, her amber eyes full of light.

Susannah met her gaze steadily, then she reached out and drew Freely close to her. The clock ticked on in the silence and two who had always cherished each other were drawn even closer together by their love of one who had left them. Gradually Susannah became aware that the sound of the clock had changed. No longer did the recurring tick-tock, tick-tock say "life-death, death life," until the words had no separate meaning, but "faith-love, love-faith" as the words grew stronger and their strength filled the room.

The next morning Freely went early to the river village with Susannah's messages—a notice to the newspaper, a note to Dr. Vernon, another to Abner Wheelman who had dug so many graves in Simonton and who, though he was old, would have felt hurt if he had not been asked to dig Benedict's, and a letter to the minister of the Millville church requesting a burial service. Freely, with the hard realism of youth, had not seen the necessity for any of Susannah's letters, but Susannah had assured her that what she was doing was not for themselves but for those who had loved Benedict over many years and looked to him to guide their lives.

Walking quickly back up the hill, Freely glanced often at the sky. It was heavy and gray. Snow was long overdue in their countryside but she had often heard Benedict pray for the weather to hold until some occasion was over. A fall of snow would not help Abner Wheelman, nor would it make it easy for any of the one-time neighbors to pay their last respects. She had passed the dell so she went on her way, praying in her heart, thanking God for the good weather they had had and suggesting that it last for another day or two.

Turning into the church, she stood there quietly for a moment, looking up at the garlands of pine she had hung over the windows a few weeks ago for Benedict's last service. Then she realized that it was Christmas Day. She wondered if she should take the garlands down but, though they had faded, they were still pretty and she decided to leave them. It made the church look friendlier.

The service had been set for two o'clock two days following. Long before the appointed hour Benedict's old friends and neighbors—those whom he had married, those whom he had comforted, and many others whose feeling for him was too sacred for definition—came up the hill, some on foot, others in wagons and buggies. Quietly they went into the church, glad for the warmth of the stove, glad for the familiar feel of the hard, wooden pews. They filled the church and they stood outside, and after the service was over when eight tall men carried the coffin to the open grave, Susannah and Freely walked behind it between rows of sober-faced people who dropped their gaze in respect. Susannah had not known Benedict meant so much to so many, and her heart was warmed by the evidence of the wide range of his life.

In the friendly fashion of earlier days when the hill had been alive with neighbors, some of the women took possession of Susannah's kitchen. By the time the people came back from the graveyard, there were pots of coffee on the stove and the table was spread with cakes and pies, doughnuts and turnovers. There was a strengthening drink and hearty food for those who had stood in the cold and had a journey to go before night.

Susannah's friends mixed sympathy with sound advice. One after another they said to her that she must soon plan to leave the hill and live in the river village, for what were she and Freely to do alone in Simonton? Susannah was tired after the long day and the rigors of the days preceding it, and she found it easier to agree with her friends' concern rather than to challenge it. Yet, in her mind was the thought, as it had always been in Benedict's, that the hill was her life and away from it she could not see herself living.

John Dexter, who had known more about the Simons than anyone in Simonton, assured Susannah that when she and

Freely decided to move down to the river village they could make a home with himself and his wife.

"The town is growing all the time," he said. "That new paper mill that got established a few years ago is doing a fine work. They're taking all the wood that people can sell them, softwood for the most part which leaves the hardwood in the forests."

"Are they apt to be interested in any wood up this way?" Susannah asked. She had been wondering where her income would come from when Benedict's small savings were gone.

"Indeed they are, and you couldn't do better than to sell to them," John Dexter replied. "They're honest and they're doing a neater job than some of the other mills. The Haven Paper Company is the name, established by Philip Haven, Senior, but the son is carrying it on now. He's a nice lad, just out of college, full of fine ideas of sparing the woodlands for future growth but they say economy won't let him carry out all his ideas."

"Haven," Susannah said. "That's a new name around here."

Dexter smiled. "That's because you don't get around much, Susannah. They've been here all of ten years. They built a big house a mile or so up the river and they're worth a lot of money, so people in the town say."

The Dexters were the last to leave. "Think it over, Susannah," John said before he left. "And, if you want me to, I'll be glad to negotiate for you any time."

Freely stood in the doorway and watched John Dexter as he took the blanket off his horse, unhitched him from the post, got into the buggy beside his wife, and picked up the reins. The buggy lurched forward as the horse started off. The Dexters turned and waved, and the girl waved back; then she went into the house. Now there was just herself and her grandmother alone on the hilltop, and enough food in the house for a week.

"A blizzard could come and close us in for days and we'd be all right," Freely commented, the tone of her voice distinctly hopeful.

"I wonder," Susannah replied, her face at the window, her eyes on the Dexters as they disappeared over the curve of the hill.

"Why, of course, we would, Grandma!" Freely exclaimed. "Look at all the food they've left us! And the cow is still giving plenty of milk and six of the hens are laying, and I'm strong as a man for any of the chores and—"

"Oh, it's not that I'm wondering about," Susannah interrupted. Her smile, as she turned to face Freely had a stiffness about it as if it had been out of use for a while. "It's whether we should move down to the river village or—"

Freely stood still. Her eyes widened and her mouth grew round until it shaped the word "No."

Susannah shook her head. "I love the hill, too. It's been my life for so long that I can hardly remember anything before it. And yet, perhaps it's not sensible, we two staying on like this."

"Oh, Grandma—" Freely began. Thoughts tumbled in her mind, words trembled on her lips, but she held them back. This was not the time for such talk. Susannah looked so frail and valiant standing there by the window with the December twilight blotting out the world. Tomorrow they could talk about their future. Not tonight.

Susannah, looking at the girl, thought, "I can sell some of the wood. That will enable us to live on here for a little while longer." Aloud she said, "I'm tired, Freely, it's been a long day." Within herself she said, "It's been a long life in one place. I'd like to finish it here if I could be sure it would be all right for Freely."

"Yes, Grandma, it's time for bed." Freely put her arm around Susannah and they went up the stairs together.

6.

⟩⟩⟩⟩⟩⟩⟩⟩⟩⟩⟩⟩⟩⟩⟩⟩⟩⟩⟩⟩⟩⟩⟩⟨⟨⟨⟨⟨⟨⟨⟨⟨⟨⟨⟨⟨⟨⟨⟨⟨⟨⟨⟨⟨⟨

DURING the winter days that followed, Freely went back and forth to school and about her tasks on the hilltop. All that Benedict had been of wisdom and goodness seemed still to be with her. Whenever a thought of his crossed her mind and she dwelt on it during the time she spent alone, it was as stimulating as his voice in her ear or the pressure of his hand in hers.

Once a week, when the snow was not too deep, Ginger would be hitched to the sleigh and Susannah would drive down with Freely to the river village. While Freely was at school, Susannah would visit her old friends and former neighbors; and she would go to the stores to replenish their supplies. In the late afternoon they would travel up the hill again, the sleigh filled with good things, among them a week's accumulation of mail, for the mailman did not include Simonton in his route during the winter months. Susannah liked the day of visiting, but on the way back to Simonton she found herself longing for the rich peace of the house on the hilltop.

Toward mid-January the winter that had been scant on snow took a turn. Freely walked up the hill one Friday after-noon under gray skies heavy with their weight of storm clouds that sagged on the tops of distant hills and veiled the out-line of more distant mountains. The clouds were as dirty as sails fouled by a smokestack and the air was still and raw. Whatever was about to happen hung brooding between heaven and earth.

Freely saw no woods creatures on her way and the only track was that of a fox that had gone up the hill a short while before her. The busyness of a few birds in their search for seeds betokened a storm as much as the grayness of the sky. Freely acknowledged the weather signs and when she reached Simonton she went first to the barn to assure herself of the well-being of the stock. Then she went to the woodpile to make certain that there was all the wood they might need for the time the storm would shut them in.

To have the right wood at hand was to entertain the right kind of company, Benedict had once said, so Freely made her choice from the woodpile accordingly. The crackle and spar-kle of wood was like good talk, he had gone on to say; the long time of smoldering like a time of pondering, and the sudden blazing up into light like an idea becoming clear and ready to be shared with others.

Freely brought in some chunks of wild cherry from a tree on the edge of the pasture that she and Benedict had cut down last summer. They would give out a good smell and burn evenly all night. Beside them she laid a piece of white birch that would burn up with an oily flame and give out a rich fragrance. Her last armful was an apple log. It would burn with orange and blue flames. There was a hole in it where once a bluebird had nested and through the hole tongues of flame would dart out as small heads once had, demanding attention. In the morning, after the apple had burned itself down, the finest and whitest of ash would cover the firebed. Freely was pleased with the sight of the logs she had laid on the hearth and the promise they held.

Freely and Susannah were sitting by the fire when the storm commenced. Susannah looked up from her mending as the first slap of snow could be heard against the window. Freely ran across the room to press her face to the glass, but there was little to be seen save a world of whirling white. The snow fell steadily all night, intermittently all the next day, and as there was no need to go anywhere or do anything, except an occasional trip to the barn to see to the stock, Susannah and Freely accepted the closing in of the storm and stayed by the hearth with books and handwork. Freely exulted in the storm, but Susannah felt vaguely disturbed by it.

Susannah broached her fears to the girl as they sat together quilting. "It's a strange life, we two up here alone. We love it, because it's what we know best, but by another year perhaps we should move away."

"Why?" Freely asked.

"Many reasons," Susannah sighed. "With Benedict gone and the church closed there's no more income, small as it was. Little as our needs are, it takes some money to live."

"What do we need money for? We have the cow and the hens. There'll be the garden soon, and there's plenty of wood to burn."

"There's more to living than eating and keeping warm," Susannah reminded her. "There are taxes to pay and shoes to buy. Why, even Ginger needs shoes! The cow will have to be bred in the summer and we can't raise all the feed we need for ourselves and the stock. Even living simply and much on the land as we do, it still costs something." Susannah smiled a thin small smile. "And it costs money to die."

Freely made no reply. She had accepted so much in life, as if it came from a natural largess in the world, that she had forgotten that some things had to be purchased.

"Until you marry, we—"

Freely would not let Susannah finish her sentence. "Don't say that, Grandma, please. I don't want to marry."

Susannah turned her gaze to the girl. "Why, dear?"

Freely shook her head. "Because I won't be myself."

"Oh, Freely, you'll be so much more yourself. Your nature will have its whole full complement and you'll be that much warmer, that much more outgoing."

Freely knew within herself that she had no intention of marrying so she said quietly, "Can we stay on in Simonton until then?"

Susannah, thinking of the trees she might sell to supplement her funds, replied, "Perhaps we can manage—through the summer, anyway." Then she smiled more easily. "We shall have to tell ourselves that or we will never leave, for when the winter comes, even with its cold and its closing in, we won't want to leave." Susannah, then, felt very firm. She would not have Freely wedded to a hilltop all her life and since the girl loved Simonton so much Susannah knew that it would be up to her to make the break away from it. "But not yet," she said to herself. "Not yet."

Freely laughed. It made it easier when she realized that Susannah loved the hill as much as she did. "Where would we go?" she asked. "To the river village?"

"Perhaps," Susannah said slowly. "And perhaps we might go to California."

Freely shivered. The fire was in no need of another log but she got up and put one on.

That night Freely was wakened from sleep by the moon coming in her window and shining full across her face. She got out of bed and looked from the window. The storm had blown itself out. The sky was sparsely patterned with stars for the moon was brilliant. The world, as much of it as Freely could see, was white and shimmering. Pine boughs bent under the weight of snow on them. Maples and oaks stood sharply outlined from the snow that clung to their trunks and branches. Looking across the clearing between the house and the church, Freely saw three deer lifting their legs delicately in and out of the snow. One, then another, they went up the white steps of the church and rubbed their noses against the wide door. Freely was glad that since people no longer came to the church the animals did.

She could not go to sleep again with the white brilliant beauty in the world, so she dressed quickly and crept silently through the house to the shed where her snowshoes hung on the wall. Taking them outside, she strapped them on, seeing the buckles clearly in the moonlight. She stood for a moment in the stillness. Never was the world so quiet as after a snow-fall; never had there been such beauty. Tossing back her head, she ran quickly over the snow, the slight swish it made as it fell away from her snowshoes the only sound in the silence of the night.

Down the hill she went, veering off the road where the white birch stood whiter than all the snow that had fallen and still as the night itself in the moon radiance. She passed it and went into the dell. The granite boulders were soft in their contours, overlain with white. The trees held her in their enfolding. She was as aware of the stillness in her heart as she was of the stillness in the dell. She could listen and, after listening, she could reply, wordlessly. The world was full of glory and she was at its heart.

Conscious of the cold around her, she was even more conscious of the warmth within that was kindled by the joy she felt when in the dell alone. Conscious that the night hours were moving on toward morning and that light would bring its changes, she was even more conscious of the eternal wonder of which she was a part. The world was hers because she was alone in it. Hers and God's.

Here, in the dell, were those things of which she was sure: flowers under the snow, trees in which birds would nest, buds on the branches that held within themselves their beauty. The earth was frozen hard but deep down it was warm and springs were running. If she brushed the snow away and put her ear to the earth she knew she would hear that voice of assurance. But she did not put her head to the ground. She looked up through the maze of slender branches to the scattering of stars in the sky, each one a world of light. In the whiteness of the night about her she was aware of the things that were her realities. And they were more evident now in the silence of the snow and the cold of the January night than when the trees were rustling with leaves and the springs were bubbling out of the earth. Was she telling herself about these things or was it her angel, she asked herself. It was hard to know in the half-listening, half-questing place that was her mind which was which, so near they both were.

A small depression in the snow caught her eye and she looked at it, thinking that a leaf must have been tossed there by the wind. She moved closer and knelt on one knee to trace the outline. But it was deeper than a leaf would have made and reaching her hand farther down she touched something soft. She drew her hand back quickly and pulled off her mittens; then she thrust her bare hands into the snow again and brought out the tiny huddled form of a bird. She held it in the warmth of her hand for a moment to make certain that life still dwelt in the feathered form; then she tucked the bird inside her coat and held it close to her.

The storm in its fury of biting wind and swirling snow had dashed the bird from its perch on a tree, Freely thought, then in strange contrition spread a white covering over the little body.

" 'He giveth snow like wool,' " Freely whispered. She could hear Benedict repeating the psalm in a voice that held words in affectionate embrace before speaking them.

During the cold of night the snow might act as wool but by morning it would be a snare to the bird. Floundering and struggling, the creature whose element was air would have known no ready way to freedom. So Freely harbored it. Then she remembered that birds in the winter and at a time of storm tended to flock together and that there might be more. She moved her bare hands through the snow, changing her position carefully. One by one she uncovered a small flock of half-frozen chickadees. She took off her jacket and made a carrier for them. Twelve she found and of them she knew that eleven had life within them. The other little one she left in the snow. Then she went back to the road, glancing up at the sentinel birch whose seeds it was that had no doubt drawn the flock to shelter in the dell.

She did not want to disturb Susannah so she went to the church. The hoofprints the deer had left were the only marks in the snow. She set down her jacket with its birds and took off her snowshoes, then she went in. There was no light but the moonlight; in its glow the gray walls gleamed softly and the high, many-paned windows gave back a brilliance from the snow. Freely built a fire in the box stove and brought the birds close to it. Gradually their huddled forms responded to the warmth; their wiry feet, curled as tightly as if they were still clinging to a branch, relaxed. The chickadees sat on the edge of a bench near the fire, making small sounds like children talking in their sleep and fluffing up their feathers until they looked twice their size.

Freely talked with them as she tended the stove. When she was assured that they would greet the morning with song and soaring wings she curled up on the floor beside them and went to sleep. Light and whirring wings awakened her and she opened her eyes in the same sudden, startled fashion that the birds had earlier, but when she realized where she was and what was going on around her she remembered the night before.

Getting up, she took the long window pole and opened one of the windows from the top. "Now you can go," she said to the birds. "But there'll always be a window open here on a night of storm if you want some shelter."

One by one they found the opening, and with ecstatic chirps they flew through it into the day that was bright with sunshine and the myriad reflections the sun was making on the snow.

Susannah was busy in the kitchen when Freely returned and she greeted the girl without surprise but with the gladness she always felt for her presence. The open bed in Freely's room had not startled her, for Freely had a way of leaving the house at unusual hours, and when Susannah had looked across the green and seen the snowshoes thrust into a drift outside the church she knew where the girl was.

Freely told her of the chickadees and how she had let them thaw out in the warmth of the church.

Susannah laughed. "Benedict would have liked that, but it's good that some of the Simonton people don't live here any more. They wouldn't have cared for anything so frivolous as a flock of birds in the church."

"If the church isn't going to be used by people," Freely commented, "the creatures might just as well have a share in it."

"They might—just as well," Susannah agreed, thinking how when you got old enough anything seemed reasonable.

It was well that Susannah's life had made her tolerant and acceptant for Freely, having found a use for the church soon found more use for it. She had always had deft hands in helping animals and she had that inner undemandingness that made them turn to her easily. But, during the weeks that followed as the year drew out of winter and advanced into spring, Freely seemed to have a special genius for finding those in need of care.

Not many days after the blizzard, when she was going up and down the hill on snowshoes, she found a cat that had been badly mauled by a fox. She carried it up to the church and made a safe place for it in one of the pews. There was nothing she could do but wash the wounds and let them heal of their own accord, feed the cat and keep the building warm, but she was happy in doing that and the cat responded to her care. She made inquiries in the river village and found that it belonged to Miss Mattie Emerson. When she told Miss Mattie, the little old lady was so pleased to know her cat was alive and being cared for that she told Freely to keep it until it was quite itself again.

Susannah wondered vaguely if there would be any objections raised by those who held the Meetinghouse in esteem if they knew what use Freely was making of it, but she said nothing.

Every week the batch of mail that had accumulated at the Millville postoffice had a letter, sometimes more than one, from Roger, or Roland, or young Mark, or one of their wives, and a great part of Susannah's life lay in reading the letters and living with her sons. Answering them was like having the boys sitting with her around the kitchen table, for she could not yet get used to the fact that they were men. In every letter they urged her to come to them and, in a quiet corner of her mind where Susannah tried to think out what was best, she wondered to herself if she should not sell everything she owned and with Freely go to California.

7.

>>>>>>>>>>>>>>>>>>>>><<<<<<<<<<<<<<<<<<<<<<

PHILIP HAVEN walked up the road from Millville to Simonton. The March wind whipping about him was
cold, but the sun was warm. Under it the banks of snow along
the road and the covering in the woods were disappearing rap-
idly. Earth was beginning to show in some places, the same
reddish brown color as the thickening tips on the trees. The
man leaned over and examined a print in the soft mud. A fox,
he thought to himself, glad that he had brought his gun. He
took from his pocket the memo he had scribbled to remind
himself of the name of the person upon whom he was calling.
*Mrs. Benedict Simon—late husband was pastor of church on
hill—owns a hundred acres or more of good woodland—
probably willing to sell.* He put the slip of paper away in his
pocket and resumed his walk up the hill.

He passed a cellar hole from which a house had been removed; only the brick chimney remained to rise like a gaunt
ghost out of the encroaching forest. He passed another cellar
hole and all that marked it as having once been a place of
habitation was the clump of lilacs that stood by the doorstep.
Crumbling chimneys looked to the past, Philip Haven
thought, but a clump of lilacs blooming each spring had a
way of looking to the future. The spirit of New England was
in them, the genius of the land. Stalwart, undefeated, they
met time and vicissitude with rugged beauty, casting their

fragrance as freely now on winds that whispered through green byways of the forest as they once had on winds that blew freshly over open fields. Philip told himself that when he had a house of his own he would have a clump of lilacs by the door.

A chipmunk sunning itself on the stone wall saw the stranger and dove quickly into its burrow. A crow flew overhead, flapping its wide wings and cawing noisily. Philip looked at the trees lining the road, sizing them up with a trained eye. It was good timber, there was no doubt about that; plenty of softwood for pulp, and some of the hardwood could be lumbered at the same time and sold to the furniture factory. He hoped Mrs. Simon would be willing to sell—but perhaps she wouldn't be. Often the older people grew the less they wanted to change the look of the land around them. It was lonely, Philip thought, and the trees made it more so, shutting the country in. With some of them out of the way there would be more light and air, more views. His eye ran appraisingly up and down a tall birch that stood near the road, estimating the board feet in it, and beyond them to the dollars and cents it would realize.

He forgot about trees when he came out on to the clearing that was Simonton. There it was, just as he had always been told—the white church on the hilltop, the confluence of the four roads leading to it, the open green, and around it a small group of clapboard houses; yet only one house had its windows unshuttered, and from only one chimney was smoke issuing.

It was true then, the story he had been told, that there had been a settlement here but that it had been gradually abandoned and the people had gone down the hill—many of them taking their houses with them—to Millville where life was easier. But one family had clung on and they were descendants of the first settler. To his surprise, Philip Haven found himself thinking that it wasn't so lonely on the hilltop. There was an air of serenity about it. He felt as if he had entered a sanctuary. He was sorry that he had brought his gun and he leaned it against a tree trunk so he might go into Simonton free handed.

The sun that had been warm on his back pushed him on and he crossed the open green to the house near which stood a massive oak. Philip looked up through its tangle of branches. "As old as a tree ever gets in this climate," he commented to himself. "A lot of living has passed under those limbs." Then he knocked at the door.

Susannah had seen his approach. Bent on business as he came over the brow of the hill, she had watched him stand still for a moment and take in Simonton with his eyes. "Perhaps he is being taken in by it," she had thought to herself, as she saw him lean something he had been carrying against a tree. Then he began his unhurried approach across the open land to the house. Expecting him, she went to the door but after he had knocked she waited a moment, standing behind the door. Then she opened it to him.

"Mrs. Simon? I'm Philip Haven. You've had my letter?"

"Yes. I've been looking for you. Won't you come in?" Susannah held the door wide. He seemed so absurdly like one of her own tall sons that it was difficult for her to treat him like a stranger.

"I'm afraid my boots are rather muddy," he said apologetically.

"That's all right. This has been a house of boys and they've brought in more than mud in their time. We'll go into the kitchen and you won't mind about that floor."

He followed her into the room that was at the left of the door, glad that his boots had given him entrance to the friendliest room in the house. In doing business with country people he had found parlors stiff places and he avoided them as much as possible.

Susannah's kitchen was a pleasant room, bright with late afternoon sun and fragrant with the smell of baking, friendly with the crackle of wood in the iron stove and the kettle singing quietly to itself.

"It's quite a long walk up from Millville," Philip ventured.

"It is if you're not used to it. We who've done it the best part of our lives think nothing of it."

"Most of the families have left the hill, I understand. Aren't you lonely living here all by yourself?"

Susannah looked surprised. "I don't live alone. Freely lives with me."

"Who is Freely?"

"My granddaughter." Susannah motioned to a chair at one side of the kitchen table. "Please sit down, Mr. Haven, and I'm sure you're hungry after that walk. I've some bread just made today and there's a jug of milk from the morning's milking."

"And you don't get lonely, you and Freely?" Philip asked as he watched Susannah pour out a glass of milk and he heard the crunch of the knife through new crust.

"When your life has been lived for a good many years in one place, somehow it still goes on around you," Susannah answered. "I don't want to leave the hill, not until I have to," she said as she put some butter on the table. "Nor does Freely. The others all wanted to go, but not Freely. She's as much a part of the hill as one of its rocks or trees."

"The others?" he prompted.

"My three sons and Freely's mother," Susannah said. Then she turned to him eagerly. "I'd like to sell some of the trees so we could stay here a while longer."

"Then what do you plan to do?"

"I'm thinking—" Susannah found it hard to speak about something she had no heart for—"we might go to California before another winter."

"That's a long way to go."

"It's where my sons have made their home."

"Oh, I see." Philip ate some bread and drank some milk.

"I'd rather stay on here but I think it might be better for Freely if we left Simonton."

"Yes, of course," Philip said, feeling inadequate and unable to say more.

Susannah leaned toward him. "Would you be interested in any of our trees?"

"Unquestionably," he replied with emphasis. "But I can't really tell until I make a survey. I suppose you have a map of your land?"

Susannah nodded.

"If you'll let me see it, it will give me an idea of the boundaries. I'll go over your land at my first opportunity, and then come back to you with my report."

"You can take the map with you if you wish," Susannah said.

"It won't be necessary," Philip shook his head. "Looking at it will give me an idea of how your land lies."

Susannah left the room to get the map. Philip watched her go with a feeling of admiration for the woman who wanted to live her life out in the place where her roots had gone down. Her face was handsome, he thought, and only her hands showed her years of hard work. He wondered where the child was. But Mrs. Simon had an air that was singularly gracious and gentle, and a child growing up in her presence was privileged indeed. The house had an air, too, he thought, as if the best of life had not left it but was still a part of it. There were shelves of books even in the kitchen, a clock ticking unhurriedly, a quilting frame in a corner, plants in the sunny window, a cat curled up back of the stove. Peace, kindliness, and patience were there, giving the place its natural atmosphere.

Once Philip had thought the hamlet on the hill must be a lonely spot, but knowing it now, he thought so no longer. Remote it might be, but it was a comfortable and a comforting life. Something that was the essence of the countryside dwelt here, capable of flowering as the lilacs were from a bedrock of simplicity. He found himself wishing that Susannah could stay on her hilltop all the rest of her life.

Susannah came back with the map in her hand. She poured out more milk for her guest and buttered generously another piece of bread; then they sat down at the table together and went over the map. It was the same one that had traced Mark Simon's first grant, the boundaries of which had never changed though the forest that had been cleared had gone back to forest again. Acre by acre the land had been made fertile so Mark Simon's family could have their living from it. Now, those who bore the Simon name and dwelt on the hilltop would have their living not from labor with the land but from the wealth that had burgeoned in its trees.

Freely came up the road singing lustily. Spring was in the air and she was conscious of its quickening. The wind was soft and caressing except, Marchlike, when a sudden gust blew sharp and cold. A grackle flew overhead and Freely stopped to watch its flight. A familiar song, unheard for a long time, arrested her attention. She searched for the singer with her eyes until she spied him—a robin sitting perched on the topmost branch of an apple tree, pouring out the joy he was feeling at his return to his nesting haunt. There was a milky softness in the light lying over the land and the feel of time growing longer as the hours of daylight lengthened.

Freely went on with her singing, looking up at the trees to

see if they were accompanying her. She stopped before a chipmunk sitting on a stone and directed her song to him. He cocked his head and listened. Then he started washing his face, shaking his paws, rubbing them back of his rounded ears and down his jowls. They looked at each other. She went on singing and he went on titivating. He could not mimic her, but for everything she did he did something in return.

"I'm late now," Freely said in explanation. "I'd like to stay here with you but the sun's getting low and you've got to go to bed."

The chipmunk did not move, and Freely went on her way. She turned after a few steps to wave to him, hardly distinguishable from the lichened stone on which he sat. Freely saw the heavy footprints made by a man going up the road, but she was less interested in them than in the prints of the fox's pads. Following them she climbed over a stone wall and lost them, then picked them up again on the checkered floor of the woods in the soft snow and earth. They led over her own secret trail that wound up to the hilltop.

Passing by certain trees she loved, she put out her hands and touched them in an ecstasy of affection. Now and again she stopped to lean against a trunk and listen to the strains that swept the bare branches. It was such music as could only be heard if it was listened for, and then Freely was never quite sure whether she heard it or imagined it. Maples and beeches, birches and oaks, hemlocks and pines, all sang in different keys, yet their combined song was the voice of the forest. The beeches still clung to their leaves and from them came a sibilant whispering. The oaks, too, bore many of their leaves, dry and brittle after the winter.

It was their music that Freely loved especially to listen for. Benedict had taught her how to listen—leaning against a trunk with hands widespread on its furrowed bark and eyes half closed, then letting the sound take her back, back over the millennia through which the oaks had lived, passing on their majesty, their power in an acorn so that when a tree was felled by nature or man, still the oak survived. "Listen, listen," Benedict used to say, "for the oaks have known the earth longer than man. Listen, listen for there is wisdom here that can't be found in books. It is—"

Freely dug her fingers into the fissured bark, for a shot had torn through the woodland, shattering its quiet. So sudden it was, so brutal, that Freely thought she herself had been shot, for she was unable to move. Her fingers, deep in the bark, seemed her only support, for her knees were trembling violently.

A moment later a fox came running through the woods and Freely watched it—pointed ears, dark slender legs, shining red coat, and long brush lying on the wind. It was beautiful and lithe, but it faltered in its flight and as it passed Freely a low sound issued from its throat, something between a cry and a squeal. Then Freely saw the blood streaming from the open wound on the fox's shoulder and the marks it left on the snow. The fox started down the trail but its gait became slower. It stumbled, going up over a rock to avoid a patch of snow, then ran on as if to reach some known shelter while life was still within it.

A passionate instinct to help a suffering creature galvanized Freely into action. Pushing herself free from the oak, she started down the trail after the fox. Another shot rang out. Freely did not stop or look behind her, nor was she sure that the sharp pang she felt was her own or because her heart was with the fox. All she knew was that she felt less sure of herself. Pain blurred her eyes and made her footsteps heavy, but she knew the way over the trail even at night and blindly, and impulsively she followed it. Then suddenly she had no more breath, no more volition. She crumpled up on the ground, drawing her right leg under her to shield it.

The sight of the open gash and the blood running down her leg revived her. Sick and faint as she had felt, she was shocked into consciousness. Looking at her leg she thought it could not be hers. Yet, she knew that it must be because the shoe was so familiar. She realized that she had buttoned it that morning when she had dressed herself. She looked at it again curiously, then her gaze left her shoe and she stared at the wound on her leg, wondering what to do. Had it been an animal she would have known instantly what to do; with herself it was different. Where something useful had been was only pain, aching and burning. She shut her eyes tight for a moment and held her teeth together.

The woods were silent now. Far back of her she could hear the trampling of someone thrusting a way through brush and low branches. But whoever it was would not find her. Like the fox, she had run over earth to break her trail. The places where blood stained a snow patch and might give direction were few and far between. The crashing behind her lessened, grew fainter, ceased altogether. Whoever it was, he had lost his quarry. Fighting for some release from the pain, Freely saw in her mind the footprint of the man and the pad of the fox on the road to Simonton; the hunter and the hunted.

Another sound came to Freely's ears; a whimpering and barking. It was like the sound an animal makes when it wants to play and cannot as the one with whom it would play will not respond. Freely saw herself as a little girl falling and bruising her knee, running to Benedict or Susannah for comfort and the assurance of cure; but there was no Benedict now to run to and Susannah was too far away to hear even if she should call out for her. There was no one but herself.

Freely took her handkerchief and doubled it over the wound, then she struggled to her feet to get her petticoat off and rip it into bandages. She wound a tight one above the wound to stop the blood and another one around her leg to protect the wound. All the while she tended to herself she was not so aware of the pain in her leg as she was of the whimpering sound that came to her through the woods.

When she could, she followed the sound and it brought her to the edge of the dell. She stopped short. Near one of the granite boulders lay the fox, a young vixen, and beside her two month-old cubs were gamboling perplexedly. They did not run away when Freely appeared but they sat back on their haunches, looking at her with the bewildered eyes of young things whose familiar world has suddenly altered. Freely knelt down beside the vixen; partly open jaw, glazed eyes told their story and yet the blood still flowed and the earth was absorbing it.

Freely could not have said which ached more, her heart or her leg. She looked around her. Yet here, in her secret place, there was peace and quiet, and beauty wrapping all four of them like a cloak. Freely smoothed her hands over the vixen's fur and tried to close the open jaw. Then she limped to the edge of the dell. With her jackknife she cut off some branches from a thickly needled spruce. She laid them over the vixen, then scooped leaves and earth in her hands as best she could to cover the spruce. It was a rude attempt at a grave, but a woods creature had the silence of the forest and that was sufficient covering. She went toward the cubs. They withdrew and snarled at the sight of the approaching hand.

"Your mother can't feed you any more and you're too young to feed yourselves," she said persuadingly. "Come along with me and I'll take care of you for a while."

They backed up against each other, watching her movements.

"Are there just the two of you?" Freely asked. "What a small family! But it's going to make it easier for me. I wonder what you like to eat."

She had her hand on one of them now and was fondling it, rubbing it behind the ears as she might a puppy. The other drew near to sniff. Freely held her hand still while the cub smelled it all over. Puzzled, but trusting, it looked up at Freely. The smell of the vixen was on Freely's hand.

In another few moments she had picked the cubs up and was holding them close to her, talking to them all the time. She made her way carefully over the rocks, conscious of her right leg and trying to keep her weight off it as much as possible. When she reached the white birch she leaned against it to rest for a moment before she started up the hill. She noticed that the birch had been notched by a knife. Wondering who could have done such a thing, she felt in the grooves with her fingers. They were freshly cut and sap was oozing from them like the blood from her leg and the vixen's shoulder.

A tide of perplexity came over Freely. This was one of Benedict's trees. It stood at the corner of his land. He had planted it himself. Who had the right to mark it in any way except a Simon?

The cubs were struggling in her arms and she began the climb up the hill. Never had she gone so slowly and never had she been less aware of the world around her, for the pain in her leg had a numbing sensation and only the urgent need of the orphans in her arms kept her from giving up. She remembered Benedict. No matter how long the way, or how hard, he used to say, it was still taken one step at a time. She took a step, knowing as she did so that she would be able to take another. Once over the brow of the hill, the sight of the church itself drew her on.

She reached the steps and paused to look at the snowdrops on the edge of a retreating snowbank. They had been just a handful when Benedict planted them; now they had become such a drift that they seemed to push the snow aside. It could not have been easy for them, she thought, to push their way up through the wet cold earth. She found a reservoir of strength that enabled her to open the door and go into the church.

Freely set the cubs down in one of the box pews and closed the small door. Then, leaning over it, she admonished them to be good. "I'll bring you some bread and milk in a little while. I'm your mother and I'll take care of you, never fear."

Leaving the church, she crossed the green to the house and pushed open the door. Susannah was sitting by the kitchen stove, rocking away. She looked happy. Freely came half in, then clung to the door wishing she could leave her leg outside. She didn't want to bring it into Susannah's clean kitchen with its feeling of peace and the good smell of dinner cooking. She entered the room slowly.

"Someone was hunting foxes in the woods—" she began, then her voice thickened.

Susannah went to her quickly, just in time to catch her before she fell.

Once Susannah saw the wounded leg she saw no reason to rouse Freely from her faint until she had bathed it and bound it up again. A cruel gash it was, Susannah told herself as she wrapped a clean linen bandage around it, but it would heal quickly.

When Freely opened her eyes she told Susannah of the cubs in the church. "Their mother is dead and they're so little they couldn't live unless someone cares for them."

"I'll take some food to them, Freely," Susannah said. "You lie back and be quite for a while."

Freely sighed. "Thank you, Grandma."

"Whoever could have been hunting in the woods today," Susannah said as she busied herself collecting some scraps of bread and a bowl of milk. "Such a pleasant young man was here this afternoon, Freely, but he didn't have a gun."

Freely heard Susannah but she did not return the conversation. Lying on the couch by the window, she raised herself up just enough to watch Susannah go into the church. Then she leaned back against the pillows and looked dreamily into the stove. It was all behind her now—the fright, the pain, the dismay, the long walk up the hill when every step seemed like the last. Around her was a pleasant daze—the warm kitchen, the memory of Susannah's skillful hands, the knowledge that there was something needing her care in the church.

A man with a gun. The words didn't belong to Simonton somehow, and yet Benedict had always said that it was just a difference in degree in philosophy whether a man carried a gun into the woods or whether he did not.

8.

SOME ten days later Philip returned to Simonton with his report on the survey he had made of Susannah's forest land. The year had moved forward into April and the world was vigorous with new life. Philip walked up the road, conscious of the naked beauty of the trees before their buds swelled into foliage, and of the rough freshness of the breeze. He had left his gun at home and he was not sorry. No matter how many foxes and rabbits he met on his way, he felt he had made a better choice for that particular day. He had a small hatchet at his belt, thinking if he had time he might mark some of the boundary trees, working in a line from the white birch; though with the contracts already made he knew that his men would not get into the Simon lot before the end of May.

Susannah opened the door to him, welcoming him. He was young and strong and she had not known until she had met him those few days ago how much she had missed the boys that had once filled her house with their eager eyes and noisy ways.

"You chose a fine day, Mr. Haven, for your walk up the hill!" she exclaimed.

He scuffed his feet politely on the doormat before coming in. "I think any day would be fine that had a visit to Simonton in it," he smiled.

He followed her into the kitchen and accepted without any remonstrance the square of warm gingerbread she offered him and the glass of milk. While he ate, he listened as she told him of the letters she had had from her sons.

"I wrote them last winter when John Dexter first spoke to me about selling some of the trees. They're all in favor of it," she said, casting her eyes toward the letters she had recently received. "They'd like me to sell everything—the house and the cleared land as well and join them in California."

"Would you like to do that?"

Susannah shook her head. "Not for myself, but for Freely perhaps. Of course, I'd like to see the boys again and their children, but they've been near me all these years. Seeing them might not be all I think it would be."

Philip Haven felt so relieved that he took another piece of gingerbread. He didn't want Susannah Simon to leave just as he had come to know her. He liked visiting with her. Her friendliness warmed something within him. Whether they ever did any business together seemed immaterial now, but he liked to have it as a reason to seek her cheery kitchen and the windy hilltop. Susannah was a person who met life with both hands open and with forward-looking eyes. It meant something to Philip to know her.

"Besides, Mr. Haven," she was saying, "it isn't just my feeling for the land. It's because sometimes we have a trust given us. I want to see Freely safely grown, and I couldn't leave the church—Benedict's church. Not just yet." She smiled at him. It was odd to be saying that to a stranger. She wondered if being alone so much of the time had made it too easy for her to make of anyone a confidant.

"The church isn't being used at present, is it?"

"No, not since the first Sunday in December, that was when the last family moved down to the river village. Freely and I have our Sunday service in it and Freely uses it during the week for her own purposes, but then it always has been almost as much her home as the house. She took care of it for her grandfather."

"She must miss him."

Susannah looked at Philip Haven with her straight gaze. It would be fitting to agree, yet she could not entirely.

"Freely and her grandfather shared their thoughts," Susannah said deliberately. "And thoughts are things you go on sharing."

Susannah looked away quickly. She hoped Mr. Haven would not ask her how she felt. It was different with herself. She and Benedict had shared their thoughts—yes, over almost more years than she could remember—but they had shared so much else. They had sat across from each other at the same table. The bed was far too big for one. Where his hands had rested there were no hands ever to rest again. Even in her most placid moments she was conscious of the ache within her; yet she would not have it otherwise, for the ache was Benedict.

"May I look at the map of your land again, Mrs. Simon? It might be helpful to have it before us when I tell you of my survey."

"Yes, yes, of course. I put it back in Benedict's desk, but I'll fetch it immediately. You will make yourself at home, won't you, Mr. Haven?"

"Indeed I will, Mrs. Simon," he smiled. "In fact, I'm very much at home already."

He moved over to the window and stood looking out. The sun was lowering in the west, gaining a richness of light and color as it neared the horizon. The distant rim of mountains made a frame for the hilltop world and against their blueness the naked trees, tipped with swelling buds, stood out. Up the road a cart drawn by a ginger-colored horse came slowly. A girl sat on the high seat with a dog beside her. The reins were lying loose on her lap as if she knew that the horse could find his way himself. Her head was thrown back and even at a distance Philip Haven could see that she was smiling. The warm mellow light of the setting sun seemed to enfold her in a sort of radiance.

It made a pretty sight, Philip thought, a country girl coming home from a day in town. He wondered where she lived. Perhaps she would stop in and call on Mrs. Simon as she passed by. He hoped not. After all, he had come on business and he begrudged the time a caller might take from his time with Susannah. Relieved, he saw that the girl drew on one rein enough to direct the horse toward the church. At the steps the horse came to a halt and the girl got down from the wagon, followed by the dog. She patted the horse and looped the reins loosely around the empty whip socket. The horse put his head to the ground and began to nibble at the greening grass. Philip noticed that the girl limped slightly as she walked up the steps and pushed open the door of the church. He turned quickly, hearing Susannah come into the room.

"Do many people pass by here during the day?" he asked, drawing near the table where Susannah was spreading out the map.

"Yes, a few, for there are still some farms on beyond and though the way over the hilltop is not the easiest in all weathers, it is the shortest. And, except for the winter months, I can always be sure of a visit from the mailman on his round. He'll stop and have a chat with me even if he hasn't got a letter to deliver." Susannah put her finger on the map. "The best timber lies halfway down the hill," she said. "The land there never could be cultivated. It was too rocky. But Benedict thinned the trees out several years ago and the remaining ones must have put on considerable girth by now."

Philip Haven checked with his survey and together they marked on the map where the cutting should commence and how far it should extend. Susannah had no mind to dispose of all her woodland. She was well schooled enough to know that so long as she had standing trees she had money at hand, and though there were such things as forest fires and hurricanes, she was willing to take her chances. After all, even a bank could fail. Ten acres was all she would agree to having cut at that time, but she assured Philip that when she felt inclined to let more of the trees go she would let him know.

The sum determined on between them seemed ample to Susannah for her needs for a considerable time and when she signed her name to the agreement she did it with a feeling of gratitude to Benedict. It was his work in the woodlands forty years ago that had made the trees the merchantable timber they were today.

Philip took from his wallet a hundred dollars in cash to seal the bargain and Susannah accepted it as a welcome token.

"Why don't you stop in and see the church before you go back?" she suggested. "The door is never locked."

"I'd like to," Philip replied.

"Come and see us soon again."

"Even when we haven't any business to discuss?"

Susannah nodded. "Even then. We'll find plenty of other things to talk about."

Philip crossed the green to the Meetinghouse. He presumed the girl was still there because the horse and cart were near, though the horse to satisfy his appetite for grass had gone quite a distance from the steps. Philip thought he would look inside for a moment and, even if the girl was resting or meditating, he would not disturb her.

He pushed the door open and stood in the entryway, but it was not the quiet of a church into which he was intruding. Laughter came from within, and growls and barks. He distinctly heard a cat meowing and a bird was singing, but whether the song came from inside or out he could not be sure. Puzzled by the sounds, he went through an open door into the small square room with its box pews and many paned windows. He noticed that the windows were garlanded with ground pine as if the church entertained the spirit of perpetual festival. For a moment he saw nothing else and he could not tell from where the curious medley of sounds came; then a girl's head shot up over one of the box pews. Her hair was rumpled and her face was wrinkled with laughter. She did not seem to be surprised at the sight of a stranger in the Simonton Meetinghouse.

"Hello," she said. "Who are you?"

"Philip Haven," he replied. "Who are you?"

"I'm Freely, and these are my children. But they won't be here much longer. They're getting strong enough to go out in the world on their own."

He advanced slowly toward her and when he got to the edge of the pew she sank down onto the floor and the two cubs gamboled around her. "So this is Freely," Philip said to himself, wondering why he had thought she was a little girl, picturing her as such whenever Susannah spoke of her.

"Freely Simon?" he asked.

She nodded. Her eyes were dancing from the game she had been playing. Her sandy hair caught the last rays of the sun as it came in one of the tall windows. She was dressed in a sailor blouse and a long full skirt; her coat was lying in a heap on the bench in the pew.

"I've just been talking with your grandmother," he began.

"Oh, that's nice!" Freely swept one of the cubs down as it tried to crawl on to her shoulder. "Have you decided on the trees?"

"Yes. Ten acres to start with. It will make a beginning."

"Grandma likes you," Freely said. "I'm glad the trees brought you to her. She loves to have people come and see her. She's here by herself so much of the day."

"Where are you?"

"I go to school in the river village. It's my last year. When I've finished school I won't have to leave the hill any more."

"Are you going to make pets of those cubs?" he asked.

"Oh no," she laughed. "They're my hospitalers. They needed care for a while and Grandpa's old church was just the place for them." She drew in her breath suddenly, "Oh, I hope you're not the kind of person who minds seeing animals in a church?"

"No, indeed," he assured her.

"I'm so glad." A look of relief came over her face and the smile that had fled momentarily returned. "Do you like fox cubs?"

"Why, yes," he replied hesitantly. "Where did you get them?"

"I found them in the woods. Their mother had been killed. They couldn't have survived without some care."

"Are you going to keep them until they grow up?"

"Oh no, that wouldn't be fair. In a few days, when the weather is settled, I'll turn them out."

"What if they don't want to go?"

"They'll go all right. The wild will call to them and they'll answer. I just wanted to keep them until they got over being fed on milk and could taste meat and hunt and live their natural lives."

"What if they loved you too much to leave you?"

She leveled her eyes at him in the same way Susannah had. "I don't let them love me that way. It wouldn't be fair to them." They were crawling up her again and she brushed them away with a gesture that was at the same time both brusque and tender. "Would you like to see my cat?"

"Of course, I would."

Freely got to her feet and left the pew, carefully closing and buttoning its door. She went to the other side of the room to a pew with a wire over the top. A demure white cat looked at them from its pillow on the bench. Freely reached in and took it up in her arms.

"It belongs to Miss Mattie Emerson and it's quite well enough to go home any day now."

"What happened to it?"

"One night it went farther from home than it should have and it met a fox. It got away but not without a mauling."

"And yet you'll take care of the fox's cubs!"

Freely looked surprised. "When a fox catches a cat it's just doing what is natural to it. I don't try to make creatures different. I just try to help them when they get into trouble."

"Oh—" Philip Haven could not remember a time in his life when he had felt so completely without words.

Freely held the cat tenderly. "The hunter who shot the cub's mother was just doing what was natural to him."

"Was he?" Philip asked. Then he looked around the church quickly. "Didn't I see you come in here with a dog?"

"Yes. She's just across the aisle." Freely put the cat down and led the way to another pew where a half-starved hound dog was cringing in a corner.

"What a miserable-looking creature!"

"Her master was beating her because he said she wouldn't mind him, but do you know what I did?"

"I can't imagine."

"I looked into her ears and saw they were both so full of wax that the poor thing couldn't have heard if her life had depended on it. So I brought her here for a while."

"And you're going to doctor her up?"

"Yes, it isn't very difficult. I put a few drops of warm oil in the ears every night—that softens the wax—and then in the morning I clean them out," Freely explained. "It may take a few days to get them quite clean but I want to keep her as long as I can to feed her up a bit and get her over being

fearful." She stroked the dog who looked at Freely with ador-
ing eyes.

"She won't want to leave you, that's certain."

Freely was equally certain. "She will when I've had a
chance to talk things over with her. Grandpa used to say that
birds knew all there was to know about education. They give
their young care, give them the knowledge they need, then
push them off the nest to fly for themselves. That's what I'm
doing. What did you say your name was?"

"Philip. Philip Haven."

"Are you going back to the river village tonight?"

"I expect to."

"Then, Philip, could you take Miss Emerson's cat back to
her? She told me today she was so lonely for it. I'll put it in a
basket. It won't be hard to carry."

"I'd be happy to, Miss—" he paused.

"My name is Freely," she prompted. "I don't think you'll
forget it. Not many people are called it. Only my mother before me that I know of, and way back long ago Benedict
Simon's grandmother and perhaps her mother, but I'm not
quite sure."

Twenty minutes later, with a cat in a basket over his
arm and the voice of the April night around him, Philip
Haven walked down the road to Millville not quite sure
whether he was walking out of a dream or into one.

9.

FREELY did not keep the hound dog long. Bess was a sentimental creature with a capacity for affection for any-one who might feed or stroke her more than once. Freely cared for the ears until she had them clean and could satisfy herself about the improvement in hearing; she fed Bess until the lean body could display curves instead of angles; and she talked to Bess as she would to a person. Then one morning, when Freely set out for school, she called to Bess to follow her. Freely had a piece of rope in her pocket which she used to tie the dog outside the schoolhouse, but there was little need. The one upon whom Bess's heart was fixed had disap-peared behind a door. The hound dog lowered herself across the step, sunk her long nose between her outstretched paws, and sighed. Nothing could have moved her from her place until the one whom she loved appeared again.

"I don't see how you knew what to do for the poor crea-ture," Freely's teacher, Miss Anderson, exclaimed after Freely had told the whole class the story of the hound dog.

"If your hands are dirty you wash them to get them clean," Freely explained with the ease that Miss Anderson might have explained a mathematical problem. "It wasn't much different washing Bess's ears except that I did it with warm oil."

"Was it from your grandfather you learned so much about caring for animals?"

"Indeed it was," Freely said. Then she went on by way of explanation, "You can't live on a farm without having to do things for your stock when they're sick or in trouble."

"But how did you know *what* to do?"

"I just do what comes natural to me," Freely said.

"Are there ever times when you can't do anything or don't know what to do?"

Freely moved her head slowly in affirmation. "There are times," she said, "but there's never a time when you can't give an animal the comfort of your presence. You just have to be sure that the hurt within you at not being able to ease their pain isn't so great that it only adds to their pain."

After school, Freely went to the small, ill-kept house on the edge of the town where she had first seen the dog. No one was in sight so she knocked at the door, opening it when a voice from within bade her enter. An old woman was sitting by the stove.

"I'm looking for Tom Slason," Freely said.

"What d'you want him for?" the woman asked gruffly.

"I've had his dog for a few days. Now I've brought her back to him."

"That old cur? She isn't worth the vittels Tom feeds her."

"Please, will you tell me where I may find Tom?"

"Where would a lumberman be but in the woods?" There was annoyance in the words.

"There are lots of woods," Freely began.

"I don't know any more than that," she muttered. "He's with the Haven outfit, wherever they're cutting. May be across the river if it isn't up Simonton way."

"Thank you, thank you very much," Freely said, withdrawing and pulling the dog with her, for Bess at sight of her old home seemed content to remain. "Come along," Freely ordered. "We're going to find your master if we have to walk to the town line."

Freely knew there was no lumbering being done on her side of the river. She crossed the bridge and, asking directions, soon found herself on the right road. There were deep ruts in the road where the wagons, laden with their heavy logs, had passed. Distantly she could hear the thudding sound as a team of choppers struck into a tree trunk. She walked more briskly. There was an excitement about it, this approach to a woodlot where work was in progress. She called to the dog to come along, telling Bess this was no time for scents that could be studied later. The road curved and bent up over the brow of a hill. Freely drew aside to let a wagon team pass her. She waved to the driver and he waved back.

"Is that Mr. Haven's outfit?" she called.

"Yup," he said. "Want to see anyone partic'ler?"

"Tom Slason. I've got his dog."

The horses were going on and the driver would not stop them for the difficulty in starting again with the heavy load, but he brandished his whip in the general direction of the forest lying at the bottom of the hill.

Freely looked and saw a shack at the edge of the cutting, and she took the gesture to imply that Tom Slason might be found in or near the shack. Suddenly the hound dog started pulling on the rope and whining. Freely saw a lumberman come out of the woods and go toward the shack. Then Bess barked—one loud high bark, as if joy had reached such an apex that it must find release in sound.

The man looked up. "Bess!" he shouted, as he saw the dog standing with the girl on the hill before him. He raised his arm and waved to them both.

Bess lunged forward. Freely loosened her hold on the rope

and the dog raced down the slope to throw herself against the man, huge paws on slouching shoulders, warm wet tongue over grizzled cheeks.

Freely ran down the hill, arriving breathless where the man and the dog were still embracing each other.

"By gory, miss, I never was so glad to see anybody before." Tom reached for his cap that the dog had pushed back on his head, and pulled it forward.

"Bess heard you all right that time," Freely said.

"By gory, you sure have fixed her up. Don't she look fat, too!"

"Suits her, doesn't it?"

"You bet!" Then dog and man went into another embrace.

"She can take a good bit more than you've been giving her, Tom."

"Well, she'll have all she can eat." Tom rubbed the dog's head roughly. "From now on it's going to be the best lap of the dish for Bess and the pickings for Tom. Isn't it, old girl?"

"Are you living on the job?"

"Yes, miss, and my shack's as nice a place as you could want, but it's been awful lonely. Now Bess is back it'll be like home."

Freely looked in the open door through which came the only light and air that the shack received. There was a bunk, and a three-legged chair was propped against the wall; on the stove stood a battered tin coffee pot. Just outside the door a broken piece of mirror was nailed onto the wall; beneath it was a bench and an upturned wash basin.

"She won't give you any more trouble," Freely said.

"I'm going to be awful good to her from now on."

Freely bent down to give Bess a stroke on the smooth head, a rub behind the long ears, and then she straightened up to go on her way.

"I'd like to do something for you, miss. I ought to owe you something for all you've done for Bess and me—"

Freely shook her head.

"Won't you—won't you have a cup of coffee, miss?"

"Thank you, I—" but, confronted by the cheerful expectancy in Tom Slason's face, the words of refusal would not come to her.

At a loss for words, it became one of those moments when she thought of Benedict, hearing his voice more than the sounds around her. If someone wants to do something for you, let it be done, he used to say. Don't ever stop the flow of goodness, no matter how it comes or from where. It's like the oceans lapping the world, holding the land in their embrace. Don't ever make a breakwall, no matter how small, to keep back that goodness. It's what the world lives in—receiving, giving, like the running in and flowing out of the tides.

Freely turned to Tom Slason and smiled swiftly, nodding her head.

"Thank you, miss. I'm that pleased about Bess that I want to do something to please you."

He went into the shack and Freely busied herself for a few moments picking a small bouquet of maple buds from the top of a tree that had been felled and had not yet been limbed.

Tom started scrounging for cups while Bess, with a sigh that came from the depth of her being, lowered herself across the doorstep and went into a wakeful sleep that would enable her to keep her eye on her master. Tom wiped his tin cup with the blue handkerchief he drew from his pocket, then he emptied soap out of his shaving mug and wiped it.

"I always keep some coffee handy," he said, filling the tin cup and offering it to Freely. Then he filled his shaving mug for himself. A can of milk stood on the floor and he poured some into both cups. A jam pot had sugar in it and Tom put a spoonful in each cup, stirring it around and then standing the spoon back in the sugar. "You never know who may be coming by."

Freely put her cup to her lips. It was hot, strong, and sweet, but it didn't taste like any coffee she had ever tasted before.

"Good, ain't it?" he asked.

She nodded.

"Mr. Haven came by here one day when I was having a cup. I offered him some but he wouldn't take none. He's too fine a gentleman."

"Is he nice to work for?"

"He pays us right. Ever seen where he lives?"

Freely shook her head.

"Well now," Tom brandished his mug, "when you go back to town you take left turning at top of hill. It's a mile longer into town that way but you'll go right by his house —and is it a sight! Haven Hall, they call it," he wagged his head and sucked his lips in. "Pretty fancy, I'd say. Have some more?"

"No, thank you. It was—" she reached in her mind after the right word for the strange brew— "it was very welcome." She leaned down to pat Bess, then she held out her hand to Tom. "Good-by," she said.

"Good-by, miss." He grinned. "Maybe Bess and I can do something for you one of these days."

Freely took the bouquet of maple buds in her hand and started off. Halfway up the hill she turned and waved.

Tom was still standing by his shack, the dog beside him. He lifted his hand with the mug in it and waved it carefully so as not to jeopardize the contents. "Now that's a lady, if I ever did see one," he murmured, then he looked down at Bess. "I guess you been living high, old girl."

Bess wagged her tail.

Freely climbed to the top of the hill where the roads

divided, but she had no desire to take the one to the left and see Philip Haven's home. She sat on the stone wall and looked back at the woodland to watch the work of the cutters, to listen to the sounds that were like a wild sort of symphony. There was the rhythmic thud of axes followed by a moment of silence when everything in her was tense and keyed to excitement, and then the shuddering crash as a tree fell; after it came a vast rippling as the rush of air caused by the fall passed through all the other trees that were anywhere near. Another brief silence, and after it the flapping of startled birds, disturbed in their woodland haunts and coming out of the trees in a frenzy of flight and bewilderment. Stillness again, and this time one that would not be broken until the thudding of axes proclaimed that another tree was destined to fall.

It was a stirring cycle and Freely relished watching it. Though lumbering was one of the activities of the countryside, she had seen little of it for none had been done in the Simonton woods while Benedict had been alive. She had often helped Benedict fell trees, limb them and work them into cordwood, but that had not had the undercurrent of urgency this had. She shivered with excitement as another tree fell.

A light gig was coming up the road. Freely turned to see who it was and Philip Haven reined his horse in to a stop.

"Well, of all people to see over here!" he exclaimed. "Whatever are you doing?"

"Watching," she said. "I like the sound of chopping. I like to see the trees fall."

"You won't have to come this far soon," he smiled at her. "We'll be cutting over near Simonton before many weeks."

"Yes, I expect you will."

He got out of the gig and stood holding his horse by the head, facing Freely who had swung her gaze around to him.

"You won't mind seeing the trees cut, will you, Freely?" he asked anxiously.

"No," she shook her head. "It just means another kind of life for them, doesn't it?"

He smiled with relief. "Some people get very sentimental."

She put back her head and laughed. "You can't live off the land the way we Simons have for generations and not know that everything has its use." She looked away as another tree crashed to earth, then she brought her gaze back to him and said, "It's good to be useful, whether you're a tree or a cow or a person."

"How are your animals?"

"I've just brought Tom Slason's Bess back to him. The fox cubs are being turned loose next week, I hope."

"Would you like me to drive you home?"

"Are you going to Simonton?"

"No, but—"

"Why should you go out of your way for me?"

"Because I like to talk to you."

"Oh." Slowly she swung her legs over the stone wall and came down to the road where he was standing. No one had ever said that to her before. She stood beside him, looking up at him. The sun was on her face. It lit up her hair and made her light-lashed amber eyes look pale. Philip wished she did not make him think so much of the fox he had been hunting and had missed in the Simonton woods.

"I think I like to talk with you too," she said simply.

He noticed her bouquet. "Those are pretty flowers. What are they?"

She laughed. "Oh, Philip, you don't recognize them and you're a forester! They're the flowers of the maple. I picked them from a big tree that had been felled." She moved them across her face. "Yesterday they were brushing the sky and today I can kiss them!" she exclaimed.

"I'm not really a forester, Freely. I just keep an eye on the cutting that's going on to be sure that the logs are being handled properly for the paper mill."

"Well, you're in the woods most of the time," she insisted stoutly.

"I never knew a maple tree had flowers."

"Everything has its blossoming," she said, looking at him and wondering how he could have lived so long and not known that.

He took her arm and led her around to the gig's left side; then, with an assistance Freely had no need of, he held her arm until she got in. The touch of his hand closing around her arm gave her a curious sensation, kin to the inner excitement she felt when a tree crashed in the forest. She had never known a man's gallantry, but she knew instinctively that it was for her as a woman to accept it. This must be what it is like to be a lovely lady, she thought, resting on a man's arm and letting him help you into your carriage. He looked at her and laid the reins in her lap.

"Will you?" he asked. "Prince is apt to be flighty."

She took up the reins, but her arms felt like water.

He walked around in front of the horse, moved the check rein, then leaped lightly into the gig, taking the reins from her. Freely moved over to her side of the seat. There would have been room between them for another person.

They trotted off, over the road rutted by the lumber wagons, across the bridge and through the town. When they turned up the long hill to Simonton, Philip drew the horse in to a walk.

"I thought you said you liked to talk with me," Freely reminded him when the familiar road made her feel more sure of herself.

"I do," he smiled at her, "but I like to be silent with you, too. Is that understandable?"

She nodded. "Sometimes my grandfather and I would go for hours without saying a word."

His eyes scanned the woods. "Every time I come over this road I look for the fox I shot one day."

"The fox you shot?" she asked, wondering what he meant.

"Yes, I was sure I hit it, but it got away from me. I followed it through the woods but I never found it."

"Oh," Freely said, conscious of the stiffening she felt within her.

The wheels of the gig crunched over the road. Prince flicked his tail and shook his head as a fly flew around him. The fly alighted on one of his ears. Philip took the whip and, with its tip, neatly dislodged the fly.

"Everything has its own secret place," Freely was saying. "I expect that's where the fox went to earth."

"I suppose that could be so," Philip replied, "for all animals do have their lairs."

"Not just animals," Freely said, turning to him and facing him for the first time since they had sat in the gig together. "People too. I have my secret place."

"Have you?"

She nodded. "It's deep in the woods and no one can find it but myself, and the creatures who let me share it with them. The trees are tall and the rocks are mossy and a spring makes music under the earth." She breathed deeply as she thought of the dell. "It's beautiful."

"Will you show it to me someday, Freely?"

She shook her head. "No. It's my secret. It wouldn't be a secret any more if I showed it to you." She turned away and looked up the road before them.

In another moment she had turned back to him. "Philip, when next you see Tom Slason will you have an eye to Bess? I think he missed her so while she was away that he's going to be good to her from now on."

"I'm not likely to see him except on pay day, but I'll have an eye out for Bess then."

"Tom says you treat your men well."

"He does, does he? When did you and Tom have so much to say to each other?"

"I stopped at his shack this afternoon with Bess. He gave me a cup of coffee."

Philip looked at her. "Oh, Freely, I—" Surprise and disapproval wrote themselves across his fine features. "That was hardly the thing for a young lady to do."

Freely stared at him. Her eyes widened. Her lips parted to speak, but no words came through them.

Philip was held by the clarity of her eyes. Looking into them he tried to adjust in his mind what Miss Mattie Emerson had said about her the night he returned the cat. And yet, if Freely could visit a lumberman in his shack as she so brazenly said she had done, it might be true. It might all be true. Philip looked away from her quickly. He directed his gaze across Prince's back, between his ears, up the road with the Simonton church rising before him in the distance. Impatiently he clucked his lips and slapped the reins. Prince broke into a trot with difficulty.

"Don't, please," Freely implored, putting her hand on his knee. "It's too much for a horse to trot up this hill. If you're in a hurry I'd rather get out and walk the rest of the way."

Philip drew Prince in to a walk again. They said nothing until they got to the house, then Philip handed her the reins and jumped out, going around to Freely's side. It was hard for Freely to restrain herself from getting out until she felt his arm under hers.

"Please, won't you come in?"

"Not today," he shook his head. "I must be back at the lot before the men stop work."

"Some other time?"

"Yes, perhaps."

He got in and slapped the reins over Prince's back. The startled animal leaped forward and trotted quickly off.

Freely stood still, one arm uplifted to wave if he turned his head at the brow of the hill, but he did not turn and look back at her. She went into the house.

Susannah called to her from the kitchen.

Freely went in and kissed her dutifully, as she always did on her return from school.

"Where have you been, Freely?"

"At the cutting on the other side of the river to return Tom Slason's dog. I've been watching them work, watching the trees come down. It was exciting."

Susannah felt a quiver within her. For a moment she thought it was her daughter Freelove standing before her and that there had been no years between. Freely's eyes looked large and fixed in their gaze and her thoughts were far from Simonton.

"Philip brought me home. He had the gig."

Freely was not her usual carefree self and Susannah was troubled. "What did he say to you, Freely, when he drove you up the hill?"

"Oh, Grandma," Freely exclaimed, "I was trying to act just like a real lady with Philip helping me into the gig, and sitting properly with my hands folded in my lap, but then he said I wasn't a lady because I'd been talking with Tom Slason."

Susannah smiled. "I shouldn't worry about being a lady, Freely. Benedict would tell you to be yourself."

Freely forced a smile. "He would, wouldn't he?"

Soon she had gathered together some food for her cubs and was crossing the green to the church. Susannah watched her go, thinking that the fox cubs would probably say more to her then than her own kind.

IO.

>>>>>>>>>>>>>>>>>>>>>><<<<<<<<<<<<<<<<<<<<<<

THE clear cool April days followed each other in a succession of changing beauty. Freely welcomed each one. The wind in the budded trees spoke clearly to her and the memory of Benedict's voice took up its refrain. Life is good, Freely, life is good, she could hear him saying. She knew it, yet during the cold of winter it was like a secret within her; now it was something that could be told. She could not remember when she had not loved the world around her, known first as seen through Benedict's eyes, then held by her own vision and cherished in her heart. But this year there was an added intensity to her feeling.

From the middle of April, the only calendar Freely and Susannah thought of was the returning birds.

"The song sparrows are here," Susannah announced one morning at breakfast.

The next day it was, "The red-winged blackbirds flew overhead on their way to the marshes."

Three days later, Freely came running across the green from the church. She stopped suddenly as a lilting melody came tumbling out of the oak beside the house. She looked up and saw—brilliant against the tree's red flowers—the plumage of a bluebird.

Breathless, she gave Susannah the news; but the look on

Susannah's face said that she had heard him long before Freely saw him.

"It is a sign," Freely announced. "Today I shall set the cubs loose."

"They're big enough to take care of themselves," Susannah replied.

"Philip wants me to tame them and make pets of them, but I'd rather they went back to their natural life."

"They were your care and it's for you to do what you think best. I've known a fox cub to be like a dog. Young Mark had one for a while. He was gentle and quick to learn whatever the boy would teach him."

Freely listened, but the only comment she made was, "I wouldn't want anyone to tame me and make a pet of me."

It was Saturday morning. After Freely finished her chores she went to the church with a sack. She fed the cubs some meat. They growled playfully and pawed at her for more.

"The next you get you'll find for yourselves," she told them. Then she put them in the sack and went down the road to the dell. Once there, she opened the sack and let them out.

They sniffed the earth, lifted their noses to the wind and shook themselves in their new freedom. They ran off a pace or two; they galloped in circles of joy around each other; then they raced back to where Freely had been standing. She had climbed up on to a granite boulder to watch them. Lifting a paw, one of the cubs scratched at the base of the boulder; the other sat back on his haunches and whimpered.

"The world is yours," Freely said to them. "All the part of it that you can run over, and you've a right to eat whatever you're clever enough to catch. Keep your wits about you so no one will catch you."

One of them barked questioningly and the other still scratched at the rock.

"Go on now. Try things out for yourselves," she coaxed. "You can always come back to the church if you get lonely or fearful. I'll leave the door so you can push it open. But I don't think you'll come back. You've got bold natures. Your legs are long and strong. Go along and see what the world is like."

They shook their heads as they often did when she talked to them, then they backed away from the rock and had one of their mock wrestling matches. Suddenly they stopped, as if neither had any more interest in a game. They began pawing at the earth, sniffing, rooting. One of them became tense and alert—ears pricked, every hair stiffening, long brush sweeping out taut. The other's nose went to the ground. Then they were off, racing through the woods, making low impatient sounds. Games had been forgotten. A scent had said something to them and they were responding.

Freely watched them until they went from her sight, but she could hear them much longer. Barking like dogs, the sound came from a distance, then drew nearer again as they wove back and forth on the scent. Freely smiled contentedly. She looked up through the lacework of budded branches at the blue April sky.

"Let them lead their lives free of fear," she said, "doing what's right for them to do."

She would miss her noisy rowdy charges with their appetites that grew with the days, but she was glad that they had gone off into their own world. Sighing happily, she stretched out on the rock and let the beauty of her secret place possess her.

Overhead the trees were waving, gracefully brushing their crowns of small new leaves against the sky. All around her were noble masses of gray boulders, some of them carpeted with wide-leaved, strong-scented arbutus just coming into flower. From the damp leaves of last year's foliage that matted

the ground, fern fronds were thrusting. So distant now that
it had gone altogether was the barking of the foxes, but near
and clear was the soughing of the wind and the bubbling of
the spring and the calling of birds.

Freely flattened out on the rock. It would be nice if Philip
came along, she thought, not with a gun in his hand looking for something to kill, not with a hatchet looking at the
trees to mark them for his choppers, but with his eyes wide
open to see what could be seen in the woodland, and his ears
quick to hear the ageless music. Then she told herself she was
glad he was not there. If he were with her, she would be aware
of him and not of the world, and on that April day all she
asked was to have the world—to hold it in her eyes and fold
it in her heart. She closed her eyes and let the dreaminess of
the day surround her. Miles away, it seemed, she heard one
of the foxes barking and then the other joining in. Like young
things suddenly come into their heritage, there was not only
joy and freedom in their bark but triumph.

When Freely started for home the sun was westerly and the
sky was beginning to gray over. The brilliance of the red
maples and the green pines against the darkening sky was
startling. The far rim of mountains was purple. There was
rain in such sharpness of color, she thought, glad that the
foxes had had good hunting. She did not follow the trail up
the hill but left the dell at the place where the birch stood
sentinel. She stopped to examine the wound that had been
made by a knife on the day she had found the vixen. She
moved her fingers over it. It was no longer soft and oozing
sap. It had begun to heal, but it would always bear the scar
of someone's carelessness or curiosity. She sighed, sorrowful
that the flawless white bark of her tree should be marked. Her
leg that had been grazed by a bullet had healed, but it would
always be marked. She stroked the tree tenderly. They had
something between them. They both bore scars.

When Freely arrived in Susannah's kitchen ravenously hungry, with a radiant face and eyes shining as if they had witnessed miracles, Susannah never found it necessary to ask where she had been. There was only one place that sent Freely back to the world with a look as if she had stood before the gates of heaven. Susannah had not the slightest idea where the dell was, nor did she want to know. The girl had found it for herself when little more than a child and Susannah had never asked to see it. One respected another's secret; a secret place was no different.

"Philip Haven called today," Susannah said casually.

"He did? What for?"

"He said it was such a fine day he wondered if you wouldn't like to go for a walk in the woods."

"I was in the woods."

"I told him that. I said you were setting the fox cubs loose. It's a pity you missed him."

"I had much more fun alone," Freely replied, sitting down at the table before the meal Susannah had put out for them.

Susannah sat down opposite her. "Freely," she said, "you can't always live your life alone."

"Why?"

"Because—" Susannah began, finding the girl's questioning always disarming, "life is lived in relation to others. I can't explain it any more than that."

"Some people are hermits."

"True," Susannah agreed. "Some people set themselves apart from the world deliberately or by vocation, but I don't believe you are that kind of person."

Freely felt uneasy. For so many years life had been simple; now it seemed she was having to think of it in terms other than her own enjoyment.

That evening a cold rain started falling. By midnight it

turned to a light snow. When Freely looked out the next morning she saw the countryside that had gone forward into spring during the past week had overnight gone back to winter. The daffodils in Susannah's garden were bowed under a wet white blanket. Birds were scratching places in the snow in search of food. Spears of grass stuck up through the snow like valiant swords doing battle with the invader. But it was Sunday morning and whatever its weather Freely greeted with joy the long day on the hill. She went to the church to look for footprints, but the foxes had felt no pressure of loneliness to send them back to the place where they had been havened.

Long before midmorning the sun was shining clear and the snow had begun to disappear. The earth absorbed it readily, drinking deep of the welcome dispensation of moisture that had come during the night. Soon only the distant mountains bore evidence of the April snow. Caps of glistening white shone on their heights and runnels of white ran down their sides. The countryside went back to green again, to earth brown, to bud red, but all day the mountains stood capped and gowned in silver. Alone, they bore the memory of a shimmering experience that had lain on all the land; a memory that was not to be tarnished by forgetfulness or dimmed by swift passage, but brightly held by those who reared themselves above the level of the land, facing the challenge of winds and the rough onslaught of weather.

Swallows were whirling through the air in their ecstasy at having reached the hilltop again when Freely and Susannah crossed the green to have their Sunday morning service in the church. Freely had filled a large stone crock with the flowers of the maple, branches trailing long green catkins and boughs with tiny leaves. The windows of the church were wide open. Sunshine and April breezes poured in as part of the service. Susannah read from the Bible. Freely played the organ and sang. Through the open windows a chorus of birds could be heard; then another voice joined the singers in the church.

When Freely heard the sound of a man singing, such an upsurge of joy went through her that it was all she could do to keep pumping and playing, her eyes on the music, her hands on the keys. It was as if Benedict were with them again; but Benedict's voice had been deep and resonant and so warm with love that Freely used to feel that the timbers of the church should get down on their knees before him. This new voice was not like Benedict's. It was a young voice, sure of itself yet not at all sure of the words of the hymn. When the last chord was played, Freely left the organ and sat in the front pew beside Philip Haven while Susannah read the blessing. Freely did not raise her eyes, but her lips were trembling with smiles. So happy she was to have him in Benedict's church on that glistening morning that she forgot that at their last meeting their parting had been strained by his disapproval and her perplexity.

Outside, in the sunshine that held the church in a warmth it had not known since the summer, Philip apologized for being late.

"The workers in the vineyard got the same wages whether they came late or early," Susannah replied.

"I'm glad you came, Philip," Freely said. "The world is so beautiful today that everyone ought to see it."

"It wasn't for ourselves then that I put that fat rooster in the oven," Susannah commented. "Freely's always hungry, but I've no doubt you'll do well by it, Philip, after your walk up the hill."

"No horse today?" Freely asked.

Philip shook his head. "I'm letting Prince have Sunday off."

Laughing and talking together, they crossed the green to the house. Soon they were sitting around the kitchen table and what Susannah had not already at hand she brought from her stores.

The meal was one that Philip thought could well rank with Thanksgiving, and he did justice to it. It filled Susannah with pleasure to be satisfying a man's hunger again. After dinner, Philip and Freely cleared the table and washed the dishes, while Susannah sat in her rocker and told them stories of Simonton.

"Mark Simon and his sons raised everything that they wore except cotton, everything that they ate and drank except tea and spices and white sugar. Almost anything that grew was cooked for greens—milkweed, horseradish, marsh marigold, dandelions, and parsley. And they were thrifty! A little girl who threw her apple core in the stove would have been rebuked and told that it should have gone to the pigs. Some of the farmers even raised their own flax, spun it and wove it into linens for their tables, their towels, and their bedding. Wool from the sheep that grazed the hill pastures was spun and woven or knitted into necessary warm articles of clothing. Tallow candles gave all the light that was needed and women saved all their scraps of cloth to be cut into different shapes and pieced into their quilts."

"But their shoes, surely they couldn't make those on the hill!" Philip exclaimed.

"Indeed, they did!" Susannah replied stoutly. "Boots and shoes were made from the hides of their cattle and a cobbler would make his rounds annually just for that purpose."

"Tell Philip about the pies, Grandma," Freely urged.

"Pies, indeed! Nowadays we bake three or four and think we've done a mite of work. In the great days of the hill it was nothing to bake thirty pies at a time and they were none too many for a husky family. One day a week would be set aside for such baking and the pies would be stored in the cool back pantry until they were needed."

"When did they eat them all?" Philip asked.

"When? Three times a day—of fruit and berries, of mincemeat or vegetables, for anything that was grown or raised or found could be used as a filler. Ah, I tell you, pantry shelves in those days were a heartening sight with their jars of milk covered with thick yellow cream, their cheeses and pies. Pumpkins would be sliced, as apples were, and hung in festoons around the kitchen to dry. And every kitchen had a small loom set up in it on which a piece of carpeting would be in the making and at which any member of the family could sit when he had a mind to busy his hands. And the pieces of the loom were always brightly colored for they got their dyes from the herbs in the gardens and the bark of their trees."

"Was there anything they couldn't make?" Philip asked, fascinated by Susannah's tales.

"Very little," Susannah said, proud of the days that though they were gone were a part of her. "Soap was one of the hardest tasks, I can well remember, but there was always plenty of it at hand. It was made from wood ashes in the spring of the year. The ashes would be dumped into barrels and these were mounted high enough so a caldron could be placed beneath into which would drop the lye produced by pouring water onto the ashes. The water filtered down and came into the caldron in dark brown streams, biting and penetrating. As soon as the lye was run out, all the grease that had accumulated from the cooking and the table was added to it, then it was boiled for hours over an outside fire until it made soft soap. It was the only soap we had for many years and it was hard on colors, but it got things clean."

Philip had listened fascinated by Susannah's tales of earlier days. He looked around her kitchen with even greater respect, then his eyes strayed out the window to take in all they could of the settlement that was Simonton; yet it was not a place, he reminded himself, so much as a way of life.

"Neither church nor house has ever been locked, Philip," Susannah went on, "and you can see for yourself that no door has a bolt on it. Mark Simon made it that way at the first and his spirit is still strong on the hill."

"He must have trusted his fellows," Philip replied.

"It wasn't that, Philip. It was because he wanted people to feel welcome."

"What if someone walked in that he didn't know?"

"Mark Simon said that was why he left the door unlocked so such a one could come in. He said he'd feel badly if any of his friends came to the door and found it locked. He wanted them to feel free, to come in, to sit by the fire and read his books or help themselves to something to eat if they were hungry."

"What if someone came who wasn't one of his friends?"

Susannah stopped rocking for a moment and sat forward in her chair. "He didn't know any such a one, Philip," she said. Then she leaned back and resumed her rocking.

After the dishes had been put away, Philip and Freely went to the woods to look for wild flowers and Susannah went to her garden. It was too early to plant yet, she thought, but not too early to plan where her seeds would go. She sat down on the bench Benedict had made under the apple tree, the bench where she often brought her sewing or a mess of peas to shell; and sometimes she went there to sit with folded hands and enjoy her thoughts. It was a wind-washed day and the sun was warm. Daffodils were nodding gaily. Johnny-jump-ups with velvet-smooth petals and small questioning faces were appearing all over the garden. Susannah's eyes dwelt on some daphne growing near the doorstep; demure of blossom and liberal of fragrance, it was the oldest greeter of spring in the garden. Mark Simon's wife, the first Freelove to live on the hill, had brought it with her and planted it with her own hands. It had never been disturbed, though slips had been taken from it by others who had left the hill.

Her eyes roamed to the herb patch and lingered on the green spears thrusting through the earth. She breathed deeply, almost able to smell the scents that would soon be coming in the hot summer sun from basil and rosemary, sweet marjoram and thyme. Slowly, delighting in all she saw whether it was brown earth or beginning green, her eyes traveled around the garden. She found an empty spot and it pleased her. That was where she would plant some lobelia, she thought. Lobelia: blue as the waves she had once watched from a ship's prow in the days when she had known where her father's ship was taking her but had not known where her own life would take her. Lobelia: for in the small blossoms of the almost scentless flower she found a memory of the sea which had nursed her early thoughts and sent them far faring. In the movement of the blossoms with the wind, she saw the movement of the waves in the wind, and beyond them the drawing of tides when there was no wind.

Lifting her eyes from the patch of earth to the lacework of leaves overhead, she saw a crow flapping idly across the sky; but at that moment it was not apple branches through which she looked, or a crow that she saw. She was looking up through the masts and the neat lines of rigging as she had done so often and it was a lone gull she was seeing. The gull banked with the wind and swerved, then catching the wind in his wings he made use of it; swerving again, he moved his wings as if he would go on his own power until such time as he chose to use the wind again. The wings became motionless and the gull glided down a current of air until he met the upcurve of a wave. With an exultant laugh, he settled in the trough of the wave. His laugh made a rift in the silence and through it the sound of bells could be heard as the ship sailed into port, buoys lining its way through the channel.

Susannah gave herself a little shake as one will when coming out of a dream, wondering why she had been thinking of ships and seabirds when she had meant to plan her garden. But beyond the blue margins of memory, where the sea rolled in lovely rhythm, stood Benedict, for the end of all voyages had been when she had met him. Susannah got up from her bench under the apple tree and walked about her garden. When she got back to the house and before she went inside, so strong had memory been, she half expected to see sea foam curling away from the doorstep where the daphne bloomed.

That night Freely said to Susannah, "Philip wants me to meet his mother sometime."

"Does he?"

"He says she may not like me at first."

"And what did you say?"

"I said that I thought I would like her just because she was his mother."

Susannah saw the gull resting on the wind, bending itself to the strongest current.

"Mark Simon's spirit is still strong on the hill and in his children," Susannah remarked, but the words had a familiar ring as if she had used them before that day. She looked at Freely and smiled, asking the indulgence of youth for the forgetfulness of age.

Freely leaned over and kissed her quickly, then she took her candle and went up the stairs to bed.

II.

➤➤➤➤➤➤➤➤➤➤➤➤➤➤➤➤➤➤➤➤➤➤➤◄◄◄◄◄◄◄◄◄◄◄◄◄◄◄◄◄◄◄◄◄◄◄

THERE was an urgent knocking at the schoolhouse door. Miss Carey, who presided over the lower grades, thought that Miss Anderson would answer it; but Miss Anderson, deep in ancient history, left it for Miss Carey. The knocking continued. Both teachers pushed their chairs back from their desks at the same time and left their rooms to meet in the hall.

"I thought you would go to the door," Miss Carey explained.

"Since I haven't, why don't you go?" replied Miss Anderson, who never liked to be disturbed, finding it too difficult to go on with her class from where she had left off.

Miss Carey opened the door.

"May I see Freely Simon?" a young man standing on the top step asked.

"During school hours!" Miss Carey exclaimed in mild horror. "Why, she is in class now."

"It's very important."

"She isn't in my room but I'll ask her teacher if she could be released. Just a moment."

Miss Anderson had not returned to her classroom for curiosity had kept her within earshot of the door. She came toward the door quickly, recognizing the caller.

"What do you want to see Freely for, Mr. Haven? Is anything wrong at her home?"

"No, not so far as I know, but there's an animal in distress at one of my woodlots and—"

Miss Anderson interrupted, "Is there no veterinarian you could call on?"

"None nearer than Concord and it's urgent."

"It would be very unusual to excuse her now, Mr. Haven. Why, the afternoon session has only just begun. But perhaps I could arrange it. Let me see, I might give her some extra homework to do and—"

"Could you possibly let her off right away?" Philip asked, trying to sound unhurried though impatience ran like a fire within him.

Then Miss Anderson grasped the need and entered into the spirit of the occasion. "Yes, of course, I'll get her immediately." She turned and went back to her classroom.

The pupils who had seized the free moment and were using it to their various advantages, subsided when Miss Anderson returned. Those who had left their desks hurried back to them and those who were chatting volubly became silent; but Miss Anderson was too full of her mission to observe the flagrant lack of discipline.

"Freely Simon," she said, "you may be excused."

Freely looked up from the book lying open on her desk. She rather liked ancient history and she saw no particular reason why she should be deprived of it. Miss Anderson met her surprised glance.

"Something has happened to an animal at Mr. Haven's woodlot. They need your help." Miss Anderson smiled proudly at this last-year pupil of hers who was already being demanded by the world and, as Freely's teacher of several years, she was ready to take due claim for any unusual ability that Freely might display.

"Oh!" Freely exclaimed. Reaching quickly under her desk for her tin lunch box, she hurried from the room too over-whelmed to say anything to her friends or teacher who watched her with admiration and a tinge of envy.

Philip took her lunch box from her. "I've got the gig, Freely. We'll be there in no time." He smiled, feeling that everything would be all right now that Freely had appeared.

Freely ran down the steps and leaped into the gig without waiting for Philip's arm. Philip got in beside her and took up the reins. Prince started off.

"What is it?" Freely asked, her face pale with excitement and her hands clasped in her lap as if to contain herself.

"It's a fawn, Freely, not more than a day old. One of the men told me about it a few minutes ago. He saw the doe forcing it out of the woods and into the clearing where the men are working."

"But why, why?"

"The fawn kept trying to go back to the doe, but the doe kept swinging around and kicking it away from her. The men wanted to get hold of the fawn but as soon as they got anywhere near it the little fellow would try to run back to his mother. They didn't want it to get hurt by her heels or lost in the woods so they stopped trying to catch it. Then Tom Slason said that you'd know what to do so I came and got you."

"Oh, Philip, I'm so glad you came. I'm so glad Miss Anderson let me go. But what a strange thing for a mother to do with her baby!" Freely drew her brows together, puzzled.

They turned the corner and clattered over the bridge and up the rutted road, Philip guiding Prince skillfully over the rough surface. They turned into the road of the wood and approached the clearing. When they could go no farther, Philip reined the horse in. Freely was out of the gig before the wheels had stopped turning. She ran toward the men in the clearing.

There they stood, a half dozen brawny woodsmen and a fawn on wambly legs not twenty feet from them where the forest rose dark and green. The fawn was bleating pitifully, sounding like a lamb or a calf or any young thing so small that only its mother could know what it wanted. Swinging on its shaky legs, the fawn turned and started back to the woods; then, remembering that only flailing hoofs awaited there, it turned uncertainly back toward the men.

Freely stood by the circle of men. Philip, after he had tied Prince to a tree, came up behind her.

"Why won't its mother have it?" Freely asked, not expecting an answer but giving herself time to think as she waited for one.

Tom Slason turned toward her. "It's got a nose full of porcupine quills, that's why."

"Oh, poor thing!" Freely cried. Then her heart went out not to the bewildered infant but to the mother who, helpless herself, had been trying to drive her fawn to those who might help it.

"If we could just get our hands on it," Slason said, "we might be able to pull them out."

"No, no, Tom," Freely implored. "That's just what we mustn't do. If it gets our smell on it the mother will never own it again." She turned to Philip. "Have you a horse blanket? fly sheet? anything? The less used the better."

"Yes, I think so." He turned and ran to the gig, opening the trap at the back.

"Tom," Freely looked into the woodsman's bearded face, "we'll need pliers or pinchers, something that will get a grip and pull those quills out. Have you got any in your shack?"

"Should have, miss. Have most every tool we need."

"Get them, will you? Where's Bess?"

"In the shack. She'd be glad to see you, I wager."

"Don't let her out whatever you do, not until this little fellow gets away safely."

"Here you are, Freely." Philip held out a blue and white check fly sheet. As he shook it from its folds a monogrammed H came into view.

"That's very handsome, Philip. It will do beautifully." Speaking clearly and quietly without any sense of urgency, Freely explained to Philip that she wanted to approach the fawn from the rear and cover him with the sheet, leaving just his head uncovered.

Philip followed Freely and they approached the fawn. Hearing them, it started to run but the six woodsmen closed their line in front of him and blocked his way. By the time the fawn had made up its mind to run in another direction, Philip and Freely had thrown the sheet over it.

Tom went up to Freely with a pair of pliers. "Just took a mite of time to fill my coffee pot, miss. Thought you might all be needing something when this is over."

"Thanks, Tom." Freely took the pliers. "Hold the fawn's legs, Philip, hold him no matter how he struggles, but try not to touch him anywhere. Let your hands be on the sheet."

"I'll hold him, Freely."

Freely slipped her arm around the fawn's neck, over the sheet, to hold his head still; then she got one of the quills between the pliers. With a swift pull, she drew it out. The fawn struggled from surprise and pain, but Philip held it firmly.

Freely drew out twenty quills, each one a minor agony to the fawn. The small black nose was bleeding from the barbs and the large eyes were glazed and beseeching. Freely looked carefully over the whole head, prying open the jaw with the pliers to be sure no quills had got in the mouth. Keenly her eyes searched until she was certain that there were no more to remove.

"You've got 'em all, miss," Tom said, who had been standing by.

"That's good," Freely sighed. "It's all right, Philip," she said as she dropped her arm from around the neck and stood away from the fawn. "Now you can let him go."

Philip loosed his hold on the legs. He jerked the fly sheet off and set the fawn free.

The fawn shook its head and stamped its feet. It lifted its legs one after the other as if to try the ground. Then, with a sound as different from its former bleating as the laughter of a child to its sobbing, it scampered off into the woods. Breathless, the six woodsmen, Philip Haven, and the girl waited to see if it would come back. After a moment or two Freely nodded as if she felt sure that all was well and walked over to a tree that had been felled that morning. She sat down on it, wiping her hot face and pushing her hair back. Tom Slason came up with his coffee pot and an assemblage of mugs, enough for them all.

"Listen!" Freely exclaimed.

There was a sound coming from the woods that meant only one thing: mother and child had met again and the one was accepting the other.

"He's getting what he wants now," one of the choppers said.

"Let him have it," another commented. "I'd rather have Tom's coffee."

"He'd have made an awful nice pet for you, miss," Slason said, handing Freely a cup of coffee.

Freely took the tin mug and shook her head. "His life is in the woods, Tom. That's where he'll be happy."

An hour later, Philip drove Freely up the hill to Simonton. They had just passed the white birch when Freely put her hand on Philip's knee and asked him to stop.

"Look, there!" she cried. She was out of the gig in an instant. "It's the first trillium," she said, a warmth of welcome in her voice.

It was growing at the side of the road, tall stemmed, its flower of three garnet red petals rising from a collar of three wide-whorled leaves. Freely knelt down beside it, content to fill her eyes with its presence.

Philip nodded. "It's really spring when you see trilliums," he said. Then his eye ran up the birch. "That's a fine tree. I put my mark on it one day so none of my men would ever touch it."

Freely sat back on her feet. "Oh, so you're the one who—" she stopped herself quickly.

"You've seen my mark?" he asked.

"Yes."

"Someday I'll tell you why I don't want anything to happen to that tree."

"Tell me now."

He looked down at her, sitting in the moss and leaves, one hand curled lightly around the trillium's stalk. He shook his head. "Not now."

Freely cocked her head at the sound of thrushes singing in the woods beyond the white tree. She got up from the ground.

"Thank you, Philip, for bringing me this far. I'm going to walk the rest of the way home through the woods."

"Freely," he said, "please—" but before he could urge her to stay she had left him.

"Good-by," she called back over her shoulder, waving her hand gaily.

He watched her go over the stone wall, making her way in and out among the trees, then disappearing from view as if the secret fastness of the forest had made her its own. Suddenly Philip felt an acute sense of loneliness. He wanted to be with her, walking through the woods, listening to the thrushes. He didn't want to go back to Millville alone. He stood still, listening, hoping; but even her footfalls had faded into the silence of the forest. He went back to the gig and put his hand on Prince's bridle, guiding the horse around until they faced the way they had come. Then he got onto the seat and took up the reins.

The thrushes in their melodious singing kept him company all the way down the hill. He let his eyes range, this time not traveling up the trees with businesslike intent but everywhere. The countryside was like a young thing, tender and trusting. Wherever he looked there were small leaves, small upthrustings, green beginnings. Freely had disappeared into the woods the way the fawn had, but she had turned back to wave to him.

Freely forgot everything—her schoolwork, the fawn, the pleasant joy in Philip's companionship—when she stood in the dell. Since the foliage had come out, it was more secret and sequestered than it had been even a few days ago. Pushing low-hanging branches aside, she entered it as if it were a small green room. She stood in it, breathing deeply.

Fern fronds that had been uncurling as the days advanced now reached high enough to touch her finger tips as she walked. Her gaze ran up the trunks of the trees that grew among the boulders. They were such straight trunks and they wore such leafy crowns, yet their foliage was still a dainty lacework and through it the blue of the sky was still visible and birds could be seen among their branches. She watched them, for the time would soon come when a curtain of green would hide their busy intentions and domestic doings. Framing the dell was a circle of hemlocks, dark masses tipped with bright new green. The ground was damp and mossy, covered with trailing pine and checkerberry, still carpeted with last year's leaves. Freely smiled widely for, where the ground began its gentle slope upward, waving pink caught her eye.

"So, you've come too!" she cried ecstatically.

And, in the light breeze, the lady's-slippers dotting the rise waved in greeting.

This was her reward, Freely thought, for not having been to the dell for a few days—these wide-open arms of spring with treasures spread before her.

She stood on the trail that led to the spring and then went on up the hill. Lovely in its hidden purpose, it was too narrow for the foot of man to tread; but, after Freely had discovered it, she had walked over it fox fashion, one foot before the other. So she had become one of the swift shy procession of creatures who used it—fox, deer, rabbit, finding their way from the spring to the crest of the hill.

Under its wide flat slab of rock the water was bubbling. Kneeling down beside it, Freely looked under the rock into the mossy cavern where the water gathered to form a tiny pool. She drew her hand across the water, kneeling lower to press her lips to it. She could taste the coolness from the depth of the earth and the forest freshness. From the wet black mire near the spring, arum lilies grew and ferns waved.

Freely knelt back. She rooted her fingers into the soil and broke off a piece of goldthread which she put between her teeth and sucked, relishing the flavor. At first, the sound of the water trickling under the rock and bubbling away was all that she heard; that and the light swaying of wind in the leaves. Then her ears began to pick up forest sounds. A thrush sang out in the trees above her and, to Freely, his song was the paean of praise her own heart was singing. Distantly, in the far reaches of the forest, the clear piercing call of the white-throated sparrow sounded, coming through the stillness and under the vaulted arches of the trees. So far distant that it was almost lost, she heard a fox barking and smiled to herself at the sound. The remoteness, the separateness of winter had gone. The world was being taken over by nature.

Freely felt almost like an intruder in it, except that it was her world too.

She dipped her hand into the pool of water and cupped some of it to her lips, then she dipped up another handful and tossed it wide. She thought of the story she had been told of Mark Simon when he found the spring on the hilltop and how he had christened his town that day; she thought of the story Benedict had told her of how he had christened her at that same spring, calling her Freelove that she might give her love freely all the days of her life.

She could almost hear the silvery tones of Benedict's voice as he told her how much there was to love. Born a New Englander, he had said, she was the inheritor of a tradition of living, but it was the world that lay before her, not a portion but the whole.

"Your life may take you far beyond the hilltop, little Freely," he had said to her one day. "But if you can remember that you once looked from a hill and if you can hold within you that height of sky and reach of horizon, you'll never be narrowed or confined."

Freely looked around her, hoping the hill would not become a symbol in her life but that she would have it always. "Thank You, thank You," she breathed. There was so much that was good that those words were often her only prayer, but she never doubted that they would be heard since the One to whom she prayed was so near.

She leaned back against the maple that grew by the spring and closed her eyes. Her being was flooded with happiness and her thoughts led her by gentle progress to Philip. Never had she wanted to show the dell to anyone, but now quite unaccountably she wanted to show it to him, to enjoy it with him. Beautiful as it was, it would be more beautiful if he were there to share it with her. A shiver of joy ran through her when she thought of his seeing it. Perhaps she would show it

115

to him tomorrow. No, not tomorrow. She remembered that he had said he was going to Boston and would not be home until the end of the week.

His words then had meant less than the breeze across her face, but now recalled they brought a sharp sense of loss. She would miss him while he was in Boston. But it would not be long, she told herself, and as soon as he came back she would bring him to the dell. It would have to be soon, for she wanted him to see it while the lady's-slippers danced on the forest floor and the arum lilies stood in dignity by the spring. In the silence Freely loved and in which she could hear her own heart speak she knew that it was right to bring Philip to the dell. To share her secret with him would only increase its value to herself.

She rose and glanced around her saying, as she always did, her brief good-by; then she went quickly up the trail. When she came out on the green she stood still for a moment to watch the swallows. They were swooping and courting in midair, swirling in circles of ecstatic joy, circling apart then swinging close, as if they wanted to fly wide and far for the delight they had in coming together again.

12.

THERE was a magic to the first of May when Freely greeted the day. A veil of warm, gently falling rain still cloaked the world and long before dawn Freely was aware of the wood thrushes singing through it. She looked from her window and saw that the clouds were lifting on the mountains. It will be fair later on, she thought to herself. She watched the swallows dipping and soaring, gliding through the rain then lining up in a row on the ridgepole of the church, their sleek feathers shining even though there was no sun to gleam on them. Freely wondered if they were discussing the rain or making plans for the day, or whether it was just their immense joy in life that filled them with such throaty chuckling and gurgling chatter. Then, as swiftly as they had alighted, all took wing again, soaring high and flying beyond the range of her eye. She sighed deeply with the joy she felt such a part of, dressed hastily, and went out to the woods to gather flowers for a May basket for Susannah.

The yellow and russet and red of the trees had almost all gone now and a canopy of green arched overhead, but the leaves were still small. They had opened like pleated umbrellas to shed the morning's rain and they were ready to open yet more when the sun came out to shield the earth from its glare. A short distance before Freely on the path a hare was washing its face, rubbing its paws around trembling nostrils, back of long ears. Freely waited until the hare had completed its morning toilet and hopped off into the woods before she resumed her way. A hawk in silent flight skimmed low through the trees, gliding on outstretched wings with eyes intent on the forest floor for any hapless small creature. Salamanders were scuttling around in the moss. Freely picked one up and stroked it, then set it down again.

She filled her basket with moss, tucking white and pale purple violets in among the moss with here and there one of the gay pink babies'-toes. She found some bloodroot with its wide leaves and small white flowers, but she did not pick any. The flowers would open slowly and their gold centers would face the sun all day; near evening the white petals would fold inward like hands in prayer. Freely did not want to disturb the little nuns of the woods at their devotions, so she went on. She stopped at the crabapple tree that stood near the Dexters' house to pick one of its buds for her basket. How old the tree was, Freely thought, almost as old as the settlement on the hill. It was twisted in its trunk, knotted and gnarled, but spring after spring it foamed with blossom, summer after summer it bowed under a weight of small tart apples. A secret of agelessness dwelt within it, a secret that it kept well through the winter but that with the coming of spring it could contain no longer. The eternal loveliness at the heart of things was the source from which its roots were nourished. That was its secret, Freely thought, and it was not content to tell it in beauty alone but went on to tell it in use.

Susannah smiled with pleasure at the sight of the May basket. Always, since she had lived on the hill, there had been some child to bring one to her door. Freely, this morning, looked as young as the youngest child that had ever run barefoot on the hill, as young as everything else this first day of May. Her eyes were shining. Rain drops sparkled in her hair. She looked taller, as if she stood tiptoe to the world.

"Happy May Day!" she cried exultantly.

"Happy, happy month of May!" Susannah replied, taking the basket from Freely's hands.

"Oh, I shall be home early this afternoon," Freely sang out. "There is so much I want to see."

"Nothing but what you haven't seen all the years of your life," Susannah commented. "But I expect you'll feel the same all the years before you."

Freely nodded, but her capacity for appreciation was now turned to the generous breakfast Susannah had set before her and which Susannah thought the girl should have before she started off to school.

"John Wheelman said he would come up the first fine day to spade the garden for us," Susannah said.

"Good. Then we can plant soon. Perhaps today, Grandma, for it will be fine by midmorning if not sooner. The clouds are lifting and you can tell by the way the birds are singing that it isn't going to be rainy long."

When Freely left for school Susannah stood, as she always did, on the doorstone to wave her good-by. Freely ran across the green, for the quick pulsation of the day was racing through her. Before the road dipped she turned to wave—a gay fling of her hand, a toss of her head, and then she was gone. Susannah felt her heart beat quickly. She wanted Freely always to be happy and yet life did strange things to people, laid such unpredictable snares. She did not want Freely to be caught in any snare, and yet if she ever were there was never anything an older person could do but keep on loving. Benedict had told her time and again not to fear for Freely, that though something in the girl was capable of soaring like a swallow in flight, she had her feet well grounded. "There may be a glint from the sun in her eyes but her feet love the feel of the earth," he used to say, and the combination pleased him.

Susannah put her hand on the door, glad of its nearness in the sudden weakness that had come over her. Holding onto the door first and then using the wall as a support, she made her way back to a chair in the kitchen and then sat down heavily, holding her hands to her heart. The kitchen clock struck eight mellow, remindful, unhurried strokes. It would be hours before Freely would be home, Susannah thought. Four o'clock at the very earliest. She sighed. Usually she loved the day with its pattern of duties apportioned neatly in packets of time, but today the hours seemed endless and the tasks so burdensome that she wondered how she would get them done. She put her head back and closed her eyes. Dan Satturlee would be along with the mail sometime before noon and there was always the chance that a traveler over one of the roads would stop in to ask directions or for a bit of sociability. Susannah hoped someone would come by, for the day that had started out brightly was yawning with loneliness.

Outside she could hear birds singing, the dripping of rain drops slowly ceasing, and far away in the forest the thud of a woodsman's ax. A sense of peace came over Susannah. Through the open window a breeze drifted, lightly laden with the scent of crabapple blossoms. She breathed deeply. Slowly she got up from her chair and began to move into the day. There were seeds to be sorted for planting, a rhubarb pie to be made for supper. She would do what came to her hand and needed to be done. By such ways did strength come back, she thought—if one waited, if one was still—strength and courage to do the things life had given one to do. She smiled as she remembered that was what Benedict had always said.

There was no inducement that could have made Freely linger in the town that afternoon and to her relief no duties were given her that would hinder her home-going. By three thirty she was on the road up the hill, swinging her lunch box in her hand and taking in all over again the sights that had given her pleasure on the way down that morning, in the misty aftermath of rain, and that now were enhanced by the golden encasement of sunshine—the shad in bloom along a brook, the reddish color in the woods that had almost disappeared before the slow tide of green, the plumes on the beech trees that were unfurling slowly.

In the distance she could hear the hollow sound of axes. She stopped for a moment to see if she could locate from where the sound was coming. It was so steady, so even, that it might have been the heartbeat of the woods, yet it was not the life of the trees she was hearing but their death. The thudding ceased. She waited for the crash. It came, and she looked skyward to see the bevy of startled birds that rocketed from the forest in the wake of a fallen tree.

But they haven't started their families yet, she thought, for though the beginnings of nests might lie scattered on the floor of the woods, no broken eggs would be among the debris. The sound was coming from the Simonton woods, she decided, thinking that Philip's choppers must have begun on the trees Susannah had sold. Freely quickened her pace. Perhaps Philip was with them. She could see him and after the men had quit work she could take him to the dell and show him its beauties.

The air was sweet with the smell of resin and sap, and the sound of the chopping grew louder. Coming down the road toward her was a team of horses dragging a scoot with a load of logs. She hailed the man as he approached her. He recognized her as the girl who had helped the fawn and he pulled in his team to a stop.

"Nice view we're opening up for you folks on the hill," he said cheerfully.

"That's good," Freely smiled. "Where are you working?"

"Up the road a few rods and in from the stone wall. We had to open the wall to get the logs out but we'll build it up again for you."

"Is Mr. Haven there?"

"No, miss, he's been away this week. Foreman says he may be back tonight. You like to walk in the woods, miss?"

Freely nodded.

"You'll find it a lot nicer when we get these big trees out of the way. You'll be able to see where you're going."

There was another silence followed by a shuddering crash and a flapping of startled birds.

The woodsman slapped the reins over the horses' backs. "Giddyup there," he called out. He waved his cap to Freely. "Guess I better get along, miss. They'll have another load ready for me before I'm back."

Freely stood at the side of the road as the creaking scoot moved on. As it passed by her she reached out her hand to touch its load, proud of the fine straight logs that had grown in the Simon woods. They would fetch a good price, she told herself. They would have many uses. Because of them she and Susannah would be able to keep their home on the hill a little longer. The land was working for them as Benedict had always said the land in time should do.

She quickened her pace up the hill, rounding a curve, drawing nearer the sound of the chopping. Excitement beat hard within her. She was breathing it in with every step. Something in her loved the sound of an ax and she could not get to the scene of the cutting fast enough.

Then she stopped still.

Coming around a bend in the road she had a sudden strange sensation of being in unknown territory. Nothing looked familiar. Could this be the road she had come over only that morning? Then there had been a forest secrecy beyond the stone wall. Now there was the open light of day. Everywhere

stood stumps ringed and tawny, oozing sap. Huge logs waiting to be dragged away lay on the ground. Near them were
piles of lopped-off branches, their small tender leaves wilted
in the sunshine. A single horse was picking its way cleverly
around and over the debris, obeying its driver's commands
but using its own judgment as it strained to draw out a log to
be piled near the stone wall. Six men were working in the cutting. They had taken their shirts off and their backs were
bronzed; their hairy chests were running with sweat and their
bearded faces were swarthy and hot.

Freely did not move as she endeavored to get her bearings;
then her eyes lighted on something familiar. It was the white
birch. Her eyes traveled up its trunk to the leafy crown, then
down again to the mark that Philip had made on it. It was the
white birch, she told herself, the tree Benedict had planted
to mark a corner of his land. But all around it was desolation.

Horror transfixed her so she could not move. All she could
do was stare with wide unbelieving eyes. Then a madness
seized her and she ran forward into the cutting.

"Make them stop," she screamed to Tom Slason who was
handling the horse.

"What's that, miss?" he reined in the heaving animal.

"Stop!" Freely cried, running toward him and grabbing
his arm. "You're cutting down all our trees." Her face was
pale with rage.

Three men who were putting wedges into the cut made in
one side of a large beech, stopped and looked at her. Two
men who were limbing branches stopped. The silence that
preceded a crash filled the cutting.

"We had our orders, miss," Slason said. "Mr. Haven
brought me up here himself and showed me the trees we were
to take. Every one, he said, except that birch, and on no condition was that to be touched."

Freely stared at him as if she had not the least comprehension of what he had been saying, but slowly her hands loosed their frenzied hold on his arm and fell to her sides.

"The trees will grow again, miss," he said, trying to console her.

"Not in your lifetime or mine," she answered fiercely.

He shrugged his shoulders. "There's thousands of feet of good timber here that shouldn't be allowed to go to waste."

"What are you going to do with the trees?" she asked hoarsely.

"They've all got their uses, miss. That ash over there will make good ax handles, and there's a lot of fine flooring in the maples, but I'm awful sorry Mr. Haven won't let us have that white birch. There's nothing better for jam buckets than birchwood."

Freely shook her head to and fro. "But the trees used to shelter song birds. They gave cover to wild flowers," she said dully. "There was a spring here from which the forest creatures came to drink." She put her hands to her eyes to take away the sight of desecration. "This was a holy place."

"I'm sorry, miss. No one ever told us that. It looked like all the woods to us."

Freely sighed. Why had she thought the dell would be safe? Because it had been her secret she had thought that it was inviolable. But to anyone else it was like the rest of the forest.

"Couldn't you save a little bit?" she begged.

Slason shook his head. "When the men get into an area they like to cut it clean. But you might ask Mr. Haven. Maybe, tomorrow—"

"Where is he?" Freely demanded.

"Might be at his home, miss, that big fancy house across the river."

Before he could tell her more, Freely had turned and was leaping over the debris, out of the woodlot, and running down the hill. Philip could save it. He would, if she told him about it. He would, he would, she said over and over to herself. Tears blinded her eyes, but her feet impelled by her passionate desire to save some vestige of her hidden world carried her over the road and through the town.

Twenty minutes later a breathless panting girl stood before the front door of Haven Hall, ringing its bell impatiently.

A servant opened the door, her face as rigid as her stiffly starched apron and cap.

"Is—Mr. Haven—here?" Freely asked, gasping for breath.

"No," the servant said, wondering if anything had happened in the woods and a child had been sent with a message. "Has there been an accident?"

Freely shook her head. "They're cutting down our trees."

The door began to shut. "You've been paid for them," the servant said. "Mr. Haven always pays in advance." The door shut and opened again. "You can't sell your trees and have them, too, you know."

Freely turned away from the door and walked slowly toward the drive. A brougham drawn by a pair of gray horses with a coachman on the box came up the drive. Freely lifted her head as it went past her. She saw the erect slender figure of a fashionably dressed elderly woman. On the seat beside her sat a small smooth-haired dog. For a moment, Freely's eyes met the eyes of the woman but Freely, frightened by the cold stare, dropped her gaze. The woman saw the uplifted head of a girl whose face was flushed and suffering, whose hair had been matted by the wind. Inwardly she shuddered and drew herself together. The carriage drove on. Freely, exhausted and heartheavy as she was, started to run again to get away from the cold eyes of the woman in the carriage.

A moment later, when the brougham drew up to her door, Mrs. Haven asked the coachman if there had been gypsies around lately.

"No, madam," he said.

"Did you see that young girl?"

"Yes, madam. Perhaps she's one of the lumbering men's children. Mr. Philip does have dealings with some rough people."

"I don't like to see a person like that around the place. You never know how safe your possessions may be."

"That's very true, madam," the coachman said deferentially as he assisted Mrs. Haven from the carriage.

By the time Freely got back to the cutting, the choppers had gone. There was a song sparrow in the white birch singing tenderly, and in the woods across the road the thrushes were carrying on their melodious courtship. Where the trees had been felled there was silence. The only sound was made by Freely as she pushed her way past lopped-off branches and over fallen logs. The lady's-slippers were flattened by the trampling of horses' hoofs, the rolling of logs, the feet of men. The maple that grew by the spring was gone, and though the spring still bubbled under the rock the sound was dull and hollow. Look as she might, Freely found no sign of arum lilies, and the ferns had been trod upon so much that only their stout roots proclaimed where they had been.

Freely threw herself face down on the ground, digging her fingers into the earth. This had been her secret world and now it was no more, she said to herself. But no matter how often she repeated the words she could not make herself believe them unless she lifted her head and looked around her; and that she did not want to do. She felt as if she had been cut off from her source and that her own blood was draining away as the sap was from the stumps.

The first impact of realization had made her feel as battered and bruised as if her own body had been the butt of saws and axes; but now there was not even the diversion of physical suffering. There was only the cold dull acceptance of what had happened, of what could not now be changed. With her secret world gone, she felt as if she stood in the midst of a void. The winds of the compass could howl around her and blow through her for no longer were there any trees to shelter her.

Twilight was settling over the world, more noticeable in the cutting than it would have been in the forest, gentle in approach, kind in intent. The shock of anguish was leaving Freely and in its place she felt the slow welling up of sorrow. A tightness took hold of her throat, a heaviness came over her eyes. She pressed her face close to the earth so she could feel the dent of a stone against her cheek, the sharp angles of a twig against her brow. With all the strength she had within her she fought back the tears; but the time came when she had no more strength to fight them back and so she had to let them come. Slowly they fell and then in a rush, as if the first hard ones eased the way for those that followed. Hot and salty, the tears flowed from her eyes, ran into the moss, and were absorbed by the earth. She cried as if there would never be an end to her sorrow, digging her toes into the earth, pressing her fingers down until they could feel coolness.

Exhaustion came over her and the tears lessened until they finally stopped. She was conscious of aching arms and legs, throbbing head and burning eyes. She loosed her hold with her fingers, her legs went limp, and she lay still, motionless and without emotion.

Twilight deepened into dusk. Small sounds could be heard among the fallen branches as forest creatures stole back to find their homes. A deer, following the trail to the spring, stopped short at the sight of Freely, wheeled, and leaped back into the woods.

Freely stirred. The agony seemed to be years behind her, but she felt weak as she had never felt before in her life and dully she wondered from where strength was summoned when there seemed no strength anywhere at all. Slowly, almost fearfully, she realized that something was coming into being within her, something was being born out of suffering and sorrow and loss.

What was it, she asked herself, lifting her head from the moss. And the voice within, that did not fail her if she could be still long enough to listen for it, said: Courage. Courage to face what must be faced.

She rolled over on her back and looked up into the sky. She saw the stars that had already appeared and she watched others that were appearing. Now there was nothing between her and the sky, she thought, and the realization brought her a curious comfort. She felt as if she wanted to lie still for a long time, enfolded in night. The terrible finality of all that had happened still ached within her, but it was like an old wound now, not something new and raw.

So soon all that was beautiful and valorous could disappear. This place that she had loved no longer existed for her; but now she could think of it without anguish and where sorrow had been, a vast kindness began to flood her being. If this could happen to trees in a few hours, it could happen to people. She wanted to embrace those she loved in the kindness that flowed around her lest in the onrush of events that doomed, sometime or other, all living things there was not enough time for kindness. Only that would be tragedy.

This must be the bedrock of life, she thought. This must be humility, the state of mind Benedict used to speak of so often. She reached back into memory to bring him near. Yes, he had said one day when they were working in the garden, that humility was the ground from which all else grew. Whether she had touched that ground or not, she knew that something was growing within her. Something clean and strong. There had been suffering, there had been pain; but it was all behind her now. Her body felt as if it had been stretched until thew and sinew ached with the tension; then, suddenly released, she could feel that it had grown. Her reach would be farther from this time on. Weak as she was and still desperately tired, she was aware of a new sense of freedom. She had found what Benedict had always wanted her to find—the secret place that was not in space or time, that was made of no substance that could be destroyed. She closed her eyes and sighed contentedly.

It was then that Philip found her, lying on her back by the spring, arms outstretched, face weary but radiant. He knelt down beside her.

"Freely," he said, and then he knew without asking what had happened. "This was your secret place! Oh, my darling, I am so sorry. If I had only known!" He put his arms under her and lifted her, holding her in his arms. He kissed her brow and her hair that was matted with moss and twigs.

"Oh, Philip," she whispered, leaning her head against his shoulder, "I wanted to show it to you and now you'll never know how beautiful it was." She sighed. She was tired, but in the haven of his arms was rest.

"I do know how beautiful it was, Freely," he said. "I know it through what it has done to you. Your secret place did much to make you what you are—and you are beautiful."

She smiled happily as if the words were a music she had not heard before but, hearing, delighted in. She put up her hand to brush away some of the leaves and sticks that she knew must be in her hair.

It was not her tear-streaked face Philip saw but the face of one whom he knew he loved. He looked at her as if he had not seen her for a long time and as if he could never see enough of her. Her amber eyes smiled at him through their light lashes; her wide lips parted; the bridge of freckles across her nose was visible in the pale evening; her thick sandy hair lay loose on her shoulders.

"I love you for what you are, Freely," he said.

He was familiar with the gay look of the child that shone in her face, but tonight there was more. The compassion of a much older person dwelt in her eyes, and with it was a quiet wisdom. He bent his head and his lips met hers that were upturned to him.

She lay back in his arms, her eyes on the stars that speckled the sky. Against the night, the white trunk of the birch stood out like a lighted thing. She curved her arm around him. "Why did you leave it, Philip, the white birch?"

"Because it made me think of you—so graceful and fearless," he smiled at her. "I was going to tell you that someday, but I had not thought to quite so soon."

"Oh, bless the fallen trees," she breathed softly, "that you have told me now and here."

She looked into his face as if she wanted to impress it on her mind for all time. It was a fine strong face with high cheekbones and a wide brow; his hair was brown and lay smooth on his head; his eyebrows were black and under them gray eyes gazed earnestly. Philip has a noble face, Freely found herself saying inwardly, and then she thought how much Benedict would have liked him.

They did not move while the evening lapped them in peace and the caroling of late birds filled the air. It seemed utterly natural to Freely to lie in Philip's arms, as if his arms had always been waiting for her. A wood thrush came to the end of its song. Freely stirred.

"Now we must go," she said.

He put his lips on hers once more, then they both stood up. He held her hand as they made their way over the fallen trees and around the branches. They stood by the white birch. Freely looked up the hill toward Simonton and instinctively Philip looked down; then they looked at each other.

"You take the low road and I'll take the high," she reminded him.

"But I want to come with you."

She shook her head. "Not tonight. I want to see Susannah alone."

He understood, but he could not let her go until he had held her close to him again, leaning against the birch, conscious of his heart beating in time with hers.

Then Freely went up the hill and he watched her until the night took her from his sight.

13

>>>>>>>>>>>>>>>>>>>>>>>>><<<<<<<<<<<<<<<<<<<<<<<<<

SUSANNAH sat in the kitchen rocking quietly back and forth. She had set a lamp in the window, knowing that its glow would reach out to welcome Freely when she came over the brow of the hill. There was a pot of stew warm on the back of the stove and a rhubarb pie on the table. Susannah put down her last piece of mending and closed her eyes, enjoying the peace of her kitchen and finding pleasure in her mind as she went back over the events of the day.

It had not been as lonely and difficult a day as it had seemed it would be when she glanced down it after the moment of faintness seized her. She had got through the household tasks in the morning. Soon after noon John Wheelman had come to spade the garden and she had relished his company. Near evening Philip had appeared to tell her that the cutting had started and that the logs coming out were fine and worthy. He had stopped long enough to have a piece of pie and a glass of milk.

"Isn't Freely home yet?" he had asked before leaving.

Susannah shook her head. "Not yet, but she'll be home by dark. She's like a bird that way, always returning to her nest before the last light goes."

So Philip, disappointed not to be seeing her after nearly a week away, had gone down the road to look over the cutting his men had done, and Susannah had gone out to the barn to do the chores Freely usually did on her return from school—milking the cow, feeding the hens, gathering the eggs, calling Ginger into his stall from the pasture. Twilight had come, and then the soft vibrant darkness of a May night. A whippoorwill called in flight. The breeze blowing across the green was warm and sweet.

The clock struck eight.

Susannah had never worried about Freely, perhaps because worry was not in her nature, perhaps because Freely was not the kind of person one worried about. She missed the girl, but Freely did not have it in her to do any wrong and there was something about her which kept harm from her. She remembered the time two years ago when she and Benedict had kept vigil in the kitchen one cold winter night. A small boy from a neighboring farm had come at suppertime with a message that Freely was helping his father with the sow's farrowing, but it was midnight before Freely returned—glowing with happiness and more hungry than tired.

The sow had not survived the farrowing and the need had been to save the litter, or as many as possible. Freely had wrapped all six little pigs in cotton blankets and put them in the warm oven, standing by until wriggling tails and snuffling snouts made it clear that they were ready to be fed. Once the farmer could get warm milk into their bodies the danger of losing them was past. There had been other times, Susannah recalled, and it was such a one tonight. Freely would be back soon and she would have a tale to tell of some adventure; and even if it were nothing unusual, Freely would still have a way of making it glow.

Susannah opened her eyes with a start, realizing she had dozed off. The front door had opened and closed. She heard Freely's footsteps in the hall, and then Freely herself was standing in the doorway to the kitchen. But it was not the Freely who had left the house that morning. Susannah put

133

her hands on the arms of her chair and started to rise, then she sank back. Her heart was fluttering—excitement, joy, or that strange malady that enforced stillness upon her at times when she most longed to be active—she could not tell which it was.

"Oh, my dear," she breathed quietly. "I'm glad you're back."

"I'm sorry, Grandma, to be so late." Freely came across the kitchen toward her.

She looked taller to Susannah, perhaps because she walked as if her head was in the stars. Her dress was crumpled and disheveled, her hands were dirty, her hair had bits of twigs and moss in it as if she had been lying on the ground in the woods, and her face showed marks of tears; but Freely was shining. A radiance preceded her as she walked, and when she stood by Susannah it seemed to enfold them both; so it was not only the girl's presence that cheered Susannah but something about the girl that warmed and revitalized her. It was as if Freely had pressed her lips to a fount of life-giving water and drunk so deeply that the water had become part of her being and anyone who came near her would be refreshed by it. How she walked across the room, Susannah thought, not with the quick excited movements of the child but with such grace and dignity.

Susannah took one of Freely's grimy hands and held it in her own, then she looked into Freely's face. The girl was smiling. And yet, Susannah thought, eyes do not shine like stars above cheeks grooved by tears unless one has gone to such depths that height can be realized.

"Grandma," Freely said, and her voice was just above a whisper, "did you feel like this when you knew you loved Grandfather?"

"Oh, dear heart," Susannah breathed, as Freely with a

swift movement knelt before her and buried her head in her lap.

Susannah's hands rested on the bowed shoulders and she bent down to kiss the top of the sandy head, while her mind hurtled back over more than half a century to a day that still shone forth in memory like a radiant jewel. It was such a day as she had never known before and it had set the pattern for all the days that followed it.

After a few moments Freely lifted her head and smiled in her old way up into Susannah's eyes. "I'm very hungry."

Susannah said dryly, "I've no doubt you are, but you're not fit to sit down before a proper meal. Go and scrub yourself and change your dress and I'll have dinner on the table by the time you're ready for it."

Freely laughed and went from the room, and all the while she was upstairs Susannah could hear her humming to herself. She was soon down again, scrubbed face shining in the lamplight, hair brushed free of the forest, clean hands and a fresh gingham dress, but the aura had not been washed away.

After she had finished her supper and Susannah had taken the plates to the sink, Freely stretched her arms across the table and sighed deeply. She looked at Susannah, who sat down across from her. The lamp at one side of the table made a pool of light which embraced them both.

"Tell me how you met Grandfather," Freely asked.

Susannah, brimming with impatience as she was, took Freely back with her over the years to the day when she had returned on the ship with her father from a three years' voyage around the world.

"I was sixteen and my father said it was the last voyage I would make with him, for he felt if I did not stay ashore a while I would never win a husband. Then I cared nothing for a husband. The sound of waves and the wind in the sails, foreign lands and the mixture of calm and bustle that was a sailing ship had been life to me and I could think of no other. Our port was Boston and I was to be sent to an aunt who lived in New York City. My education was to be that of a fine young lady—"

"But you never went to New York, did you?"

"No," Susannah shook her head, "I never went to New York. Soon after we reached Boston, my father went to call upon the ship's owner, as he always did after a voyage to make his report, and I accompanied him. A Harvard student was lodging in the house and was in the parlor with Mr.—" Susannah paused. "Now, isn't that odd but I can't remember the shipowner's name and I know it as well as my own!"

"Oh, please go on. The name doesn't matter."

But Susannah was determined to remember it and in a moment she exclaimed, "Fairbridge! That was his name. I knew I couldn't forget it. When my father and I were shown into the parlor and introduced, Mr. Fairbridge suggested that we young people go out into the garden while he and my father talked over their business. He said the bell would ring when it was time for tea." Susannah's eyes grew dreamy as she brought it back in memory.

"And then? And then?" Freely prompted.

"The bell did not ring for three hours and by then Benedict Simon knew most of my life and I knew most of his, and what lay ahead for us we knew that we would know together." Susannah sighed. "It was very beautiful in the garden. I can still see the drifts of delphinium and smell the spicy pinks."

Freely leaned nearer and put both her hands on one of Susannah's. "Tell me," she said, and her words were earnest and urgent, "when did you know you loved him?"

Susannah closed her eyes, seeing it all in her mind. When she opened them she looked directly at Freely. "I think it was when I first looked into his eyes. They were so quiet, so clear. I seemed to see myself in them—the self I wanted to be."

"When were you married?"

"A week later on my father's ship as she rode at anchor in the Boston harbor. He was a captain and could perform the ceremony, and for a ship's wedding it was not necessary to post bans."

"And then?"

"We found a little house in Cambridge near to Benedict's studies. The twins were born before our first anniversary, and young Mark came a year later, just before Benedict took up the duties in his first church. We waited fifteen years for your mother and she was born on the hill, in this house long after we came to Simonton."

"And did you love her very much?"

"Yes," Susannah nodded, "very much, and yet no more than I loved Roger and Roland and Mark. No more than I love you." She laughed to herself. "Sometimes it seems as if the heart was made of India rubber."

"I'm finding that out too," Freely said. "Once I thought I loved just you and Grandfather, the hill and the church, the dell and the animals, but now—" she stopped abruptly.

"Tell me, Freely."

So Freely told her everything from the time she had seen the dell with its desecration to the time not an hour ago when she and Philip had said good-by, standing by the white birch.

Susannah's lips were smiling but tears stood in her eyes when Freely came to the end of her story. In the silence that followed, the tears gathered and overflowed.

"Why are you sad?" Freely asked.

Susannah shook her head. "Because all you have told me is beautiful, and sometimes even beauty hurts, and because it is a hard thing you have chosen for yourselves."

Surprise was large on Freely's face. "We love each other."

"Ah, but love does not always make things easy—except that there are two instead of one to face what is difficult."

"But, if we love, then—isn't the way simple after that?"

"Sometimes, for some people; not always, not for you. His life is far apart from yours. You must realize that if you saw what his home was like when you went there this afternoon. There is a far greater gulf between you two than the distance between Simonton and Haven Hall. Yet you have bridged it."

"Then," Freely asked warily, "what do we do?"

"Give the bridge time to strengthen. It's the merest gossamer now but someday it can be strong as steel. You haven't lived on this hilltop all your years, Freely, without seeing how nature does things with such patience. The world is full of impatience, but don't let yourself become part of it or you may lose what you have found."

"If I never saw him again I could not love him more than I do now."

The lamp was flickering and Susannah reached to turn up the wick. Freely's face reflected the light and Susannah thought suddenly that the Holy Grail must have been reflected in just such a way in the faces of those who were granted its vision, those who were pure enough to behold it. But it is a Holy Grail to which she has put her lips and from this night on her life is consecrated, Susannah said inwardly. She wished that Benedict were there, knowing how wise he would be with Freely when she felt so inadequate; yet she had not shared Benedict's wisdom for years without being able to call on it in need.

"It will be easier for you than for him, Freely," Susannah said. "That is why you must be the one to be patient, to be firm."

Freely pushed back her chair. "I think I want to go and talk with my mother."

"Yes, dear heart, go, but don't stay out too long."

"No, only a very little while." Freely kissed Susannah. "Thank you, Grandma. I have it all in my heart, what you have said. There are lots of other things in my heart but I—"

Susannah stroked the strong young hand that rested on the table. "I know, Freely. Love is not only trust; it is a trust."

Freely went from the room and out into the May night, across the green and past the church, down the road the short distance and into the graveyard. There was no moon, only a multitude of stars in the sky; but Freely would have known her way on the darkest night. Aubrietia, growing through the years, had spread through the graveyard, carpeting almost all the space inside the stone walls with its masses of purple-pink blossoms. No place did it grow more abundantly than among the Simon stones, and the frail fragrance lying on the air drew Freely like an outreaching hand.

Kneeling down by the slender slate stone that bore her mother's name, she put her arms around it and kissed it; then she traced with her fingers the engraving on the stone. 'To her who loveth much, much shall be forgiven.' Whatever her mother had done then, she had been forgiven. Freely leaned back and looked up at the sky. Once she had thought that she knew what love was; but she realized now that she had not known until tonight.

Give—forgive—the words went back and forth in Freely's mind like a pendulum. She had given her heart to Philip this night, and yet when she looked back in her mind to the time when she had first met him—in the church while she was playing with the cubs, comforting them for the loss of their mother—she thought that she must have loved him then. She could not find in her mind a time since she had known him when she had not loved him, when he had not been the completion of her world.

Tonight she had only pledged her love as she gave him her

lips. Someday she would give her whole self to him and her body would be the token; but that day was not near. Dimly she saw what Susannah meant about the bridge that must be built between their lives. So that was what had happened to her mother: she had not waited for the bridge to be built, and in the giving she had plunged into a chasm that had taken her from them all.

"Oh, Mother darling," Freely hugged the stone closer. There was much that she longed to say, much that she longed to listen to, but only the wind in the pines above gave voice in the night. It was a patient sound that had eased grief for many mourners.

Freely got up from the grass and started from the grave-yard. She still walked in ecstasy and her feet trod lightly on the earth. Night, like a velvet cloak studded with stars, enfolded her. Passing the crabapple tree, she stood under it. Looking up, she could see the stars shining through its blossoms. A Bible verse that, as a child, she had thought had been spoken only for her kept coming into her mind, "Freely, ye have received. Freely, give."

She had heard Benedict say it, she had voiced it herself, and she had not realized until she was grown that the freely in the verse was not a noun and that it had no comma after it. However, she went on saying it as she always had. It was her own phylactery.

The crabapple knew the verse too, she thought, for it had received blessings of sun and rain and soil, and it was giving in blossoms that would become fruit. It was the way of nature to accept good and give it out again.

There was stillness in her heart when she joined Susannah in the kitchen.

14.

>>>>>>>>>>>>>>>>>>>>>>>><<<<<<<<<<<<<<<<<<<<<<<<

IT was long past the usual hour for dinner at Haven Hall. Philip, as he approached the house, had the same half-guilty, half-vindicative feeling he had had as a small boy when something urgent to himself but not understandable to his mother had made him late for a meal. Philip let himself in the door. He saw that a lamp was burning in the living room but no one sat beside it. He went to the bell cord on the wall and rang hastily for one of the servants.

"Oh, good evening, Sara, has my mother gone out?" he asked the maid who came in answer to his summons.

"No, Mr. Philip, your mother retired soon after dinner. She waited some time for you but when you didn't come she dined alone."

"I—I expected to be here, Sara, but I was detained. Will you find out whether I may see Mrs. Haven now or whether tomorrow morning would be better."

"Yes, Mr. Philip." Sara left the room and mounted the stairs, her shoes creaking in the stillness of the house.

Philip went in to the living room and turned up the lamp. The room looked empty in the sudden bright glare and he turned the lamp down again almost as quickly; full of furniture as the room was, heavy with ornamentation, it was curiously devoid of life. He heard Sara coming down the stairs and went out again to the hallway.

"Mrs. Haven says will you please come up now, Mr. Philip."

"Thank you, Sara." Philip took the stairs two steps at a time, impatience speeding him. "Mother—" he cried as he crossed her room to greet her.

Mrs. Haven, dressed in a negligee, was sitting by her writing table. A small pug dog lay on a cushion near her.

"Philip, my dear boy," she held out her arms to her son. "You've had me very worried for the last two hours."

He kissed her. "Sorry to be so late, Mother." He sat down near her. The little dog got up to sniff Philip then, satisfied, returned to his cushion.

"Where have you been? We thought you were getting home by the afternoon train and I waited dinner half an hour."

"I did get back on the train but I walked up to the cutting to see what the men had been doing. They started on a new piece while I was away and I wanted to see that they knew the boundaries."

"Philip," she leaned toward him, "did anyone get hurt today?"

He looked surprised. "No, not as far as I know. Why?"

"Sara said a wildly excited child came here asking for you."

He shook his head. "I'm sure nothing happened. Slason would have told me. I saw the men before they left the piece. I'll find out tomorrow. Probably one of the men drank up his wages last week and his wife sent a child to protest."

"Have you had any dinner?"

"No."

She reached toward the bell to summon Sara.

"Mother, please, I'm not hungry. I stopped in to see Mrs. Simon for it's in her woods we're cutting. She gave me something to eat. Mother, I—"

"Philip, dear, are you feeling quite yourself?" Mrs. Haven

142

leaned toward her son, aware of his flushed face and the brightness in his eyes. "You're not feverish are you, dear?" She took one of his hands in hers and held it for a moment. It was quite cool and the pulse was even.

"I'm all right, Mother. I've never felt better. And I—I'm terribly happy."

She smiled at him fondly. "I'm glad, dear. Things went well for you in Boston, then."

"Yes, I suppose so, I wasn't thinking about that. Mother, I—" he put his head in his hands to hide the uncontrollable smile he felt coming over his face, part of the tidal wave of happiness that was submerging his whole being. Then he moved his hands up and ran his fingers through his hair.

Flushed cheeks, disheveled hair, bright eyes, he looked then to his mother like the small boy just come from his bath instead of the capable young man of twenty-five who had succeeded to his father's place in the paper business.

"What is it, Philip?" An uneasy foreboding came over Mrs. Haven. She hoped her words did not convey the dread that was in her heart.

But had they, Philip would have been oblivious to them. He was lost in his own dream, so absorbed by its wonder that he thought anyone with whom he shared it would feel as he did.

"Mother, I'm—" he smiled again— "I'm in love."

"Oh." Mrs. Haven leaned back in her chair. So it was that, she said within herself, the announcement she had dreaded for years and yet knew must one day come; the event she had tried to steel herself to face ever since Philip's father had died.

"Isn't it wonderful?"

"It may be, if she is the right one."

Philip laughed. "But how could there ever be anyone but the right one to make me feel this way?"

"You are very young, Philip," his mother reminded him.

"Have you known her long or did you meet her during this last trip of yours to Boston?" Mrs. Haven was tormented by the possibility of his answer. If he had known her long it was painful that he had not told her before; if he had met her within the last few days it was obviously a dangerous infatuation.

Philip looked at his mother but he did not see her. His eyes were seeing Freely. "Sometimes I think I've known her all my life, and all the other lives I may have lived before this one."

Mrs. Haven sighed. Philip was in no mood to talk sensibly. "Where did you meet her, Philip?"

With an effort he focussed his eyes on his mother and smiled apologetically. "She lives in Simonton, on the hill above Millville, and she's the great-great-granddaughter of its founder, Mark Simon."

"Simonton? The village that everyone left?"

"Not everyone, Mother. She and her grandmother still live there in the house Mark Simon built."

"Oh—" the sound was long and drawn out as Mrs. Haven began to recall stories she had heard of the village on the hill. A bit of gossip here. A tag end of rumor there. An odd piece of scandal. "Oh," she said again, then brought her lips tightly together.

"Shall I tell you about her, Mother?"

"If you wish."

"She's beautiful—with amber eyes that are as clear as mountain water and tawny hair that's thick like a fox's coat. She has a way with animals. It's like a magic in her hands. And there's something so wise about her. She has ideas that are all her own. I've never met anyone so stimulating and yet everything seems to resolve itself to such a simple equation when I'm with her."

"She sounds most unusual," Mrs. Haven commented, her voice edged with sarcasm.

"Oh, Mother, I know you'll like Freely when you get to know her."

"What is her name?" Mrs. Haven queried.

"Freelove. Isn't it beautiful? It's an old, old name with the Simons."

"It's a dangerous name to give a child."

Philip stared at his mother.

"How long have you known her?"

"All this spring," Philip answered quickly. He might have said as easily, "All my life."

"All this spring—" Mrs. Haven repeated. "Philip, do you realize that today is the first of May?"

He stared at her again, wondering what a date on the calendar had to do with his feeling for Freely.

Mrs. Haven sighed.

Philip looked at her solicitously. "Are you tired, Mother? Shall I leave you now?"

"Yes, Philip, I am tired, very tired, but before you go I would like to get to the bottom of this. After all, I must do for you what your father would do if he were here. Tell me more about this girl, you say she is the daughter of the woman who still lives in that hill village?"

"No, Mother, granddaughter. Freely's mother died when she was born. Freely was brought up by her grandparents. She and her grandmother live in the old house. Benedict Simon was pastor of the church. He died last Christmas. He was her grandfather."

"What was her mother's name?"

"Freelove Simon. You can see her grave in the old cemetery."

"I mean—what was her married name."

Philip paused. Something had begun to crumble around him. "She didn't have any other name," he said quietly.

"Then who was this girl's father?"

"I don't know. No one knows."

"Does she know?"

"I never asked her."

"But you must find that out, Philip."

"Does it matter as much as all that?"

"Philip, you are a Haven. You will inherit your father's fortune as you have his business. You can't give your heart to just anybody."

"Mother, she isn't just anybody. Can you realize what it is to be a Simon? Long before any of us were heard of, Mark Simon founded the town on the hilltop and Millville is just an offshoot from it. The Simon roots go deeper into the soil than ours into family trees. They've been farmers and pastors for four generations. It's the oldest kind of American stock and it's as noble as—" Philip reached desperately for words — "as an oak tree."

"That is all rather unnecessary, Philip."

But Philip was determined to have his say. "How long have we been in this countryside? Fifteen years! Making our money by stripping the land of trees the first settlers spared and cared for."

Mrs. Haven moved her hand irritably as if she had listened long enough. "How old is this girl?" she asked.

"Eighteen. She's in her last year at the Millville school."

"The Millville school!" Mrs. Haven exclaimed. "And you have had a college education! Oh, Philip, Philip, I had hoped for something better for you," she sighed, "and I shall go on hoping."

Philip stood up. "Mother, may I bring her here to see you sometime?"

"I haven't the slightest desire to meet her but I suppose, for your sake, I shall be obliged to."

"Thank you." Philip stooped over to kiss her goodnight. "I'm sorry if I've upset you, Mother. Please don't let it

146

disturb your rest." He smiled at her pleadingly. "Are you ready for bed now? Shall I tell Sara to come up to you?"

"Yes, tell Sara to come up to me."

Philip bent down to stroke the dog who wagged his curl of a tail. Leaving the room, he went downstairs to deliver his message, then he went outdoors.

The night air was cool and caressing, but nothing could still the impatience in his heart or take the edge of anxiety from his mind. Once before, he had come up against the stone wall that was his mother. That had been when he had started off to college. He had longed with all his heart to study to be a doctor, but his father had recently died and Mrs. Haven was determined that her son should take over the paper-mill business. Philip had not been strong enough then to hold his heart's desire against her will. A chill of fear passed over him when he thought of what his heart's desire was now.

"God help me," he groaned, smiling ironically. It was so easy for a man to pray when there was no other help at hand, yet Freely prayed all the time.

Sara, assisting her mistress into bed, knew that words must have passed between Mrs. Haven and her son. Mrs. Haven said nothing, but her hands were trembling and the set of her lips spoke for her.

"Mr. Philip doesn't look too well to me, madam," Sara began hopefully.

"No, he isn't well at all. He's working too hard. I hope to get him to go away this summer."

"That will do him good," Sara said soothingly. "Everybody needs a change now and then."

"Sara, do you know many people in Millville?"

"A few, madam."

"Who are some of the people who used to live in that little village on the hill?"

"I couldn't rightly say, madam, but I've heard that Miss

147

Mattie Emerson lived there most of her life and knows about all the people. They say she has a great memory."

"Miss Mattie Emerson—where does she live?"

"In the white cottage just at the corner where the Simonton road comes into Main Street."

"Thank you, Sara. I shall call on Miss Mattie. There are things that only someone with a long memory can tell me."

"Will there be anything more, madam?"

"No, Sara, good night."

"Good night, madam. I hope you will rest well."

15.

≫≫≫≫≫≫≫≫≫≫≫≫≫≫≫≫≫≫≫≪≪≪≪≪≪≪≪≪≪≪≪≪≪≪≪≪≪

THE next day at school Freely had to pinch herself to keep her mind on her work, and more than once Miss Anderson had to rap sharply on her desk and call Freely by name to get her attention. But Miss Anderson prided herself on being understanding and she had always sensed a poetic quality in Benedict Simon's granddaughter. It was not surprising that on this warm May day, when the birds were singing their hearts out and the trees were full of blossoms, that Freely should lapse into reverie. However, it was one thing to understand and another to condone, and Miss Anderson felt that mind wandering could not be encouraged in a classroom.

"Freely Simon!" she rapped her desk with her ruler.

Freely started and transferred her gaze quickly from the open window to Miss Anderson's desk. "Yes, Miss Anderson?"

"Please answer the question."

"What question?"

"The one I just asked the class."

Freely shook her head and smiled, acknowledging her fault. "I didn't hear it, Miss Anderson."

Miss Anderson sighed. "Wandering minds gather no learning. When was the eruption of Mount Vesuvius that resulted in the destruction of Pompeii?"

Several hands shot up with a ready answer but Freely shook her head. "I don't know."

"Please pay attention to the work of the class," Miss Anderson said. Then she accepted the answer from another scholar and went on reading and interpolating remarks to do with the last days of Pompeii.

Freely, with a supreme effort, riveted her attention to Miss Anderson for fully five minutes, then the temptation to let her mind and her gaze stray again was too much. History had been one of her loves at school, but today it had withered into unimportance. There seemed little reason to read history now when she was making it herself.

On the whole, Miss Anderson was lenient with her. Freely had been a good student, attentive, applying herself well. Her teacher was willing to allow her a time of grace—such a time as everyone needed now and then, Miss Anderson thought to herself—when daydreaming takes ascendance over actual thinking. Then, too, it was Friday, always a difficult day for boys and girls in the spring of the year since the diversions of the coming week end were so many. Miss Anderson had no intention of indulging Freely, but she thought that by Monday the girl would have adjusted herself to the advent of spring. Inevitable as the event was in the year's calendar, it was always inclined to be disturbing.

That afternoon, when school was dismissed and the boys and girls of all ages and sizes went trooping out of the schoolhouse, Freely was not surprised to find Philip waiting for her with the gig. In fact, she realized with a start, as she got in and waited for him to get up into the seat beside her, that she would have been surprised if he had not been there.

"Shall we go for a drive," Philip asked, "along the river and up the other road to Simonton? It's a few miles longer but Prince hasn't been out for a week and he's ready for anything."

"Yes, that would be lovely," Freely said. The greater distance would mean that she would be with Philip longer.

They went at a brisk trot down the Main Street of Millville and along the river road. It was like driving through a fairytale world, Freely thought, for the river was rippling and dancing in the sun. The fields were green and laced with flowers. The blossoms on the fruit trees looked as if small white clouds had come to rest near the land for a while. The leaves on the maples lining the road were so new that they shone in the light. A medley of song came from the birds who, having concluded courtship, were deep in the business of nest building.

Freely sat dreamily with her hands folded in her lap while they drove through the town. Once they had passed the last house and were out on the country road with only Prince to hear them and only birds to see them, Freely unclasped her hands and laid one on Philip's knee, looking up at him. She hoped he would understand it was not that she would not have others see their love but that she wanted to keep it secret for a while.

He leaned toward her quickly and kissed her. "Do you love me, Freely, today?" he asked. He knew there could be only one answer for it was already in her face and in her eyes, but he wanted to hear it from her lips.

"More than ever."

They drove along in silence for a few minutes. Then Freely said quietly, "I told my grandmother last night."

"I'm glad."

"But, Philip, I don't want to tell anyone else just yet. It's too wonderful. I want to have it for us to live in for a little while."

"I'd like to have it that way too," he agreed. Then, after a pause he added, "I told my mother about you, but she isn't apt to say anything."

"That's good." Freely settled back into the seat.

"Are you happy?"

She nodded.

"So am I, but, Freely, it isn't even a whole day yet that we've known we loved each other."

She sat up straight and looked at him. "Oh, Philip, it's more than that. It's weeks and weeks. It's since the first day we met in the church when the cubs were little."

"That's a long time."

"A very long time." She leaned back in the seat again, half closing her eyes. "I like to remember," she spoke reminiscently, "how I saw you, then you saw me, and suddenly we saw each other. We weren't strangers any more after that."

A cart was coming along the road. Freely folded her hands in her lap until it had passed them, then she put her right one again on Philip's knee. They left the river road and turned up the road that wound hillward toward Simonton, past bright green fields with sheep and cattle newly turned out and reveling in the freedom of pasture after a winter in the barn, past orchards white with blossoms, heavy with the drone of bees, past an occasional farmhouse, and then the woods began closing in on either side of the road.

Prince was walking slowly now, up the long hill, the reins lying loose on his back, the murmur of voices in the gig behind him going down to silence. Philip and Freely had had much to say, and then there was nothing to say for somehow they knew it all and what remained could be conveyed with silence. Freely wondered if there would ever be need of words between them except for the most trivial of matters.

The land they had discovered was new for both of them, the land that was their love, yet there was nothing foreign about it. It was as if on entering it each had been given a passport which had made everything familiar. So much had been different in their lives, yet the essential things were the same, and to Philip and Freely on that May afternoon they were all that mattered.

When they reached Simonton, Philip tied Prince to the hitching post under the oak tree. Tired from his long pull up the hill, Prince was willing to stand quietly, nibbling the new grass at his feet and swishing an occasional fly with his long tail.

Hearing their voices, Susannah came to the door to greet them. Her glance rested on Freely for a moment, then she turned to Philip and, just as if he had been Roland or Roger or Mark come home at last, she put her arms around him and kissed him warmly. Philip blushed with embarrassment and pleasure. Lost for words, he followed Susannah into the kitchen. Freely, safe in her own surroundings and sure that Philip was there for a while, became matter of fact.

"I've a cow to milk and eggs to gather," she announced, "so, if you'll just excuse me, I'll leave you two to look after each other."

"Can't I help?" Philip asked eagerly.

Freely smiled. "I'm willing to wager your hands don't know the first thing about milking a cow."

"They don't," Philip laughed. "Will you be long?"

"I can't get Brownie dry in under fifteen minutes," she said, "but I'll be as quick as I can about the eggs."

After she had left the room, Philip turned to Susannah. "Do you know how much I love her?"

Susannah shook her head. "No one can say that for another. All I know is that she is worthy of much love."

Philip spoke quickly, "I want to be worthy of her."

"Sit down," Susannah said, knowing Philip wanted to talk with her.

Suddenly Philip found himself telling Susannah about his mother. Susannah listened and at the end of the story said, "I thought it might be that way."

"What can I do?"

"Have you ever watched a good seed grow out of good soil?"

"I suppose so, but never seriously."

"You've not worked in the earth with your hands then?" she looked at him quizzically.

He shook his head. "No, there's always been someone else to do things like that, a gardener or—or someone."

"Freely's life has been the kind where she has done the chores herself and looked to others with whom to enjoy the time of leisure."

"Yes, I realize that. Does that make any great difference between us?"

"It need not."

"You were going to tell me something about a seed," he reminded her.

She spoke slowly as if she were telling a story to a child. "I've watched seeds grow, every year when I've put them in the soil. For days and days there'll be no sign at all, but the sun and the rain are working and in the earth the seeds are stirring. They are breaking their pods, reaching out, thrusting up, reaching a little farther, breaking the soil, growing every day, yet never hurrying. They are resting in the laws that govern growth, the assurance that full stature, fruition, is part of all being—" she looked at him more closely— "as it is for anything. What is planted rightly, Philip, has within it its own ability to come to fulfillment."

Philip glanced at the clock, thinking of Freely. She must have almost finished milking the cow. Soon she would be gathering the eggs. He turned to Susannah.

"What shall I do?"

"I'd be happy if you didn't ask anything of Freely until she finishes school next month."

"Not even ask her to meet my mother?"

"I think it would be better if you waited."

Philip thought for a moment. "It will be hard, but I'll do as you say."

"None of the way is going to be easy, Philip. It will help if you get used to its being hard now."

Philip was silent again. Freely would be back soon and in this moment alone with Susannah he knew there was something he must ask her.

"Can you tell me anything about Freely's father?"

Susannah caught her breath. She had been hoping it would not come, that question, while knowing all along that it would have to come; yet it was not Philip who was asking but Mrs. Haven.

"Very little. He was a French Canadian, a foreman of a lumber crew working near Chessington when the woods there were being cut. That was almost twenty years ago."

"How did your daughter meet him?"

"That," Susannah breathed deeply, "I will never know. She lived with him after she left the hill and until their baby was born. He had a wife and two children and he evidently had no desire to have this baby. Freelove must have known she was dying for she sent for us. I could not go. Benedict went. It was the closest moment those two ever had, and yet she was dead when Benedict got there."

"Where is the father now?"

"No one knows. He was moving off into New York state when Benedict saw him."

"Could he ever return and lay any claim to Freely?"

"No. He signed a paper for Benedict, waiving all rights and claims forever in his child. I have the paper. I will give it to you if—" Susannah corrected herself— "when you and Freely are married."

"Do you know his name?"

"Yes. Raoul de St. Pierre. Benedict told me he was a handsome man. Fair, thickset, with a face that might have been almost noble had it not shown the marks of rough living. Benedict said he was a good man but that life had gone hard with him. I can not tell you any more. No one can."

"Why didn't Freelove come back to you when she learned he had a wife and children?"

Susannah lifted her shoulders in a gesture of inscrutability. "The Simon pride was strong in her. Perhaps love held her. Who can say?"

It had been hard for Susannah, this story, and Philip knew it. He reached toward her and took her hands, pressing them between his. "Thank you for telling me," he said.

"Freelove was so different," Susannah went on, speaking more easily as if from her heart instead of from her memory of events. "And I loved her so. She was my only daughter, my youngest, and she was born long after I had given up hope of having another child. But there was always something she was reaching for, something we could not give her. For years after her death I could not bear to think of the anguish she must have lived in, the suffering—and not the physical suffering alone—she must have endured during that one year of marriage that was not marriage. My only comfort was in thinking how she must have loved the child she was carrying. How it was I do not know, but I feel certain that Freely came into the world with an endowment of love such as few children have."

They could hear Freely's footsteps as she returned from the barn, her cheerful humming preceding her through the woodshed.

"Look!" she exclaimed, as she entered the kitchen, "Brownie must have known you were here Philip—the pail is nearly up to the top! And look again," she held out her basket. "Eleven eggs—and we've only got ten hens!"

Susannah smiled. "Brownie has been in pasture these last few days."

"Oh, and Grandma," Freely cried excitedly, "the radishes we planted three days ago are showing!"

"That's good soil and they were good seeds," Susannah commented, as if to ask what else could one expect from such a combination.

For supper that night Susannah made an omelet out of seven of the eleven eggs. There were glasses of milk and biscuits hot from the oven and bowls of rhubarb pink and fresh and sweet. They sat around the kitchen table, laughing and talking, while Susannah told them stories of Simonton days.

"Do you remember the dress I made for you when you were ten years old with the buttons down the front?" Susannah asked Freely. "Meg Dexter was playing with you the first time you wore it and she started to count out the old rhyme on your buttons—richman, poorman, beggarman, thief, doctor, lawyer—"

"I do!" Freely exclaimed, her eyes dancing. "But you had sewed just four buttons on the dress and that made it stop at thief."

Susannah took up the story. "Nothing would do, Philip, but for me to sew another button on right away so Freely would not marry a thief but a doctor."

Freely and Susannah laughed as if the joke were an excellent one on themselves.

"But I always wanted to be a doctor!" Philip said.

"Why aren't you, then?" Freely asked.

He shook his head. "My mother wanted me to carry on my father's business."

In the early evening that as yet had no darkness to it, Freely drove down with Philip as far as the white birch. The cutting had been progressing. There were slash piles waiting to be burned on a rainy day and a pile of logs waiting to be removed the next day. Freely winced inwardly as she thought of the beauty that had once been there and of which she had thought only she was aware.

Philip looked into her face longingly. "I didn't know it was your world. I wouldn't have let it be cut had I known."

She placed her hands in his. "You are my world now," she said simply.

The dell had gone, but it had been like a sacrificial lamb and from the sweet savor of its going their love had arisen.

He put his arms around her and held her close to him, heart beating near heart, lips meeting the curve of lips. He put his arms on her square, straight shoulders, then let them slip down her body. She tipped her head back to look into his eyes. The glow of evening in the sky caught the gold in her eyebrows and on her sandy hair and made her eyes pale with light. He held her tightly again.

"Freely," he whispered, telling her all that he had said so often, all that she could not hear enough.

"And tomorrow—and tomorrow—and tomorrow—" she whispered back.

Prince gave a short whinny. It might mean that someone was coming over the road or that he was impatient.

"Sunday I shall come up to go to church with you and Susannah, but on Monday I'm going away."

"Not again?" she asked quickly, almost fiercely, as if she would not let him be taken from her.

He nodded. "Boston first, then New York. I may even have to go farther than that."

She clung to him. "Will you write to me?"

"Every day."

"When will you be back?"

"By the middle of June, I hope."

"Oh, Philip, my graduation is the twenty-fifth of June. You must be back by then."

"I will, Freely. I promise you that I'll be back by then."

She breathed deeply. It was something to hold to. "I'll be my own self after June twenty-fifth."

He laughed. "Who are you now?"

"I'm Freely, but I'll be free Freely after graduation."

"Or Philip's Freely?"

She put her hands against his chest and pushed him back gently. Love him as she did, seeing the future before them as she did, she still had not thought of being his entirely. "I'll tell you then," she whispered.

She placed a quick kiss on his lips and he released her. She turned and ran up the hill, stopping to wave to him, then spinning around and making her way light of foot, strong, eager, over the road she had traveled so often.

Philip drove slowly down the hill. Prince stepped carefully, for the road had been roughened by the lumber wagons; the breeching rubbed against his black coat as he held the gig back, making a white lather that foamed around the leather.

"Easy there, easy," Philip crooned, drawing in on the reins.

It was slow going and it gave Philip time to think, but that was what he wanted; for a plan was taking shape in his mind. There was something he intended to do; something which, in fairness to his mother, he felt bound to do. It would take him away from Freely for a while, but it might be the means of bringing them even closer together.

Philip had not thought of time in its relation to hours and their occasions, but as he approached Millville he became conscious of the fact that for the second night in succession he would have kept his mother waiting for dinner. A clucking sound and a flick of the reins sent Prince into a trot. The horse, eager for his own stall, clipped speedily through the town and over the bridge, disregarding the sign that admonished all horse-drawn vehicles to cross at a walk. Prince lengthened his pace the nearer he got to his stable.

"I thought you'd be back before dark, Mr. Philip," Hawkins said, putting his hand on the bridle and stroking Prince's head.

"Thanks, Hawkins, for waiting for me. I've been running Prince rather hard but I had a good bit of ground to cover."

Philip hurried from the stable to the house. His mother had not sat down to dinner yet and he went to his room to wash first and change his clothes. He still felt well fortified from Susannah's ample supper but he knew that he would have to make a good attempt to eat dinner as well or face a barrage of questions which he was not ready to answer.

It was not until they had finished dinner and had gone into the adjoining room, well out of range of servants' ears, that Philip and his mother spoke of anything but conventionalities.

"I had a most interesting time today," Mrs. Haven began, "calling on one of the oldest residents of the town."

"Good," Philip smiled. When they had first moved to Millville, his father had urged his mother to call on her neighbors and integrate herself in some way with the life of the community; but, except for a chosen few who came up to her rigid standard, she remained aloof and austere, sheltering her shyness behind a wall of formality. Philip was delighted to know that something had made her willing to call on one of the townspeople. "Who was it?"

"Miss Mattie Emerson."

"Oh, I know her. Cheerful little body, but quite a talker."

"Yes, she said she knew you. She told me you brought her cat back a few weeks ago, that your—your friend had been taking care of it."

"I did indeed. How is the creature?"

"It seemed quite all right. It was sitting in a sunny window and paid no attention to me. Of course, you know I've never liked cats."

"I'm glad it's been keeping out of trouble. I must tell Freely that you saw the cat."

"Philip," Mrs. Haven looked at her son seriously, "Miss Mattie told me that she gave you a piece of her mind the day you brought her cat back."

Philip laughed. "Was that what it was she gave me!"

"Philip, since you seem unable or unwilling to find out anything about the girl, I took it upon myself to make some inquiries and this afternoon I found out all I need to know."

"Mother," he said leaning toward her, "will you take the word of a ninety-year-old woman, who has not heard properly for half a century and whose tongue has a twist in it, against my word?"

"That is beside the point, Philip. Miss Mattie has a keen mind. She seemed to hear me very well and her memory includes the days long before we came to Millville. I knew no one else to ask."

"You might have asked Freely's grandmother, Mrs. Benedict Simon," Philip said. It was not easy for him to disguise the bitterness he felt at what his mother had done, at her lack of faith in him.

"I will not compromise you to the extent of calling on Mrs. Simon."

Philip put his head in his hands. He wanted to hold onto the memory of strength, simplicity, serenity that breathed from Susannah in her kitchen, that the church stood for, that shone out in Freely's eyes, but they were all slipping from him like a dream before the time of waking.

"From what Miss Mattie told me, I must urge you to reconsider about this girl," Mrs. Haven said, trying to speak gently, knowing her attitude was alienating her from her son but wanting to do everything she could to keep the rift from widening.

"What did she tell you?"

"Well," Mrs. Haven began, going back in her mind over her long conversation with Miss Mattie and trying to pick from it just those nettles that might prick Philip most, "she said that the Simons had always been a headstrong lot, and that old Mark Simon ruled like a king on his hilltop. She said that the generation to which your friend's mother belonged was the most headstrong of all, that there were three boys who went West against their parents' wishes and that no one has ever heard of them since, and there was a girl who had no use for home or parents and ran away as soon as she was old enough. Apparently she ran off with a dissolute woodsman —a drinker, a man of bad blood—and her life with him was a torment.

"Mercifully, no doubt, she died when this child—the girl you tell me you love—was born. The child's natural father disowned her and moved away. Somehow or other Benedict Simon found her in the hovel where she was born and brought her back to his home, but he couldn't adopt her legally as he should have done if her father had not disappeared."

"Oh, Mother, Mother," Philip said hoarsely.

"Can you say that it isn't true?"

He shook his head. "It isn't that. It's the light that's put on the whole thing."

"Philip, be firm with yourself and rid yourself of this infatuation," she said sharply.

"Did Miss Mattie have anything good to say about the Simons, about Freely?"

"She said that—that the girl you are interested in had a remarkable skill with animals, but—"

"So," Philip exclaimed angrily. "She even had a 'but' there! And yet her white cat wouldn't be sleekly sunning itself in a window now if it hadn't been for Freely." He stood up abruptly.

162

Frightened by his reaction, Mrs. Haven looked at her son. "Philip, what are you going to do?" She hardly recognized him as he stood before her. His face was set in a mold of determination and his eyes would not meet her gaze.

"I am leaving Monday on a business trip. I may be gone several weeks."

"Are you going alone?"

He smiled bitterly. "Yes. I'm going alone."

She sighed with relief. "What is it now—more buying or selling? You've just got back from a trip."

"Yes, I know, but this is important. I am going to try to find a lumberman to put in charge of my crews. I've recently learned of a fine woodsman who can do a good job for me if I can get him. His name is Raoul de St. Pierre." Philip approached his mother and bent over to kiss her dutifully. "Good night, Mother. I have a great deal of work to do before I leave Monday morning."

"Philip—" she called after him— "Philip."

He did not hear her or heed as he left the room. She listened to him going up the stairs and into his own room, shutting the door quietly but firmly behind him.

"But that," she said aloud, "that *was* the name. Surely I can't be mistaken. One doesn't make a mistake with a name as distinctive as that."

16.

>>>>>>>>>>>>>>>>>>>>>>>><<<<<<<<<<<<<<<<<<<<<<<<

FREELY went out to the barn and gave Ginger an extra measure of oats. While he was eating, she took the harness down from its pegs and put it on him. She combed his mane and tail, talking to him all the while. This night of her graduation from school was exciting and her anticipation spilled over in eager words to the horse who flicked his ears and switched his tail in brief comment. She led him out of the stall and backed him into the shafts of the buggy that stood in the middle of the barn floor. She wrapped the tracings neatly around the shafts and made sure that every buckle was tight.

"Now, Ginger," she admonished, "you stand there quietly and we'll be out in a little while. I had to get you ready before I get myself ready." She reached into a pocket for a lump of sugar.

Ginger whinnied softly in pleasure and then more emphatically, stamping his hoof on the barn floor. Freely gave him another lump of sugar, putting her arms around his neck and standing on her toes to whisper into his furry dusty ear.

In the rafters above, swallows were busy with their first families. Peering down over the edges of their nests and twittering throatily, they watched the girl and the horse, then just the horse as the girl left the barn. Freely went up to her room to dress for the occasion, and then she joined Susannah in the kitchen as the clock was striking six.

"Do I look all right?" she asked.

Susannah smiled, for Freely, who had cared little all her life how she looked, had of late become concerned with her appearance. Susannah surveyed her carefully. The sandy hair had been washed that afternoon and brushed so vigorously outdoors that it shone as if the June sunshine itself had been caught in it. Her skin was tanned from the long hours outdoors, not deeply, but with a soft glow under it rather than on it, and the little bridge of freckles across her nose had widened. The long white dress Susannah had made for her hung well and seemed to make her look taller. She wore no ornament of any kind. Her eyes were dancing, and excitement had brought a flush of color beneath her tan.

"You look as nice as I've ever seen you," Susannah said. "Neat and clean and healthy."

"Do you like my hair?" Freely asked eagerly. "I've pinned it up." She turned around so Susannah might see it better.

"It gives you some height," Susannah said.

Freely threw her arms around her grandmother. Her heart was tumbling over inside her and but for the quiet of Susannah's presence she felt she could not have contained herself. They went out to the barn and while Susannah got into the buggy and took up the reins, Freely opened the door; then, careful of her full white skirt, she climbed up beside Susannah.

They drove out of the barn. Freely looked at the house as they went by it, then at the church. The places she loved she wanted to see for one last time as she had always seen them since her eyes had first taken them in, for she felt that when she returned with her diploma in her hands she would be a different person. Her eyes rested on the other houses grouped around the church. One or two of them were showing signs of life—curtains fluttering in open windows, smoke rising from long unused chimneys, as their owners came up from Millville to spend the summer months in Simonton.

Ginger drew the buggy slowly down the hill. Susannah surveyed with interest the cutover woodland at the left of the road. The logs had all been removed and the brush piles had been burned during a succession of rainy days early in June. The whole area was gradually being taken over by a weedlike growth of hurrying green. It still looked denuded, but it no longer looked raw and desolate.

"There'll be good berrying in that piece in another year," Susannah commented. "Nature's wonderful that way; take one thing and She gives you back something else, and always more than you expect."

Freely said nothing.

"There'll be good berrying all through the country this year," Susannah commented again as her eyes lingered on the blackberry bloom that was white along the roadside and over the stone walls.

"I hope I'll remember my piece," Freely said.

"If it's in your mind—and it must be by the way you've been saying it all these weeks—it'll come out all right." Susannah flicked the reins over Ginger's back. "But don't get your mind all clutered up with thinking how you look or wondering what others are thinking of you; if you do, you'll forget your piece."

"I won't," Freely said, the tone of her voice solemn with promise.

It was only the third week in June, but the full tide of summer had come over the land. The year grows up as quickly as all young things once they start growing, Susannah thought to herself as they drove along in silence. The gaiety of blossoms had gone, the many shadings of color, the quaint pattern of wild flowers, they had all gone with the fragrance of the lilacs, and a density of green was everywhere. The woods bordering the road looked impenetrable, but they were not silent. They had been taken over by the birds. The lush melody of wood thrushes, pierced now and again by the clear sweetness of the white-throated sparrow, made a rich tapestry of song. Susannah always stopped whatever she was doing when the white-throat sang. Tilting her head, she would listen to hear his song, for to her it was the song of one who had known sadness but had turned it to praise.

"Grandma, will he be there?" Freely asked earnestly.

Susannah slapped the reins across Ginger's back. The horse, made mindful that a destination lay before him, shook his head and walked more briskly.

"He told you he would be," Susannah said.

"But that last letter was from such a long way away, could he ever get from there to here by tonight?"

"I think so."

"I never knew he was going so far when he left," Freely went on. "He never said he was going to California, but wasn't it nice that he could see Uncle Roger and Uncle Roland. Think of Uncle Mark being a grandfather!" Freely laughed. "I always imagine him to be about my own age. That's because you call him 'young Mark.'"

Susannah nodded. "Yes, I suppose he'll always be that to me. He was just about your age when he left the hill and I've not seen him since."

"You must have missed them!" Freely exclaimed. She had never thought a great deal of how Susannah had felt about things, but something had been happening to her the last few weeks that had made her aware of another's capacity to feel intensely. She had begun to outgrow the self-absorption that was the armor of her adolescence.

"They've been with me in their letters," Susannah said, "and I've always been proud of them."

"It's strange that they all left Simonton." Loving it as she did, it was hard for Freely to understand how anyone could ever leave it.

"There was a great pull to the West in those days," Susannah said. "New England was like a mothering place. Her sons and daughters took what she had given them and planted it elsewhere, just the way they took roots from the lilacs. It's men like your uncles who are the bones and sinews of this America."

It was still daylight when they reached the Town Hall where, for reasons of space, the graduation exercises were being held. A row of horses were already standing by the hitching posts. Some had light blankets thrown over them; others wore old straw hats with their ears sticking through holes cut in the wide crowns; others wore fly sheets with gay-colored baubles dangling from them. Susannah tied Ginger to a post and threw a sheet over him to protect him from flies. Freely took a bundle of hay from the back of the buggy and put it down before him, stroking him in affectionate good-by; then they went toward the building. At the door they parted. Freely kissed Susannah impulsively, longing to stay with her but knowing she could not. Susannah straightened a fold in Freely's dress and smoothed her hand over the sandy hair.

"God bless you, dear heart," she whispered.

Freely's eyes filled with tears and she clung tightly to Susannah's hands. "I wish Grandpa was here," she said.

"He is," Susannah replied, "in all that he has given you. Stand forward then in the things he taught you."

Freely nodded.

People were pushing past them, around them, eager to get to their seats. Freely hurried to the stage at the end of the hall where her classmates were sitting and Susannah found a seat in the second row from the front. She was glad to sit down, for the June night was warm and she was feeling tired.

A brougham drawn by a pair of high-stepping gray horses drew up to the Town Hall. The coachman got down from the box and held the door while a tall, elegantly dressed woman got out, followed by a tall young man. But the hall was full and no matter how important the latecomers might be there were no seats for them except in the last row.

The exercises began with the singing of the National Anthem. The twelve graduates, seven boys and five girls, sat stiffly on the platform that was flanked with large blue hydrangeas and pine branches standing in tubs filled with sand. One by one the graduates spoke their pieces, sang their songs, or played the piano. Each one had the opportunity of revealing some particular skill to the townspeople who were gathered in the hall, more particularly to the admiring group of family or friends who were there and for whom one graduate was the sole reason for the evening. As the entertainment went on, no names of the participants were announced as presumably each one was known to all who were in the audience. Each in turn, in an order arranged through many rehearsals, the graduates left their chairs, moved to the center of the stage, bowed, did what their teacher had trained them to do, bowed again and sat down. Applause followed every performance, but the applause depended for its volume on the number of friends in the audience.

Susannah half closed her eyes when Freely stepped to the front of the platform, bowed her head, and made the merest suggestion of a curtsey.

Philip gripped his hands together. It was the first sight he had had of Freely for more than six weeks. He felt his mother raising her lorgnette. His hands were cold. His throat was dry. He could not have answered if Gabriel himself had called him by name.

Freely looked into the sea of faces, seeing them all, yet none in particular. The wild tumbling in her heart had ceased, the knocking of her knees that had made her wonder if she would ever get to the front of the platform had stopped. An immense stillness had come over her. She heard the familiar voice within herself and she knew that she could obey its prompting. She was in the Millville Town Hall facing a multitude of people; but she might have been standing in the dell with the trees arching overhead and the moss springy beneath her feet for at that moment there was no one in the world but God and herself.

"Portia's speech from *The Merchant of Venice* by William Shakespeare," she announced. She heard her own voice and its sound gave her something to hold onto:

> *"The quality of mercy is not strain'd,*
> *It droppeth as the gentle rain from heaven*
> *Upon the place beneath. It is twice bless'd:*
> *It blesseth him that gives and him that takes.*
> *'Tis mightiest in the mightiest: it becomes*
> *The throned monarch better than his crown;*
> *His sceptre shows the force of temporal power,*
> *The attribute to awe and majesty,*
> *Wherein doth sit the dread and fear of kings;*
> *But mercy is above this sceptred sway,*
> *It is enthroned in the hearts of kings,*
> *It is an attribute to God himself;*
> *And earthly power doth then show likest God's,*
> *When mercy seasons justice."*

Freely paused. In the room, as far as she was concerned, there was not even the sound of a hundred people breathing. There were only words, deep toned, clear winged, and behind the words the invincibility of truth. She smiled and went on,

> *"Therefore, Jew,*
> *Though justice be thy plea, consider this,*
> *That in the course of justice, none of us*
> *Should see salvation: we do pray for mercy;*
> *And that same prayer doth teach us all to render*
> *The deeds of mercy."*

Freely bowed and walked back to her chair. There was the small sound of her feet on the wooden platform, the faint creaking of the chair as she sat on it, but no other sound filled the room in which the words seemed still to be echoing. It would have been like clapping in church, some thought; but applause was her due and in time it came, not only from a quiet-faced country woman in the second to the front row and a young man at the back of the hall, but from everyone —even from the graduates sitting on the platform who had not previously applauded their fellows. Surprised and delighted, Freely smiled at the sound, glancing into the wings at Miss Anderson who stood there with the book in her hands from which she had been ready to prompt. Miss Anderson beamed at her pupil.

Mrs. Haven had put down her lorgnette to wipe her eyes. During the applause she leaned over and whispered to her son, "I've seen many a Portia, but that girl—that simple country girl! I wonder who she is."

Philip could not hear all that his mother said but he sensed her approval. He nodded vigorously and warmed his hands by clapping.

Freely's piece was the last. Miss Anderson had planned it that way and she was glad she had. Portia's speech was a fitting climax to the entertainment and it set the right tone for the graduation address.

The Superintendent of Schools spoke with appreciation and warning. In grandiloquent words he reminded the graduates of all that had been given them through the years of their schooling. He urged them to realize that it had not been given them for their own enjoyment, but that they might carry into the future wisdom, good judgment, and high vision. He reminded them that they stood on the threshold of a new century, that already great changes had come to the mechanics of human living, but that greater ones were bound to come before many more years had passed. "Power may well be the keynote of the new century," he concluded, "but may I ask you all to remember, as tonight you go forth from the portals of learning, that it is the power in your own minds that will carry you far and make useful citizens of you, boys and girls."

One by one he handed out the diplomas, calling a graduate's name as he did so, but such a tumult of clapping followed each presentation that the names went unheard.

"Isn't she beautiful, Mother?" Philip asked as he took his mother's arm and guided her through the crowd to her carriage.

"You mean the one who spoke Portia?"

"Yes, Mother. That's Freely. Freely Simon."

"Oh." Mrs. Haven hesitated as she felt herself rallying. "I'd never call her beautiful, Philip, but I will say she has considerable character in her face."

Philip was so overflowing with joy at the sight of Freely that he scarcely heard what his mother had said. He helped her into the brougham, then he shut the door and spoke to her through the window.

"Mother, I'll be home in a little while. I'll come to your room to say good night if your light is still on. Thank you for coming with me."

Startled, she leaned forward to call him back, but he lost himself quickly in the crowd of people near the steps of the Town Hall.

"Shall we go on, madam, or wait for Mr. Philip?" the coachman bent down to ask.

"We'll go home, Hawkins," Mrs. Haven said, leaning back against the padded walls of the brougham. "Mr. Philip is coming later."

Philip pushed through the crowd until he stood near Freely and Susannah. Friends were congratulating friends, good wishes were being exchanged, farewells were being made. Everyone seemed to be closely linked with everyone else. Philip felt unrelated and out of place, longing to be near Freely but not sure how to press his claim in such a gathering. Then Freely saw him. Crying his name, she broke away from the group of admiring school friends that had surrounded her. She held out both hands to him.

"Oh, Philip," she cried, "you're back. I'm so glad to see you."

He took her hands in his and looked at her—flushed face, shining hair, long white dress. Then it seemed as if there had been no time away for him, for the miles that had lengthened between them had only drawn them closer.

"I'll wait," he said, dropping her hands so that others with more urgent demands could speak to her. Once he had seen her, and seen that she was the same, only far lovelier than he had remembered her to be, he knew he could wait.

Susannah put her hand on his arm. "Philip," she said, "I'm very tired. Let me go out with you to the buggy and we'll wait there for Freely."

They went out together and Philip thought with a start how much frailer Susannah looked than when he had last seen her, and how heavily she leaned on his arm. Near the row of horses they stood in the warm night air with the hub-bub of voices resounding from the Town Hall behind them.

"You have much to tell me," Susannah began.

"Yes, enough for a whole day in your kitchen."

"The boys? Young Mark?" she asked, so eager to hear in brief that she could not wait.

"They're marvelous. They've loaded me with messages and presents for you, and a few new photographs. I'll come up tomorrow with them all."

"And Freely's father? Did you find any trace of him?"

"Yes," Philip said, "but I want to tell it just to you sometime."

Susannah shook her head. "Freely must know it too. When did you get back, Philip?"

"This afternoon."

"You must be tired."

"Not tired, Susannah, happy."

Susannah smiled understandingly. "I'm going to sit down in the buggy, Philip. I'll wait there for you to bring Freely to me."

He saw her safely up onto the seat, then he went back to the hall to wait for Freely. She came soon, calling goodbys behind her to school friends and teachers, holding her diploma tight in her hand. She let him put his arms around her, there on the Town Hall steps. She lifted her lips to his, feeling the warmth and sureness of his love in a quick, impassioned kiss. Then, arm in arm, they went down the steps and started off across the lawn toward the horses by the hitching posts.

They had not gone half the distance when they stopped by a large shadowy spruce and stood still to look at each other.

"You've grown since I've been away!" Philip exclaimed.

She put one hand up to her hair to see if it was still in place. "I've pinned my hair up. Do you like it?"

He nodded. "You're beautiful."

She held up her diploma for him to see. "I must be wise, too. Look at this."

"So," he laughed, "it's free Freely now!"

Amused that he had remembered what she had once said about her graduation from school, she nodded.

Looking into her radiant face, Philip longed for words of assurance from her lips. "Or—" he asked, dropping his voice as if the words said too loudly might break the dream they were both in— "or is it my Freely now?"

"Perhaps," she said, unwilling to commit herself. Suddenly overcome with shyness she looked away from him. "Perhaps," she said again, her words just audible in the night.

He reached into his pocket. "I brought you something, Freely. It's very little, the merest token, but I wanted you to have something from my travels."

She looked at the ring he held between his fingers. In a silver setting a small, curiously cut stone burned with pale luster.

"It's lovely," she said. She touched the ring as if she could scarcely believe that it was for her. "It's like a bit of moonlight caught in a tiny glass box."

"It is a moonstone," he said. He held her hand, the ring poised between two fingers of his other hand. "May I put it on your finger?"

She looked up at him, her face expressionless, her eyes serious. Then, with a catch of her breath she whispered, "Yes."

He slipped it on her outstretched finger and pressed her hand to his lips.

She held her hand off and looked at it. "Thank you, Philip," she said quietly. Then, in a natural voice, "Where did it come from?"

"I got it in a little mining town in the Sierras. A town named St. Pierre. I'll tell you about it when I see you tomorrow."

She put her hands together quickly. "Oh, then you are coming to Simonton tomorrow?"

"Yes, I told Susannah I would be up in the afternoon. I have so much to tell her about her sons."

"And me, too."

"Yes," he laughed, "I'll tell it to you too."

They walked over to the buggy. Philip helped Freely in.

"Have I kept her too long?" he asked Susannah.

"If you hadn't someone else would have," Susannah said as she picked up the reins that were lying over the dashboard.

Philip took the sheet off Ginger and folded it, handing it to Freely. He went to the hitching post and unfastened the chain that was attached to Ginger's bridle. Freely sank back against the seat. There was no longer any need to sit upright and keep her white dress clean.

"Good night, Philip," she said.

Susannah clucked to the horse and waved to Philip as they started off creakily.

Philip stood by the hitching post watching them until they had become part of the soft darkness of the June night.

Freely and Susannah went over the road in silence. There was little need to speak for each had much to think about. Susannah looked at the road ahead, thinking of her sons. Freely looked at her hands folded in her lap. By the time they reached the top of the hill, the rising moon had just begun to burnish the white church.

"I knew I would not be the same person when I saw the church again," Freely said.

"So much has happened in these few hours?" Susannah asked.

Freely laid her hand on Susannah's lap and for the first time Susannah saw the dull luster of the moonstone.

"Oh, dear heart," she whispered softly.

Freely nodded.

Susannah placed her hand on the girl's, covering it. The

buggy wheels turned slowly; the harness squeaked, and Ginger's hoofs thudded against the night.

"So you have chosen," Susannah said. "You have chosen the high road."

Freely shook her head but her lips were smiling. "I haven't said anything to him yet."

"Ah, but you would not wear his ring if you were not sure in your heart."

They drove into the barn. Susannah got down from the buggy and went into the house, carrying Freely's diploma to safe keeping, while Freely tended to the horse. After she had given Ginger a half measure of oats and a long caress, she went over to the church. Standing on the steps, she could see that the moon had preceded her, for a wedge of light had gone in through the half-open door. There was no sound anywhere but a whippoorwill distantly calling and the wind in the trees. Freely went inside. Never had the church seemed so holy. The moonlight, coming in through the high, paned windows, made squares of light on the floor and across the pews.

Freely shivered with excitement, anticipation, wonder, for though she had said nothing in words she knew that she had given herself to Philip. So, she was not the same as when she had left the hill earlier in the evening, nor would she ever be the same again. Always she had been herself. Now her life would be lived in terms of another. Until she knew Philip, she had not thought that she wanted to belong to anyone but herself; now that she knew him and loved him she felt differently. Her mind was free of uncertainty and questioning. She felt sure of herself. She sat down in one of the pews.

Tentatively her thought went ahead, but she drew it back. It was no use. She would have to wait and talk with Philip. All she knew now was that she was as sure of him as she was of herself and the sureness made her willing to wait. She thought of Susannah with new understanding—her life so rich and warm with love, so deeply satisfying that parting and sorrow and loss had not been able to dent it—and Freely prayed that her own life might grow as Susannah's had. Her school days, her child days, were behind her and before her reached the length of her life to live as best she could, doing honor to Benedict's teaching. Thinking of him and looking at the pulpit from which he had spoken for fifty years, she could think only of the generosity with which he both gave and received and the strange and wonderful mercy that he showed to all people. It had not been in him to condemn, either himself or another. Portia's speech started to repeat itself in Freely's mind and she whispered it into the moonlit stillness of the church.

Outside the whippoorwill ceased calling; far down in the cutting a fox barked; the droning of insect voices merged with the wind in the pines. The excitement Freely felt had gone down to calm. It was as if time had stopped, for there was no hurrying, no hungering. Such was the gift of the church, its benediction, Benedict had always said. Freely felt encompassed in a silence as filled with bliss as the church on the hill was filled with moonlight.

17.

PHILIP found his mother in the garden that led out of the house and went down toward the river. The warm June air brought out fragrance from the flowers and the darkness was heavy with the scent of roses and honeysuckle.

"Well, Philip, I hardly thought to see you home so soon!" Mrs. Haven exclaimed.

He sat down in a chair near her and the moonlight washed over his face. His mother, looking at him, thought how absurd young people look when they are happy.

"Thanks so much for going with me, Mother. I did want you to see Freely for yourself."

"And, of course, you didn't want to see her at all!" Mrs. Haven chided playfully.

"Six weeks is a long time to be away," Philip admitted.

"You've not yet told me a thing about your trip, dear. I had no idea, when you left, that you were going so far."

"Nor did I."

"Was it successful?"

"Very."

"Did you locate the man you wanted for a foreman?"

"I located him, but his services were not obtainable."

"What did you do with yourself all the time?" she asked, an edge of impatience to her voice.

"I saw Freely's uncles and I found out something about her father."

"But Philip, I thought you were going on business."

"That was business, of a kind." He sat up in his chair and looked at her. He had made the trip to satisfy her more than for any other reason and now he was eager to tell her about it. "Mother," he began impetuously, "I love Freely Simon, but if I marry her I want it to make you happy too. I thought you would have a better feeling for her if I could find some trace of her father and that was the quest I started out on."

"And did you?"

"Yes. Picking up a clue here and there, from saw mills and lumber camps, I followed him across New York State. Then I lost my remaining clue for a while, and didn't pick it up again until Chicago. It kept leading west and I got as far as the Sierra Nevada Mountains before I could satisfy myself fully. When I was so near Freely's uncles as that, I decided to go a little farther—for Susannah's sake this time, not yours."

"Who is Susannah?"

"Freely's grandmother. I thought to go on and see her sons so I could bring back news of them to her."

"How old are they?"

"They are men in their fifties, men with families, well established, well regarded. Mark Simon, he's the one Susannah always calls 'young Mark' for he was such a lad when he left the hill, had his first grandchild while I was there."

Almost in spite of herself, Florence Haven listened eagerly to her son's tale of these New England men who had gone West at a time when the country was expanding, when the lure of land and gold was like a magnet. Leaving New England far behind them, they had taken with them all that it had given them—a feeling for the soil, an understanding of animals and a closeness to nature, as well as the ability and the desire to work with their hands not only in their chosen ways of livelihood but in shaping beauty. Each one was a craftsman in his leisure hours and there were few skills to which they could not turn their hands.

"In the midst of a world pushing and straining for success and power it was a delight to meet Susannah's sons. There didn't seem to be any frenzied striving for what they were doing. I think their quiet contentment was the gift of their hilltop and they have grafted it into their new ways of living."

"But the girl's father?" Mrs. Haven pressed. She was willing to agree that Susannah's sons might be good stock, but it was this other element that had entered into the girl which might blight her son's life.

"Ah, yes—" Philip leaned back in his chair. His face was in shadow now as the moon had moved on. He was beginning to feel very tired. The West and all that he had seen and done seemed oddly remote and unreal. What mattered was his longing to be with Freely, to look into her eyes and hear her voice and feel the pressure of her hands in his.

"I'm listening, Philip," his mother reminded him.

" 'I give you the end of a golden string, Only wind it into a ball,' " Philip said, as if to the night rather than to anyone listening to his words. "But it wasn't a golden string, it was good coarse hemp, and it didn't lead me to Heaven's gate, though it did lead me to a door in a mountain. I followed it to a little town by the name of Lost Cause—"

"That wasn't the name of the town you wrote me from."

"It wasn't the name, but it was the same place," he explained. "Lost Cause was a town that had a mushroom growth near one of the mountains from which gold was being drawn like water from a spring. Just after an army of prospectors had moved there and the town had built houses and laid out streets, suddenly there was no more gold. Up to that time, the town had been only a dot on a surveyor's map;

after that it was called Lost Cause. Some of the more impatient prospectors began to move away, but plenty stayed on hammering away on the lode. However, there wasn't enough work going on to warrant much care of the mines, nor were there people to do it.

"The skilled workmen had gone to other, more profitable mines. At Lost Cause, when props rotted they weren't replaced; when they buckled and fell in a whole tunnel would be cut off. Accidents happened as inexperienced men handled dynamite that exploded at the wrong time. But the prospectors went on looking for gold and they never closed a gallery until they were sure to the last man that it had been worked out. But sometimes they struck a vein of water that drove them out of a mine and closed it forever."

"How dreadful it all sounds!" Mrs. Haven exclaimed.

"Among the prospectors at Lost Cause was a Raoul de St. Pierre," Philip went on. "He was living in the town with his daughter, who had gotten enough education to be a schoolteacher. His wife had died and his son had moved farther West, but though he had been moving like a rolling stone across the country his days were not so active as they had been. He'd lost a leg in a lumbering accident in Minnesota and though he got around on a wooden one, he wasn't the man he used to be. Then, one day, a prospector working at Lost Cause discovered a vein of feldspar. They began hacking it out and found some sale for it. It was only a semiprecious gem, a moonstone, but it seemed to be peculiar to that one place and the demand for it increased. It began to look as if Lost Cause might not be so lost after all.

"But they went too fast in the mine and few of the men were experienced. One day they struck a vein of water. They thought it was a spring and someone went back for a pump, thinking they could handle the seepage into the mine that way. St. Pierre must have thought differently. Taking one look at the crack in the wall through which the water was flowing he must have known that the mine would be flooded in a matter of minutes. He grabbed the flat sledge they used to drag through the mine with their tools on it and he held it up to the rock where the water was—"

"Why? Why?" Mrs. Haven was leaning forward in her chair.

"To hold the rock back so the force of water behind it would not shatter it until the mine had been cleared. He was a powerfully built man, everyone who knew him said, and as strong as an ox. He put the sledge against the wall of rock that was already beginning to show signs of crumbling, and he braced himself. Then he shouted—and they say his voice echoed down the mine and through all its galleries like the voice of God itself. He called to them to clear the mine, and they did.

"The man who told me the story and who had been working beside St. Pierre said that he didn't know why they obeyed him but that they did. There was something in his voice that made them act, leaving all questioning till later. They dropped their tools and ran. 'Clear the mine!' they shouted, as they ran from it, echoing St. Pierre's words. They got out, but only just in time for the waters of an underground river were at their heels. They clambered to some rocks outside the mine entrance and watched the river go on its way, down the rocky slope to join another river."

"And the man who held it back, de St. Pierre?"

Philip shook his head. "They never saw him again. He was lost in the rising waters, but forty-six men owed their lives to him."

There was silence in the garden.

"They named the town after him," Philip went on, "and they called the river St. Pierre too. It's still flowing, and beside it where it issues from the mountain, at the place where men used to go in to work, they've built a little stone chapel. I spent a whole afternoon there. It was the end of my search and," he added slowly, "the beginning of my life."

"What a strange story! And this de St. Pierre is the girl's father?"

Philip nodded.

"He couldn't have been such a worthless man after all," she admitted, more to herself than to her son as she tried to make sense from the story and link it to what she had already been told about Raoul de St. Pierre.

"A man who, at the last, will give his life for his fellows has not been entirely heedless of them up to that time," Philip added.

Mrs. Haven shivered and drew up the shawl that had slipped from her shoulders. Her eyes rested on the flowers of her garden that were almost without color in the moonlight, but it was not cool stately irises and opulent poppies that she was seeing.

Philip was leaning back in the chair again; his eyes were closed. He felt he had no more to say. His thoughts were with Freely. He wondered what she would say when she heard the story of her father. She had the capacity to see nobility wherever she looked and it would not surprise her to know that her father had possessed it. Neither Benedict nor Susannah would ever have spoken to her of her father except as someone of whom she could be proud. She must have met her share of curious questioning, lifted brows, innuendoes and outright words, but they had not touched her. She had learned to hold her head high before she met them so when they came they passed over her like a warm wind that, though it might ruffle the surface, left all else undisturbed.

"Have you asked—" Mrs. Haven could not bring herself to call the girl by name—"this girl to marry you?"

"Not in so many words, but we have given each other our

love." Philip answered. He could hear Freely's breathless whisper as he had held her close to him, "Perhaps"; he could see the look in her eyes when she accepted the moonstone. Then Philip, unable to stand the tension and longing for approval from his mother, burst out, "Didn't you really think she was lovely, Mother, when you saw her tonight, heard her?"

"Yes," Mrs. Haven agreed, "I do think she is a nice-looking country girl, and she spoke her piece very well indeed. However, I wonder if with her background—or lack of background—she can possibly be a fit wife for you in your position."

"Background!" Philip exclaimed. "How many young men have the opportunity to marry a girl whose great-grandfather named a township and whose father gave his name to a town?"

Philip could feel his mother marshaling her arguments. He sighed. The moon was moving across the sky but they were getting nowhere. Talking about Freely would never change his mother; only Freely herself could do that.

"Mother, please ask her here for a visit. You'll feel differently when you know her for yourself."

"Very well, Philip," Mrs. Haven agreed, surprising her son with the alacrity of her decision. She drew her shawl around her and stood up. There was nothing she could do, she knew, to change her son's feeling but she had every confidence that what she could not do his home might. Take the girl from the simple country setting in which he saw her and place her against the background where her life would have to be lived if she was to be his wife, and Philip would see her for what she was.

Philip rose and stood by his mother. He slipped his arm through hers as they walked back to the house together.

"You'll like her, Mother, once you know her," he said persuadingly. "And she likes you already. She's got the kind of nature that embraces everything. She's just as polite to a spider walking over her hand or to a rabbit she meets in the woods as she is with people."

"What a curious accomplishment!"

"It's not an accomplishment, Mother, it's—it's Freely."

Mrs. Haven's laugh had a brittle sound. "That is all very well, I'm sure, for the life on a remote hilltop, but your wife should have more to her than that."

"What, for instance?"

"A certain elegance. A *savoir-faire*. You know what I mean, Philip."

"I think that what Freely is will come out in whatever Freely does."

"We shall see. However, for your sake, I am willing to invite her to Haven Hall. Any time next month would be pleasant for a visit. I'll write a note for you to give to the girl's grandmother when next you see her."

"I'm going up to the hill tomorrow," Philip said eagerly.

Mrs. Haven looked at him and smiled. "Dear boy, how difficult it is for you to see anything in your own home any more."

At the door, Philip bade her good night, then he turned quickly and walked back into the garden they had just left. Impatience fretted him. He longed to be with Freely, to hold her in his arms again; he yearned for the time when she would be wholly his. He felt frustrated at being held back and deep within him he felt afraid of what his mother might do. He thought enviously of Freely's father doing something as tangible as holding back a wall of water, for he felt so helpless, so ineffectual, and yet so desperately sure of his desire.

The next afternoon when Philip went up the hill to Simonton he felt more hopeful. His mother had been charming in her assurance of welcoming Freely as her guest during July and he knew that she had written a warm invitation. The hours spent in Susannah's kitchen were happy ones. Knowing that Freely was in the same room was pleasure sufficient, but it was an added joy to be able to tell Susannah about her sons, to watch her face light up with memory and satisfaction as he showed her photographs of the tall men, the different grandchildren, and the newest child, Mark III. Philip already felt himself to be a part of this family that had dug its roots deep in New Hampshire land, but whose branches were spreading far.

It was Freely who spoke of her father, asking for the story that Philip had saved to the last. She listened wide eyed and grave, but she was detached from it. It was the story of a lonely man who had been seeking a dream, going from one place to another, driven on by hard work and suffering. Then, at the last, the whole plan of his life was made clear as in one terrible moment he lived for others rather than himself. It was a moving story, but it was the story of a stranger. Freely looked down at the small blue-gray stone on her finger.

"And this came from that very mine," she said wonderingly.

"Yes, so I was told," Philip answered. "The vein they were working on before they came to the water."

Freely pressed it to her lips, but it had nothing to do with that unknown man who was her father. It was the token of Philip's love.

Susannah was smiling to herself, nodding her head in time with her rocking, as if much that she had puzzled over for years had come clear at last. "Then that was what Freelove saw in him," she said. "That was what she loved—a man capable of a moment of high courage. I'm not surprised," she went on, softly as if she were talking to herself, "for Freelove had courage too. The same spirit was in them both and called to the other across a world of differences."

After supper, just before Philip left, he gave Susannah

the note his mother had written. Susannah read it to herself, then she read it aloud to Freely, whose face paled as she listened.

After Susannah had finished reading, Freely shook her head. "No, no," she said.

"But you must come, Freely. I want my mother to know you," Philip urged.

"Will you be there? All the time?" Freely asked.

"Yes, and when I have to go out to the woodlots or the mill you can come with me."

Freely turned to Susannah, but she saw that even with her there was no escape. Susannah merely nodded her head. Freely got up quickly from her chair and walked across the room to look out the window. She felt the first sudden realization of how love made things difficult, and before it she had no ready response.

When Philip went down the hill a half hour later it was with a note from Susannah in his pocket. She thanked Mrs. Haven for the generous invitation to her granddaughter, which her granddaughter would be pleased to accept. She added that it would not be easy to spare Freely with the garden coming on and summer with its round of chores, but that she would manage.

After Philip left, Freely clung to Susannah. "What shall I do when I'm there?" she asked.

"Just what you always do. If you can't be yourself at Haven Hall you've got no right to think of marrying Philip Haven."

"Marrying!" Freely echoed the word as if she had not heard it before.

"You have known all along that it was inevitable for you and Philip," Susannah reminded her.

"Yes, I have known," Freely said.

And she had, she told herself, but it was the curious sequence of steps leading up to it that she had forgotten. This then was marriage—this growing into each other's lives so that the thing that was love was not the delight of a moment but the gradual acceptance of a new way of life and the duties that went with it.

"Then of what are you afraid?" Susannah asked.

Freely's head went up a little higher. "I am not afraid," she answered.

18.

>>>>>>>>>>>>>>>>>>>>>><<<<<<<<<<<<<<<<<<<<<<<

ON the first day of July, Mrs. Haven sent the carriage for Freely. The grays came up the hill and to the square white house that looked cool under the mass of shade cast by the oak tree. Hawkins got down from his seat. He felt no concern about the horses' standing as they were, tired from the long pull. He went up to the door. Susannah had seen him coming and stood there to meet him.

"I've come for the young lady," Hawkins said, touching his hat.

"My granddaughter is ready. Here is her box. Would you like some water for your horses, or for yourself? The well is just beside the house. It's a warm day."

"Thank you kindly, ma'am, but the grays have taken it easy up the hill and they'll need no water until we get back to the stable. I'll just set the young lady's box in the carriage and then I'll get a drink for myself."

Freely came to the door. "Isn't Philip here? Oh, Grandma, I did so hope he would come!"

"His mother thought it was better for you to arrive this way, as if you were her guest. She thought it was more dignified."

Freely swallowed quickly. Dignity: that was a word she had been hearing lately and which she had not heard often before.

190

Susannah put her arms around Freely. There was so much she longed to say, so much she wished to spare the girl, for Freely seemed young to be facing this test of love; yet if her love for Philip was real, if it was to endure, she would have to face it.

"You've not lived on a hilltop all your days for nothing," Susannah said, releasing Freely from her embrace and starting out to the carriage with her.

Freely nodded. Benedict would have said the same, she thought, challenging her to be true to what had been hers, what would always be her own.

Hawkins held the door of the carriage open. Freely threw her arms impulsively around Susannah, then she got in. Hawkins shut the door and mounted the coachman's seat.

"You're sure you'll be all right?" Freely asked.

"I have been all these years," Susannah answered with a smile. "There's no reason why anything should happen to me now. Two families are living on the hill this summer so I'll not lack neighbors, and John Wheelman is coming every day to do the chores. We'll have a barn full of hay and an upstanding garden by the time you're back." She withdrew a few steps from the carriage and raised her hand. "Now go," she said, adding quietly the words that were in so many Bible stories, "and the Lord be with thee."

Hawkins flicked the reins and the grays started off. Freely waved until the drop of the hill took her from sight, then she leaned back against the seat. She wished she were sitting on the coachman's seat and could talk with Hawkins. She wished she were seeing the road across a horse's back as she was used to seeing it; but she could not. There were many things now she could not do because she loved Philip.

Almost without asking or seeking it had come upon her, this love. In accepting it, she accepted also the fact that she must embrace a new way of living. She looked at the small stone in its silver setting. She had never worn a ring before, but this one had become such a part of her that she thought she could not be without it. She turned the ring on her finger, wondering what lay before her. Susannah had told her to give herself time in the new life; that the pull back to the hill might often be great but that she should not think of returning until she saw her way clearly.

"You can't balance yourself in the middle of the scales," Susannah reminded her. "Sooner or later you'll have to throw your weight on one side or the other, and then be willing to accept the consequences of your decision."

Freely had not thought, then, that she would be called upon to make any particular decision and Susannah's words had seemed needless.

Susannah stood by the kitchen window long after the carriage had disappeared down the hill. She was proud of Freely, sitting there so demurely in her neat gingham dress, holding her wide straw hat in her hands, with her dark blue coat folded on the seat beside her. In her box were sufficient clothes for any occasion—the white graduation dress for best, the linen skirts and blouses for daily wear, and the three gingham dresses, the two pairs of shoes, the cotton nightgowns with their picot edging at cuff and neck. Even her underclothes were in good order, Susannah thought with gratification. A few bore darns, but they had been carefully and lovingly done during the last few days by either Freely or Susannah as they sat in the evenings by the kitchen table in the pool of lamplight. Freely had taken pride in the assembling of her clothes and she was happy about them.

Susannah felt that she was sending the girl out in the best way she could and though that best was a long way from what Haven Hall knew or expected, it was Freely Philip loved, and Susannah had no wish to change the girl. Susannah felt safe about Philip. If he did not believe in Freely so much he would not want her to come to his home. The way might be open to a good life for Freely, Susannah thought, and she would ever cease to be grateful to Philip for stirring something in Freely that made her conscious of the world away from the hill. Wherever Freely's life might lead her or however Freely might live, it mattered less to Susannah than that Freely's life be one wherein she was loved and could give her love in return. That was what Susannah had prayed for since she had first held in her arms the child that had cost her mother's life and been rejected by her father. Susannah had prayed that she might be near until Freely was grown and that, to Susannah, meant until Freely was loved.

But whatever might happen during the next few weeks, Susannah found it necessary to face certain facts. She and Freely could not live another winter on the hill alone. No matter how much each one loved it, the rigors of life were not to be born without a man's strength to share them. Even in the few months they had been without Benedict, much had gone undone: there had been no boiling down of the sap that year, except the small amount Susannah had done on the kitchen stove; the woodpile was dwindling alarmingly. There was hay to be cut and stored, manure to be spread. Even with all her willingness, there were tasks that Freely could not do and have anything left of her life, and to employ someone to care for the place would mean selling off more and more timber until there were no reserves left. When Freely returned, Susannah knew she must tell the girl that before the first cold came they would have to prepare to leave the hill. And whether they would go to California or Millville remained to be seen.

Susannah suspected that Freely would not want to go far from the Simonton country. So, though they had stood their ground longer than anyone else, the river village would draw them as it had drawn everyone else who had once lived on the hill. They would find a little house, or a part of a house, and Freely could get work in the mill. Perhaps they could keep a few hens, but the horse and the cow would have to be sold. And the house? Susannah felt the strength of the house that had sheltered so many Simons and from which they had gone forth like scions from a tree to be grafted to other trees in other parts of the land. They might do what other families had done—tear it down and sell the good material, saving what they needed to erect a smaller house where life could be lived without such rigor.

And the church? Susannah shook her head. It would stand where it had stood for a century, where the first Mark Simon and his three powerful sons had built it; and if only the animals and birds came to it for refuge from storm and a brief safety, if only the winds were its worshippers, it would still proclaim its essential truth. A passer-by could find rest in it. A troubled person coming up the hill road—that would soon, for lack of use, have grass growing down its center and trees crowding in from the side—would find quiet near the church. In the Middle Ages, men's longing after God and desire to worship flowered in great cathedrals. Stone had yielded its harshness to the hands of men, and stone would stand for all time to proclaim to the world what marvels the desire to honor God could call forth. Here, on this deserted New England hilltop, the church would stand, not for all time because of the nature of its fabric, but for a long time. Some would see it, some would remember it; but it would be there to declare to all when doubt swept over them that there man had sought to honor God. And, so desiring, the cleanness of his hands and the pureness of his heart had expressed themselves in this building that stood four square, as stout in structure as it was in purpose. Men would know, if only for a moment, that where people had once been sure they could be sure again.

Susannah turned back to her work, comforted. She was old and had not many years before her. Freely was young and strong and could adapt herself to anything. The house that had served three generations well could go on to other ways of usefulness; but that the church should continue to stand was strength to her heart. A tree in the woodland lived its life independent of man; so the church would continue to live its life, white and serene on the hilltop though the forest was crowding in on every side. It would stand and its message would remain unchanged, though it might no longer be valued.

Philip was waiting to greet Freely when she arrived. At sight of the carriage coming up the drive, he ran out to meet her, opening the door himself. Freely had imagined that Philip would take her in his arms, but when he held out his hand to her as she got out of the carriage she took it readily.

"You've grown again!" he exclaimed.

"It's just my hair," she laughed. "I'm going to wear it up all the time now."

"It makes you look like a young lady."

His words pleased her. That was what he wanted her to be.

"Mother's waiting for us in the garden," he said. "Would you like to go to your room first or shall we go to see her?"

"Let's go to her. I've waited so long to know your mother, Philip."

"Hawkins, please put Miss Freely's box in her room," Philip said. Then, slipping his arm through Freely's, he led her to the garden that fell in a series of terraces from the house to the river.

Freely saw well-kept beds of flowers; she breathed the scent of roses; she walked on the rich green turf of a long-established lawn. And, except for Philip beside her, it would have seemed like a dream. In a summerhouse backed by evergreens, she caught sight of an erect gray-haired woman with a piece of needlework in her hands. Freely's impulse was to run across the lawn and throw her arms around the person who, because she was Philip's mother, had already won Freely's love; but Freely felt Philip's hand on her arm, restraining her. They walked slowly across the grass. Mrs. Haven did not look up at them, but she was conscious of their approach as she thrust her needle through the silk and laid the piece on the table. She lifted her glance when they stood before her.

"Mother, this is Freely," Philip said.

Freely had pictured herself embracing Philip's mother as she would Susannah, but when Mrs. Haven looked at her she had a curious feeling within her as if flowing water had suddenly been dammed. She held out her hand and bent her knees in a brief curtsey.

"I'm glad to meet you, at last," Mrs. Haven said, dropping the girl's hand and reaching out to pick up her needlework.

"Thank you, ma'am," Freely replied. "It was kind of you to ask me to visit you."

Philip moved away to bring some chairs from another part of the lawn. Freely felt lost without him standing beside her.

"You must be tired."

"Oh no, I'm not at all. I haven't done anything to get tired," Freely said. The thought crept into her mind that, for purposes of conversation, it might have been better if she had been tired. "It was a lovely drive. I've never sat behind two horses before. It—"

"Is your grandmother well?"

"Oh yes." Freely's face brightened. "She—she's always well."

"How nice for her."

"Yes, it is," Freely agreed. There seemed to be nothing more to talk about. If Susannah were not well, Freely thought, there would be a great deal to talk about. But that would have been no bargain for Freely.

Philip came back with two chairs. Freely smiled swiftly at him. He saw something in her smile that he had not seen before and he came to her aid with a flow of small talk. He knew that it did not matter what he said. Anything would help to ease the way between these two at their first meeting. In the midst of relating an inconsequential event that had taken place that morning at the mill, Philip smiled to himself as he thought irrelevantly how two women never could love the same man without becoming tense with each other.

Sara appeared with the tea tray and set it down on the table. She said in a confidential tone to Mrs. Haven, "I've unpacked the young lady's box, madam, and if there's nothing else you wish me to do I'll just run an iron over her dresses."

"Oh no, please," Freely started to rise from her chair. "I can take care of my own clothes."

Mrs. Haven went on talking with Sara as if she had not heard Freely. Philip leaned toward Freely and put his hand on her arm. "Let Sara do it, Freely. It's what she expects to do."

Freely smiled weakly and sat back in her chair.

On the tea tray there were tiny sandwiches cut in fancy shapes and daintily iced cakes, but delectable as everything was it went down to a dull tastlessness in Freely's mouth. Mrs. Haven was charming in addressing conversation to her guest, but Freely found little beside yes or no to say in answer. Philip came to the rescue more than once, amusing his mother with his chatter and asking Freely questions about things on which he knew she could converse. He was determined that she should speak for herself, even though the things that were real for her had little meaning for his mother.

After they had their tea, Mrs. Haven suggested that Philip take Freely for a walk about the place while she went back to the house. "But don't be too long, let Miss Simon get to her room in time to have a nice rest before dinner." Mrs. Haven threw her shawl over her arm. "I'll see you later, my child. Don't let Philip take you too far away."

"Yes, ma'am, I mean, no, ma'am," Freely murmured.

Mrs. Haven got up from her chair and patted Freely on the shoulder, smiling at her. Her smile was very sweet, Freely thought, yet looking into it she could see nothing that was familiar, nothing that was warming. It was like a mask covering all that Mrs. Haven was feeling within herself.

They stood by the summerhouse watching Mrs. Haven go toward the house. Freely turned to Philip. "I do wish your mother would call me by my name."

"She will in time."

"Why in time, why not now?"

"It's such an unusual name. She has to get accustomed to it, and—" he paused.

"What, Philip?"

"Well, to tell you the truth, it embarrasses her just a little."

"Oh—" Freely felt as if her heritage had been challenged and she must rise quickly in its defence. "But it's a beautiful name. Those who bear it give their love freely." She looked at Philip, putting her hand in his. He smiled at her and her longing to be understood was satisfied.

Together they walked through the garden, down the terraces and toward the river, but the tropical plants, the formal setting out of flowers, the tight arrangement of the beds were not like a garden to Freely; even the roses seemed restricted in all but their fragrance.

"It's like a park," she commented appreciatively.

Philip laughed. "I like Susannah's garden better where flowers spill all over as if they were having a good time growing."

"Your mother is very beautiful, Philip. She is like her garden."

"Formal? That's because it's been her life to be like that. Don't be frightened by her. She's really desperately shy and wants to like people. There's a very tender strain in her, too, but sometimes I think the only one that ever sees it is her little dog."

"Her dog?" Then Freely remembered she had seen a dog sitting beside Mrs. Haven in the carriage on the day she had run in such panic to Haven Hall, but no one remembered having seen her and she was glad to put from her mind that part of the day.

"Yes, she has a little pug. He's been a great pet for years, most intelligent, understands mother better than anyone else —except perhaps Sara."

"Where is he?"

"In the stable. He was injured a few days ago and Hawkins has been taking care of him. Would you like to see him?"

"Oh, please."

They approached the stable and when they stood alone in it Freely breathed deeply as if here were a world in which she felt at home. Hawkins had gone and the horses were quietly munching the last of the hay he had given them. The rows of carriages stood clean and waiting for the next day's needs. She went into the tack room with its rich smell of leather; admiringly she looked up at the saddles hanging in readiness, at the polished harnesses. Freely visited each one of the horses —the two grays, Philip's black Prince, and a fat Shetland pony Philip had ridden as a child and which was kept on as an old pensioner. She stroked the curve of each strong graceful neck and ran her hand over one velvet nose after another.

Philip watched her, delighting in her as he had not done since her arrival. When she had come from the last stall, he held out his arms to her and with a cry of joy and surprise she ran into them, receiving his kisses and then resting her head on his shoulder, blissful in her tranquility. This was what she had thought would happen when she arrived. Like a starved person, she fed deeply on the joy that it had happened at last; not that she had doubted Philip but it was good to be assured that his love surrounded her and her place was at its center.

She put back her head and looked into his eyes. "The little dog?"

"I almost forgot." Releasing her reluctantly, he went to one of the box stalls and opened the door.

A blanket had been spread in the corner and on it a small dog lay. Opening his eyes, he looked at them but made no move.

"He must be lonely," Freely said.

She crossed the stall quickly, ankle deep in straw. Kneeling down beside the blanket, she ran her hand across the dog's back. The curl of tail wagged—briskly for a moment, then more feebly—and a pink tongue drew itself across Freely's hand. A deep sigh could be heard as the pug's head sank back on the blanket.

"What happened?" Freely asked, more to the dog than to Philip as she slipped her hand under it and drew the limp little body to rest against her knees.

"Mother was coming home from a drive one day and Dombey jumped out of the carriage before it stopped. Somehow a wheel went over him. He was injured internally. Hawkins has done everything for him but he says Dombey hasn't much longer to live."

"Couldn't we bring him to the house? To my room? I'll take care of him. If he can't get well, at least he can die more happily."

Philip shook his head. "Mother has a strong feeling about sick animals. She thinks their place is in the stable."

"But isn't Dombey her pet?"

"Yes, he is, but all the same it makes mother nervous to have something sick around. She's always been that way. She even feels like that about people. Dombey might die and she couldn't stand seeing that."

"But it's not wrong to die if you can't live any more. Everything dies sometime."

Philip shook his head. "Dombey is a sick animal and mother won't have such in the house."

Freely held the dog closer and addressed herself to him. "I'll come to see you as often as I can, Dombey, and I'll bring you something to eat. You shouldn't be so thin."

The tail wagged again and the pink tongue reached out to kiss the cheek bent near him.

When Philip and Freely went back to the house, Freely felt happier than she had since her arrival. There was an animal that needed care and that was all she needed to feel that the days at Haven Hall would be well spent.

Philip took Freely to her room. "Mother always thinks people should have a rest before they dress for dinner," he said, then he left her.

Freely had no intention of resting with all there was to see and discover. There were magazines lying on the table for her to read and look at. There were framed pictures and photographs on the wall and she gazed long and earnestly at each one. That must be Philip's father, she thought, as she saw in the older man's face much that she loved in Philip's. There were five different chairs to try and there was the carved oak bureau with its silver toilet set to admire. There was much to examine and much to fill her with awe before she got to the wardrobe with her own clothes hanging in it. Her dresses looked lonely in such a large space and she put her hands on each one in turn, promising them that they would soon be worn. Everything at Haven Hall was different from the house on the hill with its plain furniture that had been stout enough to stand the living of a hundred years, and its many books. Different as it was, it fascinated Freely and she handled the objects in her room with respect and admiration.

After dinner that night they sat in the garden for a long time. Mrs. Haven talked about Dombey, telling Freely what a companion he had been to her for many years. Freely listened earnestly and Philip watched intently, thinking that it seemed easier for these two to understand each other now that they had a dog to talk about.

When they came in from the garden, Mrs. Haven and Freely said good night to Philip downstairs. Mrs. Haven went with Freely to the door of her room. A lamp was burning on the bed table on which had been placed a glass of milk and some crackers. The bed had been turned down and the cotton nightgown had been laid on it.

Mrs. Haven ran her eyes around the room to make sure that everything was in order, then she directed her gaze to Freely. "Sara will bring your breakfast tray at nine o'clock. Good night, child. I shall see you at luncheon time. I think you will find plenty to entertain yourself with during the morning."

Words leaped to Freely's lips—tray—nine o'clock—what did it all mean? But before she could formulate a question the realization came over her of what she was expected to do.

"Yes, ma'am," she said.

"And please, don't call me that. It makes me feel as if you were a servant."

"But what shall I—" Freely began, then she knew. It sounded distant to call Philip's mother Mrs. Haven and yet that was what she wanted—distance, between them. "Yes,

Mrs. Haven," she said meekly. Longing as she had been to kiss and be kissed good night, she took Mrs. Haven's outstretched hand in hers, then turned into her room and closed the door behind her.

Her eyes roamed around the cluttered strangeness, then she ran to the bed and threw herself on it, sobbing as she had the day in the dell when she discovered its desecration. How was it possible, she asked herself, to be in Philip's home, under the same roof, and yet feel farther from him than when she was in Simonton and he was here.

19.

>>>>>>>>>>>>>>>>>>>>>><<<<<<<<<<<<<<<<<<<<<<

FREELY woke before six. She lay still in bed, watching the sunlight slowly flood the room, listening to the birds in the vines outside, letting her eyes rest on the unfamiliar, fascinating objects. At Simonton, at such an hour, there would have been the small brisk sounds Susannah made in the kitchen, the smell of wood smoke, the fragrance of coffee. The busyness of the birds and the light on the distant hills would call to her to come out, and she would leave her bed, wash in the basin of cold water, dress and be downstairs and about her early chores in a matter of moments. Here there was silence. Life was not beginning with the day but waiting for some moment when the day could begin.

She looked at the clock on her table and thought what a long time to wait for breakfast. But there was no reason why she could not go out and do whatever she liked and get back in time for breakfast; no reason at all, she told herself.

Quickly she drew a small amount of water in the bathroom adjoining her room and washed, then she dressed. Putting the crackers from the plate on her bed table in her pocket, she tied her shoes together, hanging them and her stockings around her neck; then with one hand she carried the glass of milk and with the other she opened the door. There was no sound anywhere. Somewhere down the corridor was Mrs. Haven's room, somewhere was Philip's. But they were still asleep. She did not care what Mrs. Haven did but she was sorry that Philip should miss the early morning, the wonder time of the day.

She crept down the stairs and out the front door. Heavy as it was, it swung noiselessly open and shut for her; like everything else in this well-trained household, it did what it was expected to do in its appointed place. Leaving the glass of milk and her shoes on the step, she ran barefoot across the dewy grass, through the garden to the river. A heron stood on a flat rock near the bank. He observed her curiously, then flapped his wings and flew off down the river in search of breakfast. Freely felt as if she had found a friend and from that moment on everything seemed friendly. Even the trees seemed to lean toward her in a comradely way and she laughed at herself for having felt lonely the night before.

"I shall get up and come out like this every morning," she said exultantly.

She ran back across the lawn, making another trail of footprints that showed dark in the silveriness of the dew. At the doorstep, she sat down to put on her shoes and stockings. Then, taking the glass of milk in her hand, she went out to the stable.

Dombey wagged his curlicue of a tail when he saw her approach and he responded to her greeting by licking her hand.

"I've brought you some breakfast, Dombey," she said.

At first he merely turned his head away when she offered him a bit of cracker, as if he could not be bothered to think of food; gradually, as she persuaded and cajoled, he ate a little, then a little more. He lapped a few drops of milk from her palm. Freely went on coaxing and talking to him. The glass of milk was half gone and the cracker all gone when Freely stroked the dog and got up to leave. Turning, she saw Hawkins leaning over the door of the stall, smiling at her.

"He's taken more from you, Miss Freely, than he will from me."

Freely laughed. "If we can get some nourishment into him he should mend."

"You like dogs, I can see that."

"I like all animals," Freely corrected him. "And people too," she added hastily. "Only animals are easier to understand."

Hawkins nodded in agreement with her. "That's what I always say, Miss Freely. Now, you take these horses, I say all I want to them and not one of them ever answers me back."

Freely stayed with Hawkins until it was time to go back to the house. She watched him feed and water the horses, and when he led them into the yard to groom them she sat in a wheelbarrow and listened to his rambling talk, tucking away in her heart any reminiscence he had of Master Philip. When she returned to the house the front door was open, though there was no one around. She went in and ran lightly up the stairs to her room. She was making her bed when Sara arrived with her breakfast tray.

"Good morning," Freely said. "Isn't it a lovely day?"

"Most young ladies have their breakfast in bed," Sara said disapprovingly as she set the tray down on a table.

"Oh!" Freely exclaimed, thinking that was one price she could never pay.

"Mr. Philip said to tell you that he was going out in the gig at ten o'clock, if you would care to go along with him."

"Yes indeed. I'll be downstairs long before ten."

"That won't be necessary," Sara replied stiffly. "Ten o'clock is the time."

The hour before her seemed incredibly long, but Freely dared not leave her room before it had elapsed. Something in Sara's manner had conveyed to her the fact that she should not appear downstairs except at the proper moment. She looked at the clock reproachfully. On the hill, hours were marked so simply. They merged into each other and made a day. Here they were set apart and carefully relegated.

But the restrictions of the new life fell away from Freely when she sat in the gig beside Philip, talking to him, listening to him, feeling his hand on hers, and then sitting quietly with the reins in her lap while he talked with his men at a cutting. When he went into the mill she waited for him contentedly, not caring how long he might leave her for the joy of knowing that he would be back again. But in all they said, as they drove over the roads under leafy archways with a little cloud of dust trailing behind them, they did not speak of the life at Haven Hall.

This was their life, Freely thought, as she sat beside Philip, sharing their plans, building their togetherness; this was their home. But deep within her she was beginning to wonder if that other life could ever be hers. On the hill, when things had troubled her, she had gone to the dell to reason them out. Sitting on a rock or lying flat on the moss, she had thought and she had listened; and she had not left the dell until she had been able to bring her thoughts to Benedict's equation that life was good. Whatever it was, it was good. Then everything had become simple and lucid and she had gone on her way. But now something that was disconcerting was in her mind and it was trying to get out, like a bird that had flown in through the open window of a house and was beating itself against the walls because it could not find its way out. Every hour she was with Philip made her love him more; yet she found it difficult to reconcile her life with Philip and his life at Haven Hall. Then in a remote part of her mind the question began to loom: did she have to? If she could find the answer to that, she might be able to give freedom to the bird that was imprisoned in the room.

"What are you thinking about, darling?" Philip asked. He

had been watching Freely's long gaze on the road ahead and the reverie that had come over her face.

She shook her head. It was nothing that she could tell him just yet.

"You do love me, Freely?"

"Oh yes," she cried, turning swiftly and facing him, honest eyes wide with surprise that he could ask such a question.

"That's all that matters," he said with a sigh.

"Is it?" she asked, her voice low. There had been a time when she would have reversed the words and made a statement of them. Now, doubt was creeping in around the edges of her mind and what should have been a fact had become a question.

After luncheon Mrs. Haven told her son politely but firmly that she had her own plans for Freely and that he should go off about his affairs and not expect to see them until dinnertime. Mrs. Haven then asked Freely to make herself ready for a drive at three o'clock.

Make myself ready, Freely thought, as she stood in the middle of her room, wondering what Mrs. Haven meant. She couldn't be expected to change her dress for she had put on her newest gingham, and her white dress she was keeping for Sunday. In the time remaining, she slipped over to the stable to talk to Dombey and see if she could get him to eat the piece of meat she had saved from her luncheon.

At three, she stood on the doorstep waiting for Mrs. Haven who appeared in a gray silk dress with a little flowered parasol over her shoulder. She smiled at Freely, but there was neither warmth nor approval in her smile and Freely realized with a sinking heart that she should have made some change in her costume.

Once they were in the carriage, Mrs. Haven said to Hawkins, "I shall not call on the Templetons after all, Hawkins. Just take us for a drive. But first, tell Sara that we will be back for tea, Miss Simon and I, and will she serve it in the summerhouse."

"Very good, madam."

Freely knew she had done something wrong, but it was not until they had returned from their drive and she was having tea with Mrs. Haven in the garden that the full extent of her wrongs became apparent.

"I heard that you were in the stable at an early hour this morning."

Freely nodded, opening her lips to say how Dombey had taken some food from her.

Mrs. Haven waved her hand as if she would be heard without interruption. "I do not wish to have a guest at Haven Hall converse with any of the servants as you did with Hawkins this morning. It is not dignified. What is more, you are to remain in your room until Sara brings you your tray."

"Please, Mrs. Haven," Freely leaned toward her beseechingly, feeling that even Mrs. Haven would not want her to give up those morning hours if she knew how beautiful they were.

Mrs. Haven smiled as if in an endeavor to mitigate her reproof. "I know you've been brought up to be helpful, my child, but I do not like to have you make your bed. That is one of the duties of the servants and I prefer not to have their work interfered with."

"Mrs. Haven, I've always looked after my own room, my own clothes. It makes my hands feel empty not to do that much."

"At Haven Hall you must learn to conform to others' ways of living."

Freely drooped her head. "I'll try," she murmured, but there was no heart in her words.

"Sara told me," Mrs. Haven went on relentlessly, "that you brought very few clothes with you. I realized that this afternoon when you obviously had nothing suitable to wear and so I put off one of my regular afternoon calls."

"I brought my best clothes," Freely said defiantly. A wave of stubbornness came over as she stood ready to defend what Susannah had put so much heart and handwork into. She did not feel in the least sorry that Mrs. Haven had had to change her afternoon plans and nothing would make her offer an apology.

"And they are charming, your little frocks, such ones as I have seen," Mrs. Haven said. Again her smile, crisp and placating, curved her lips. "And I am sure they are exactly right for your country life. For this life they are neither adequate nor sufficient."

"But—" Freely began, wondering what she could do.

"I have a little plan, my child," Mrs. Haven went on. Her voice was persuasive for she knew that she would have to win something over in Freely for her plan to succeed. "I propose to take you to Boston for a few days to have you properly outfitted."

"Oh!" Freely exclaimed. "But my grandmother—"

"I shall write to your grandmother tonight. You can be quite sure that she will approve."

Freely saw Philip coming across the lawn, walking quickly. She raised her hand to wave to him. He started to run.

"Will Philip come to Boston too?" Freely asked.

"Oh no, my child, he has his work to do here."

"Freely," Philip called, "do come. Mother," he said when he reached them, "Hawkins is worried about Dombey. Freely, perhaps you can do something."

Freely rose quickly from her chair.

"My little Dombey, oh my poor little dog," Mrs. Haven clasped her hands together. "Has he taken another bad turn?"

Philip nodded. "Hawkins says he can't last much longer."

"Won't you come, Mrs. Haven?" Freely asked, looking at her eagerly. "It might mean everything to Dombey to see you this once."

"No, no, my child. I couldn't stand it. You go. Do what you can. Perhaps you can save him for me. Philip says—" her voice fluttered off into silence.

"I'll do what I can," Freely promised. Impulsively she leaned over Mrs. Haven and kissed her, then she started running across the lawn in the direction of the stable.

"Can I get you anything, Mother?" Philip asked. "Shall I tell Sara to come to you?"

"No, no, Philip," she leaned back in her chair waving her handkerchief before her face.

Philip started off, but she called to him to come back.

"Send Sara to me, Philip. I'll go upstairs with her. I really feel quite faint—all this worry—the excitement—I do hope that girl can do something—"

"I'm sorry, Mother, to have upset you, but Hawkins thought you would want to know. He thought you might want to see Dombey."

"Oh, never mind about what Hawkins thought," she said irritably. "Please go and get Sara."

Philip hurried to the house to deliver his message to Sara, then he went to the stable. He found Freely sitting in the straw beside Dombey. Hawkins was leaning over the door to the stall, his cap in his hands. He shook his head at sight of Philip.

Freely picked Dombey up in her arms and the little dog, struggling for breath as he was, looked at her gratefully. Dombey's eyes saw the two men leaning over the door of the stall but he gave no indication of recognition; his whole attention was on Freely, with his ears cocked to the sound of her voice as she held him close to her. Very low, very gentle was the voice as it crooned over the dog. Freely's hands held the wasted little body tenderly, but her eyes looked across the stall and out the small barred window above the manger.

"Dear God," she said, "I do thank You for all Your wonderful works, for the sun and the moon and the stars; for trees and birds and flowers. All that praises You and rejoices us. And I thank You for little Dombey who has praised You in his own way, loving and giving all these years."

Philip walked quietly through the straw to kneel down beside Freely. "Ask God to save Dombey, Freely, ask God to do something for him." There was an earnestness in Philip's tone. This moment when he knelt beside Freely in the straw with the dying dog between them was to him the test of Freely's time at Haven Hall. If she could save Dombey, he knew that his mother would believe in her.

Freely turned to him, scarcely seeing him for the tears that glazed her eyes. "This is the way Benedict taught me to pray," she said, and her voice was unsteady, "to give thanks—in everything to give thanks." She looked down at the dog and smoothed her hand comfortingly over his body. "And praying is one thing I must do in my own way," she whispered.

There was no sound in the stall but the convulsive breathing of the dog, the breaths becoming shorter and shorter. Freely held him close to her, stroking his head, rubbing his ears; but there was no urgency in her movements, only the comfort of love. Then a shudder ran through the dog and a sudden gasp could be heard. Freely looked down at him. She shook her head. She laid him on the straw while one hand moved across his head to close the eyelids down over the filmed eyes and the other hand came up under his jaw to close the mouth from which the last breath had escaped. She drew the blanket over him, then she turned to Philip.

"He's gone," she said, while the faint light of a smile moved across her face. "But it made him happy to know that we were near."

She got up from the straw, shakings wisps of it from her skirt. At the door to the stall she looked at Hawkins. "Thank you," she said, "for all you've done for Dombey." She held out her hand to him.

He took her hand in his and shook it. "If you'd been here sooner, Miss Freely, to help me with him we might have got him well." He withdrew his hand quickly and put the back of it against his eyes.

"Perhaps," Freely murmured. She turned to Philip and slipped her hand through his arm.

Hawkins watched them leave the stable, walking down the drive and going toward the house. "There goes as true a lady as I've ever seen," he observed. Then he put his cap on his head and went to fetch a spade.

Before they reached the house, Freely said, "I think I should go back to Simonton."

Philip turned to her and his hold on her hand tightened. "No, no," he said fiercely.

She shook her head. "But I'm not what your mother wants for you, Philip, that's so, so easy to see."

"But you're what I want, Freely," he implored. "Oh, Freely, you make everything worth while and so much has been meaningless for so many years. You mustn't go, you mustn't ever go."

She smiled at him wanly and stroked his hand as she had the little dog, giving him the comfort of her love. "All right, Philip, I won't go, not for a little while. And I'll try to do what will please your mother."

Freely left him and went to her room while Philip went to find his mother. He found her in her bedroom, lying down, with a bottle of smelling salts beside her. He approached her and stood beside her.

"I'm sorry, Mother. Dombey is dead, but he died happily, in Freely's arms, and if ever a dog could smile I think Dombey did."

"I thought you said she had a way with animals," Mrs. Haven replied, bitterness in her tone.

"She has helped many, Mother, but isn't it helping them too when they die happily?"

"It's just like everything else you say about her, Philip, highly exaggerated."

"Don't you like her at all, Mother?"

"It's not a question of liking or disliking, Philip. She's a pleasant country girl. I find her quite restful to be with for a while, but she has absolutely no social grace. However, I propose to do what I can to remedy that."

Philip sat on the bed and took one of his mother's hands in his. "What are you going to do?"

"I'm going to take Freely to Boston for a week or two."

"Oh Mother," he exclaimed reproachfully, "she came to visit us here, not to go away with you!"

Mrs. Haven smiled as if to say that she knew what she was doing.

"Does Freely want to go?"

"Any young thing likes diversion," Mrs. Haven replied, "and that child is very young, you must realize that, Philip."

In her own room, Freely stood by the window looking out. Within was all that could be asked for comfort; without was all the beauty that could be desired—velvet lawns, great trees drooping their shade on the hot July day, a carefully tended garden. She knew that she was surrounded by ease and beauty, yet a sense of desolation was slowly coming over her. She felt, for the first time in her life, as if she had lost her hold on God.

Always she had been able to look within her mind and in the stillness that was there respond to the promptings of an inner voice. Benedict had said the voice was her angel that always dwelt in heaven no matter where she might be. But now there was no stillness within in which to hear the voice. There was only the clashing of wills and the struggle to know what was right in this life where things were done not for the love of God—the standard Benedict had set—but for conformation with custom.

20.

FREELY went to Boston wearing a gingham dress and a wide-rimmed straw hat with a velvet ribbon; she returned to Millville in a modish traveling suit with a trim little hat perched on top of her head. No longer were the braids looped around her head; her hair was brushed high into a pompadour in front and turned into a neat coil at the back. She had gone with misgivings but with a determination to do everything she could to try to become the person Philip's wife should be.

The few days lengthened into a week, the week into three. Mrs. Haven divided the time between trips to shops and hairdressers and visits to museums, galleries, points of interest, plays, and concerts. She was as eager to have Freely's mind adorned with the ornaments of living as she was to have her person speak of styles and modes. To Mrs. Haven's surprise, Freely responded far better than she had thought possible. Freely had a child's delight in the new world, in seeing things she had read about or Benedict had told her of. The subtleties of flattery had begun to make her conscious of her own beauty. Clothes were no longer merely functional. She realized that they graced her figure or set off her coloring. They had even begun to become a background for the pieces of jewelry that Mrs. Haven took pleasure in giving her to mark some small occasion. Mrs. Haven was still acutely aware of the lack of refinement her charge showed in many ways, but a certain delight in the girl's company was increasing with the days. No matter how flurried or wearied she felt, there was refreshment and a kind of peace in Freely's presence.

Freely found it difficult to adjust to tight shoes and corseting, but she accepted them as part of the restrictions and formalities of living that now existed for her. She began to feel that life on the hill belonged to some remote past and as she saw herself being transformed into a young lady of fashion she tended to look disparagingly upon the self she had once been.

It puzzled her that in this new world people so often said things they did not mean. One day, when Mrs. Haven met an acquaintance in a store, she greeted her as if she were a bosom companion. After the woman had gone on her way, Mrs. Haven exclaimed, "What an insufferable person! Such a bore. I really don't know how her husband stands her."

"I thought she was your friend," Freely remarked.

Mrs. Haven's laugh had a tinkling sound to it. "That, my child, is a front one puts on in the world of society. You will soon learn."

Freely could not dull the edge of disquiet that ran around her mind and that seemed always with her, even in the midst of rustling silks and shining satins, of jewels that flashed in the light, of smart hats and flattering attentions. A thrill of delight would run through her at each new excitement, while at the same time a question would pose itself to her. She was not sure yet whether she wanted to make this world hers, though she was enjoying it.

She knew that she was learning a whole new vocabulary from contact with Mrs. Haven. Words like charming, enticing, delectable, ravishing began to fall off her tongue easily because she heard them used; but uttering them sometimes gave her a feeling of guilt when she remembered that Benedict had always told her not to use a word unless she knew its meaning. However small her vocabulary, he would say, it was better for her to know what she meant; in that way honesty lay. But she shrugged off the memory, for there was an enchantment to the new life and the old had a way of pricking her uncomfortably.

She looked at her hands after their first manicure, and wondered if they were the same hands that had planted Susannah's garden and milked the cow, split wood and cared for animals. They were the same, of course, but they belonged to another Freely. This was the new person. The person she was to be as Philip Haven's wife. Her hands would be beautiful as they handled a silver teapot, as Mrs. Haven's were, or as they did fine embroidery on a silk scarf.

On their first Sunday in Boston, Mrs. Haven took Freely to one of the fashionable churches, and though Freely was not yet wearing her new clothes with complete ease, Mrs. Haven was proud of the figure she made. Freely sat back in the pew, pleased at the thought of hearing a sermon again. It fascinated her to make acquaintance with a God who apparently ruled through fear. Benedict's God had been so different, and for the first time in her life Freely began to turn over in her mind the possibility of there being more than one God. After the service was over they spent some time in sociability, as Mrs. Haven met many of her friends and exchanged her news with theirs.

"What a great many people you know, Mrs. Haven!" Freely exclaimed as they walked through the Public Gardens back to their hotel.

"Our life was lived in Boston for a good many years," she replied, "and I always plan on spending some of the winter months here. That will be something we can do together, next year."

"It was pleasant to see so many people after church,"

Freely commented, not sure what Mrs. Haven had meant by her last remark and preferring to let it go unnoticed.

"Yes, indeed. It always seems to me that the most important part of church-going is seeing one's friends after the service."

Obedient and agreeable, Freely gave Mrs. Haven little cause for criticism and the two had amiable times together. Freely was especially happy whenever Mrs. Haven spoke of Philip when he was a little boy and she would try to maneuver the conversation around to him as often as she could. Freely had a letter from Philip every day, but during all her stay in Boston she heard only once from Susannah.

She was getting on all right, Susannah said, and Freely was not to feel any concern for her. Philip had been up to see her. The garden was growing well. She had had Brownie bred so there should be a new calf next spring. Ginger had cast a shoe and she had taken him down to the river village to be shod. She was at work on a new quilt that she was making from the bits and pieces left over from Freely's dresses. It was to be a Dove in the Window pattern. She had seen one like it only once before and had always wanted to make one. The boys were well. Mark III had cut a tooth. Most of the birds had had second families. She had found a humming bird's nest the other day. It had been very hot and dry the past few weeks and the pasture grass was as brown as an old mat, but the zinnias in her garden were thriving. She missed Freely, but she enjoyed her letters, though it was hard to tell from them just what kind of a life she was living. "You haven't the skill with your pen that your uncles have, but perhaps it will come in time."

Freely read the letter and put it away, for it tugged at her heart. The oddments of country news sounded remote and strange in the noise and excitement of Boston. She wondered how the life she had known and loved for so long could possibly have fallen into the background so quickly; and yet, it had.

Up on the hill Susannah watched for Dan Satturlee's coming, and she greeted him with a smile whether he had a letter for her or not.

"I hear they're making changes in young Freely," he remarked one day after Susannah had slipped into her apron pocket the letter with the Boston postmark.

"Who told you that?"

"I got it in the town. Seems that woman Sara Jenks was in Boston last week to see Mrs. Haven about one thing or another. She saw your Freely and she's telling everyone the girl's so changed you wouldn't know her."

"No one could change Freely," Susannah said stoutly, "unless Freely wanted to be changed."

"I wouldn't be so sure, Susannah Simon."

"I've got some fresh-made doughnuts and a pot of coffee on the stove," Susannah suggested.

"Now you're talking," Dan Satturlee said as he climbed down from his buggy and dropped the reins so his horse could eat too.

He followed Susannah into the kitchen, but no matter how many doughnuts she gave him it could not keep him from talking.

"Who are these Havens anyway," he asked rhetorically, "that they want to make over a nice girl like Freely Simon to be like them?" He took a large bite off a doughnut and washed it down with some coffee. "They came here a few years ago from Lord knows where; they buy our trees, cut them down and make a lot of money with their paper mill, then they act as if they owned the place. Got some more coffee?"

Susannah filled his cup, adding cream and sugar generously.

"Why, I tell you, Susannah Simon, it's folks like you whose

forebears sweated over the land who really own it. They're newcomers, those Havens, that's all they are. And that's what they'll always be until a few of them lie buried down in the cemetery at Millville. I tell you, if that Philip Haven does anything to make our little Freely unhappy I'll—I'll—"

"Philip wouldn't do anything to hurt Freely," Susannah said quietly. "Philip's a fine boy. He's like one of my sons. If anyone does anything to Freely it will be Mrs. Haven."

"Well, whoever it is, I'll—I'll—"

"You better hold your words, Dan Satturlee," Susannah said, offering him another doughnut. "You know as well as I do that she'd be more than a match for you."

Dan grunted and contented himself with his coffee. When he got up to leave he said vehemently, "When I was a boy and they sewed pink patches onto one of my blue shirts I was told to be grateful, that they were better than holes; but I don't want anyone sewing any pink patches on our Freely."

After he had gone on his way, Susannah settled down to her letter, but the contents were read almost as soon as the address on the envelope. It was no news to know that Freely was well or that Mrs. Haven was kind to her; it was no news to know that Freely loved her. Susannah folded the letter and put it in her pocket. There was no news in it at all, and yet it was all that Freely could say.

Susannah got up from her chair. She was glad she had work to do. The garden needed a ruffling of the soil to make a mulch against the dry weather. She would go across to the church and sweep and dust it as she always did once a week; then she would be free to spend the day's remaining hours at her quilting frame. It was pretty, the pattern she was making. She would like to have it done by the time Freely came home.

Mrs. Haven was insistent in her wish for Freely to have a French lesson every day.

"But we're only in Boston for a little while," Freely remonstrated, "and how could I ever go on studying French when I'm at home—there's so much else to do."

"You can manage somehow," Mrs. Haven said. "Once the groundwork is laid you can continue with a weekly lesson when we get back to Millville."

"But, French!" Freely exclaimed, unable to see the necessity for such an accomplishment.

"Every young lady should speak a little French," Mrs. Haven said. "It gives a certain charm and elegance that nothing else does. It is especially important for you to speak French because of your heritage."

"My heritage?" Freely asked, thinking of the hilltop and the white church.

"Your father was a famous French mining engineer."

"I thought he was a lumberman."

"He was Raoul de St. Pierre." Mrs. Haven rolled the name richly off her tongue as if it accounted for much.

Freely shook her head. "I never knew him. Benedict and Susannah have been my parents and their name is Simon."

Freely knew that once they returned to Haven Hall Mrs. Haven had planned to give a tea at which she would formally introduce her to the neighborhood. After that, they were to make a round of calls on the neighbors who would be Freely's friends.

"In that way you will have an opportunity to meet the people among whom your future life will be passed," Mrs. Haven explained.

When Mrs. Haven had first informed Freely of her plan, Freely had not welcomed it; but the weeks in Boston had been slowly readying her for her presentation to society. She even found herself looking forward to showing off her new clothes and she was glad that, at last, she would be able to stand before the world as Philip Haven's fiancée.

"I'm beginning to feel quite proud of my future daughter-in-law," Mrs. Haven said as they were journeying back to Millville on the train. The seats near them were piled high with their boxes and bags, though most of their luggage had already been sent ahead.

Freely turned to her, her amber eyes clear and shining. "I wouldn't be your daughter-in-law unless Philip asked me to marry him, and he hasn't done that yet."

Mrs. Haven smiled charmingly. "He will, my child. When he sees you now he won't be able to resist you."

Freely felt herself blushing. In a small voice, because it was for some unaccountable reason the old Freely speaking, she said, "But I would have to say yes."

Mrs. Haven rapped Freely's folded hands playfully with her fan. "That won't be difficult with all Philip has to give you."

Philip met them at the station. He kissed his mother, then he took Freely's gloved hand in his and held it to his lips. Freely had dreamed during the days away of what his first embrace would be like. It would be strong and sure, she had thought, and in it would be the realization of all that his letters had promised. Meeting him, as she stood with Mrs. Haven on the station platform, Freely had not thought that he would look at her, however adoringly, and merely put her fingers to his lips. She wanted to cry out to him in the old way, to leap over the wall of formality that had risen between them; then it struck her that, because he was Philip Haven, he must be doing the correct thing and she must act accordingly.

"*Je suis très contente de vous voir, Phillipe,*" she said, with a coquettish tilt to her head.

Philip looked surprised. "Well, you have done a lot in a few weeks!"

"French comes naturally to her," Mrs. Haven murmured. "Doesn't it, *ma chérie?*"

The first smile Freely ever received from Sara greeted her when they arrived at the house. There were roses in her room and Freely welcomed with a glance all the objects that made up the room—the stuffed chairs, the pictures in their gilt frames, even the tasseled curtains at the windows. It was good to be back in the big house, she thought, with its air of order and efficiency, with its well-trained servants treating her as if she belonged. Joyously she dressed for dinner, putting on the long-sleeved green silk with its smart little bustle. Opening her wardrobe door she felt a sudden shock when she saw her old clothes hanging there. She gazed at them, fascinated to think that she had ever worn such dresses; then she shut the door hastily.

The rustling of her silk skirt preceded her down the stairs to the drawing room and she knew that Philip and his mother had been talking about her by the sudden way their voices ceased as she approached, then resumed their conversation in a higher, more impulsive tone.

"Isn't she adorable?" Mrs. Haven said as Freely entered the room.

Philip nodded his head and smiled as he offered a chair to Freely, but in his heart was a sudden longing for someone whom he had once known.

It was not until after dinner, as they were having coffee in the garden in the sultry August darkness, that Mrs. Haven disclosed the plan she had been discussing with Philip. His silence while his mother was speaking was evidence of the tacit agreement he had made with her.

Freely listened, her eyes wide, her lips parted; aware of Philip in the chair beside her, she was even more aware of the distance between them. She had always known that Mrs. Haven had not approved of her name and that she had used it as little as possible. Since the French lessons had started, it had amused Freely that Mrs. Haven had taken to calling her Simone. The name had meant nothing to Freely at the time, but she realized now that it was all part of a plan, as everything in this new life seemed to be. Freely put her hands to her heart in the little gesture she had seen Susannah make in moments of agitation; then her hands crept up to her throat as if she would hold back as long as she could any words.

Mrs. Haven brought her long dissertation to a close. Suavely and charmingly she said, "And so, next week at the garden party when I introduce you to society, it will be as Miss Simone de St. Pierre."

Philip nodded mechanically. "A pretty name," he said to the night.

Freely's hands were on her throat. She said nothing.

"I knew you would see the wisdom of it, my child," Mrs. Haven went on. "In fact, I was so sure, that while we were in Boston I left an order for the invitations for the garden party."

"No, no," Freely said. Her voice sounded muffled as if it were being choked within her, yet her hands had left her throat and were gripping the arms of her chair.

"But why, my child? When you have the right to a beautiful name, why not use it?"

Philip turned to her. "I think Mother is right, Freely. It is a beautiful name and it really is yours." He tried to smile into her eyes, but she would not look at him. "You'll always be Freely to me, no matter what everyone else calls you." He put his hand out to touch one of hers, but she withdrew hers quickly and held it in her other hand as if she could trust only what was hers in this strange moment.

"It—it wouldn't be me," she gasped. "I'm Freely Simon. Everyone in the river village and on the hill knows me as that."

Mrs. Haven laughed and the sound was like the tinkling of

ice in a tall glass. "That everyone is not so very many. The people who really count, whom you will be meeting next week, have never known you before. To them you will be a new person. Why not have a new name? A name—" Mrs. Haven hesitated— "a name without any aspersion to it."

"Mother!" Philip exclaimed.

Freely stared before her. So many new words had come to her ears lately; this was only another one.

Mrs. Haven turned to her son. "Philip, my shawl, please. The night air is cool."

Philip got up and went to the house. The night felt distinctly hot and close to him, but he was too used to complying with his mother to question her request.

Mrs. Haven leaned forward in her chair. "Simone, listen to me. As long as you do not bear your father's name you bear the stamp of illegitimacy, and that is a very terrible thing."

Freely shook her head, almost wishing Mrs. Haven would speak French for even with her few weeks' knowledge of it she felt it would be more intelligible.

"Believe me, Simone, I am doing this only for your good."

Freely went on shaking her head, evenly like a pendulum.

"I should be sorry to have my son carry that cross all his life," Mrs. Haven said, leaning back in her chair with a resigned air.

Philip was coming across the lawn, his mother's shawl over his arm.

"You mean—" Freely asked hoarsely— "it would be better for Philip if I used my father's name?"

"Yes, decidedly."

"But I never knew him."

Mrs. Haven laughed and took the shawl from Philip. "That hardly matters. Thank you, Philip, dear. And now, if you children will excuse me, I'm going to the house. I find myself a little tired after the weeks in Boston." She crossed to where Freely was sitting. "Good night, dear," she said gently. "I knew I could depend on you to see the wisdom of my decision." She patted Freely's bowed head with her fan.

Freely leaned forward and covered her face with her hands. Almost silent were the sounds of sobbing, but they were unmistakable.

"Oh Mother, whatever did you say to her to make her cry?" Philip asked as he accompanied his mother back to the house. "Freely doesn't cry easily."

"She's just a little nervous tonight. You'll find all women are like that at times, Philip dear."

"But not Freely. She's so solid, so certain."

"You're just like any young man in love. She's all perfection to you."

At the door, Mrs. Haven said good night to her son. "You know, Philip, the garden party next week will be officially to announce your engagement. Don't forget that you should ask her to marry you before then, will you?"

Philip smiled. "We've been so sure of each other, Mother, we haven't thought of marriage."

"She probably has, Philip. Women do, you know. Good night, dear.

Philip hurried back across the lawn. Freely was still sitting in the same position, hugging her sorrow to herself. Philip knelt down in front of her and put his arms around her, drawing her face to him, kissing the tears from her eyes, steadying her quivering mouth as he placed his lips on it. Only when he held her close to him did Freely feel the loneliness of the big house with its formalized living fall away; only when she felt his love around her could she trust herself to speak.

"Oh, Philip darling, I've missed you so. I've been hungry

for your love. When I got back today I wanted you to take me in your arms and all you did was hold the tip of my fingers to your lips."

Philip wanted to explain why he couldn't give way to his feelings on a station platform, but the words withered before the sorrowful honesty in Freely's eyes.

"After we're married, Freely—" he began.

She shook her head. "Sometimes that seems further away than when you first told me you loved me—do you remember, standing by the white birch?"

He nodded, putting his hand lightly on her head so as not to spoil the pompadour effect of her hair. "Can you really agree to use your father's name?" he asked.

"Yes, I think so," she answered with difficulty, "if—if it's better for everyone."

"It will please Mother."

"Philip," Freely asked suddenly, "will it be this way always —doing things just to please your mother, to suit her way of life?"

"Oh no, darling. We'll have our own life after we're married. We'll have our own home. It will be different then."

Her face was shining. "Our own home! Oh, Philip, I was afraid we would have to live here."

"No," he shook his head. "We'll build a house of our own, white and strong like Susannah's, with lilacs by the door. There'll always be a fire in the kitchen stove and there'll always be the smell of baking, and not a door in the house will have a lock on it!"

"Where, Philip, where shall it be?" Her heart was beating wildly. With this new hope she felt she could hold out against anything.

"The place I love best in the world. The place where I feel most myself."

She knew the place, but she wanted to hear it from his lips. "Say it," she commanded.

"The hilltop," he smiled. "Simonton."

She put her arms around him again. Oh, the joy of it, the sureness of it she thought, and yet she had always known it; and the days at Haven Hall, trying to conform to his mother's ways, trying to fit herself into a pattern of living, would soon be behind them and she would be her Freely self again.

Before they said good night she said to him, "It doesn't seem right, changing my name, and yet—if it was my father's it could be mine, and Simone is almost Simon, isn't it? Besides, I'll be changing my name soon again anyway."

"You will," he assured her.

"But isn't it odd that your mother doesn't like my first name? She has never called me by it."

He shrugged his shoulders. "I told you that it embarrassed her." He laughed. "My mother is a very righteous woman."

Freely laughed too. "Yes, I know. We went to church every Sunday when we were in Boston."

That night, before she went to bed, Freely leaned on her window sill for a long time, looking out into the darkness. There was no quiet within her any more, no place of retreat, only jangling questions and confusing answers. Mrs. Haven had said that if she changed her name it would be better for Philip; and Philip had said that if she did it would please his mother; yet no one thought of Freely. She supposed she didn't matter. Benedict would have thought differently. He would have said she must feel right about it herself to be honest with God. How remote and old-fashioned, as if it belonged to another day, such thinking seemed; but there was nothing remote about Benedict. She could see him sitting in the lamplight by the kitchen table; she could hear him reading from the Bible to her. He was reading one of her favorite stories, the story of Samuel when he was sent to find a king among the sons of Jesse. How rich and full Benedict's voice was as he read the words, " 'The Lord looketh not on the outward appearance, but on the heart.' " He had no need to read them for he knew them so well, but he loved the book and preferred to keep his eyes on the printed page.

Freely tried hard to reconcile the wind-blown honesty of the Simonton hilltop with this life where people lived according to a pattern and not from the heart. Yet she loved Philip, of that she was certain; and Philip loved her, of that she was equally sure. And that was from the heart.

"Hold the high way," she whispered into the night, "and God shall thee deliver."

21.

>>>>>>>>>>>>>>>>>>>>>>>>>>>>><<<<<<<<<<<<<<<<<<<<<<<<

THE richness of summer was upon the world and the August days moved on—slow, long, hot—each one with its wealth of bloom and fruitage. The flower garden was vivid with color, the kitchen garden was heavy with produce. Grapes were swelling. Berries were ripening. Apples were changing their hue. Freely knew that in the old pastures the blueberries would be hanging on the bushes in clean heavy clusters. If she were back on the hill she would go off in search of them, a tin pail over her arm. Standing by a bush she would reach up to gather the fruit and the first few to be dropped into the pail would make a musical sound as they landed on the tin. But she was learning to be a young lady and such excursions were no part of the pattern into which Mrs. Haven was weaving her slowly.

Now she lay in bed of a morning waiting for Sara to bring her breakfast tray, listening to the birds, letting her eyes roam around her room. But the more her physical self became integrated with the fashionable life at Haven Hall, the more something within her yearned for the wind-swept simplicity of the hill, the smiling friendliness of Susannah's kitchen, and Susannah herself—her arms so enfolding, her eyes so unasking and yet believing.

One morning, as she lay in bed waiting for Sara, it crossed her mind that in the woods the blackberries must be ripening.

She remembered a place she had discovered last year where she had stood in bracken and brambles waist high to get at the fruit. She had had to reach above her head for the heavy blackberries that were shining with the dew still on them. Her arms had got scratched and her clothes had got soaked with dew, but her pail had soon been full. As she went back with her treasure, her heart sang like the gayest kind of bird. She knew that she walked with God and she talked to Him fully about whatever came into her mind. That was the day she saw the first stalk of goldenrod edging the road. Loving it as she did all growing things and welcoming it, she saw it with a start, for goldenrod was the hinge on which the door of summer swung. Ahead was the fall with its brisker tempo. The golden stalk swaying in the breeze reminded her that she could not go on endlessly enjoying earth's bounties; that a time of garnering was at hand, soon to be followed by a time of readying against the winter. Nature never let man pleasure himself for too long, Benedict had always said. A little while he might bask in bliss, then the ancient injunction came upon him to gird up his loins and be ready for the fray.

There was a light tap at the door, then Sara came in with the breakfast tray.

"Good morning, Miss Simone. Did you sleep well?"

"Yes indeed, Sara."

Sara set down the tray, surveying it to be sure that everything was as it should be.

"Mrs. Haven wanted me to tell you, Miss Simone, that Mademoiselle Antoine would be here for your French lesson at ten o'clock."

"Thank you, Sara."

Sara left the room. Freely leaned back on her pillows and looked at the tray. Everything on it was dainty and tempting, yet it did not make her feel hungry. She poured half a cup of coffee and broke a portion off a piece of toast. She glanced at her clock. Today would be like all the other days, she supposed—a French lesson, a music lesson, luncheon with Mrs. Haven and Philip; yet it would not be the Philip she knew when they were alone together. In the afternoon there would be a fitting on her dress for the garden party and a drive with Mrs. Haven. She had been spending an hour or more every afternoon addressing the invitations to the party that was now only two days distant. Mrs. Haven had approved of her handwriting as being sufficiently well formed and flowing to grace the large heavy envelopes, but every time Freely's hand moved across an envelope she felt that she was tightening a noose from which she would never extricate herself. *To meet Miss Simone de St. Pierre*——— the invitations had said, but who was she? As the days went on and the garden party drew nearer, Freely felt increasingly uneasy about her.

Philip had said everything would be different after the party. His mother would be satisfied because Freely would be formally introduced to society. He knew that Freely would have to make a round of calls with his mother, and there might be a few parties which they would all have to attend, but after that life would soon return to where it had been before the garden party and he and Freely would begin to make their own plans.

"Of course, Mother doesn't want us to be married too soon," he had said one day.

"Are you quite sure it will be me you will be marrying, Philip?" Freely asked. "The me you first loved?"

A puzzled expression came over his face. "Why, of course, darling. I couldn't love anyone else."

She shook her head. She was unsure about so much these days and there seemed no way to stabilize herself. Her times alone with Philip were growing rarer as the demands made by Mrs. Haven increased. She longed to talk with Hawkins or one of the gardeners, but that had been forbidden, and she would not talk with Sara. She knew instinctively those whom she could trust.

Freely pushed the tray aside and sat up in bed; then she threw back the covers quickly. Beautiful and well ordered as the life at Haven Hall was, she had a feeling that in trying to make herself something other than what she was she was drying up the springs of her own being. Go to your source, Benedict used to say. What it is may be different for every-one, but each one knows his own and should seek it out. Benedict had always loved the story of Antaeus, Freely re-called, Antaeus whose contact with the earth had been his strength. In other days Freely would have gone to the dell, but it was no more. She shuddered inwardly, glimpsing to herself something of what tragedy was. She shook her head. Not yet, not yet, she said within herself, would she admit that her sacrifice had been in vain.

At luncheon she asked Mrs. Haven if she might go to see her grandmother that afternoon.

Mrs. Haven seemed surprised. "But I had other plans for you, Simone."

Freely looked imploringly across the table to Philip.

"Mother, I could drive Freely up this afternoon and have her back by teatime. I'd like to see Susannah myself."

"Philip dear, you know that I prefer not to have you and Simone seen together too much until she is introduced as your fiancée."

Freely remained silent. She had learned that any persuasion she might offer could be offset by Mrs. Haven.

"You would rather go, Simone, than spend the afternoon reading to me?"

"Oh Mother," Philip interrupted, "don't—"

"Philip, I am talking to Simone."

Freely looked clearly at Mrs. Haven. "I would like to go very much," she said.

"Very well, then, if that is your desire. I'll tell Hawkins to be at the door at two thirty, but I must ask that you return in time for tea. A guest is coming whom I particularly wish you to meet."

"Yes, Mrs. Haven."

The open carriage and one of the grays was waiting at the door at half past two. Freely had changed into the simplest of her Boston dresses, but it had its elegance—a tiny silk ruffle edged neck and wrists of the cream-colored taffeta, black patent-leather shoes peeped out daintily from a long skirt that rustled as she walked. She carried a parasol as Mrs. Haven wished her to do so the sun would not tan her skin, but as soon as she was out of sight of Haven Hall she folded it up and laid it on the seat beside her. She sat stiffly against the cushioned seat as Hawkins sat on the box, and the gray stepped smartly over the road.

The country looked dusty from the August heat, and the leaves were drooping. There was goldenrod along the road-sides and at the sight of it Freely felt a sudden pang within her that summer could so soon be nearing its end. She had been away so long from the life of the hill and the joys of summer that were a part of it. To have them she would have to wait for another year to come around. She would tell Susannah that she had seen autumn's first color and that it was a sign she would soon be coming home. At the thought of Susannah she held her hands tightly together. She had written to her about the garden party and of the new ac-tivities in her life and Susannah had replied simply, honestly, speaking out of her heart, yet Freely knew that between the lines lay all that she would not say.

She leaned forward impulsively. "Hawkins, do you see that white birch?"

"Yes, miss."

"Will you stop there, please? I—I want to get out."

Hawkins reined in the gray and looked around at his passenger anxiously. "Are you feeling quite all right, miss? You're sure the sun hasn't been too much for you?"

"I'm all right, Hawkins, thank you. It's just that that is a place I used to love to go to when I was free, when I was Freely. I'd like to visit it again."

She waited for Hawkins to get down from the box and open the small door for her; then, while he stood by the gray's head, she went through the opening in the wall left by the lumbermen and toward what had once been her cloister. But she had not reckoned on heeled shoes and a tight skirt. She found the going difficult and she tripped more than once. Only memory could make the dell familiar, for its outward aspect was so changed. Dead, brittle branches crackled underfoot and rose up to whip against her skirt. The spring had long since dried up and only hard, cracked earth surrounded the flat stone under which the water had issued. The rocks were warm with the sun's heat. Leaning against one, she put her cheek to the lichened stone, cherishing the rough caress. New green had covered many of the scars left by the lumbering, and looking down the hill her eye could range widely. Once she had seen only trees in the dell, but now she could see sky and distant hills.

Behind her, at the edge of the cutting where the forest began again, the trees rose in seriate lines to the hilltop that was Simonton. Somewhere beyond the green density of the forest was the white church and her own home. Her heart ached as she thought of them and she turned quickly to face the wide spread of country that fell away before her down the hill. Across the billowing crests of trees she could see the rooftops of Millville and the river winding its way. Beyond the river were fertile fields, green pastures, and roads linking farms together, and still farther, the place where Haven Hall lay secluded and protected in a folding of the hills. The land below her was brisk with use and activity; the land behind her was secret and silent, and it would always be so long as forest trees climbed the rising of the hill to its summit.

This was her world, she thought, as she looked around it fervently, giving it to her heart through her eyes in all its desolation coupled with the green of upsurgent growth. She had an almost uncontrollable desire to throw herself down among the debris on the forest floor and cry to ease her heart, to wash her eyes clean. But one could not do that in fine clothes and, what was more, the life at Haven Hall was teaching her to put a rein on her emotions. Slowly she was learning not to show all that leaped and longed within her. Picking her way carefully through the clearing, she went back to the carriage.

Hawkins heard her coming and held the door open for her.

Freely stroked the gray's head for a moment, placing her cheek against the velvet muzzle; then she got into the carriage.

"And now, miss?"

She shook her head. "I'm not going to see my grandmother, Hawkins. We'll go back to Haven Hall."

"Very good, miss." He shut the door slowly, but he did not take his hands off it. He kept his eyes down for he did not want to embarrass her by looking at her. "Miss Freely," he began, "I've been with Mrs. Haven since Mr. Philip was a little chap. I wouldn't say anything against her, but as long as I've known her she has lived his life for him. I'm thinking, miss, that one day Mr. Philip will have to learn to go his own way." He took his hands off the door. "Beg pardon, miss, for saying so much, but I know how you feel about Mr. Philip."

"Thank you, Hawkins," Freely said. "I—I think we should go now."

"Very good, miss." He mounted the box and took up the reins, turning the gray slowly.

Freely put up her parasol, not against the sun but because she could not trust her eyes as they drove down the hill and she would not be seen crying as they drove through Millville.

Sara met her at the door and said that Mrs. Haven was in the garden and would Miss Simone please come as soon as possible as she did not want to keep Mr. Montague waiting.

"As soon as possible—" Freely murmured. That meant she was to change her dress. She started up the stairs. "Who is Mr. Montague, Sara?" she called down.

"I'm not the one to say, Miss Simone, but he came with a portfolio of pictures he's been showing to Mrs. Haven."

Freely washed her face, hoping her eyes would not be telltale, then she brushed her hair back into the high pompadour and put on a pale blue dress with a lacy collar and a narrow velvet sash. The high neck bothered her, but it was becoming. She smiled at herself in the glass, then she hurried downstairs and out to the garden.

"Ah, Simone," Mrs. Haven held out her hand to her. "Did you have a nice time?"

"Yes, thank you, Mrs. Haven."

"And did you find your grandmother well?"

"She is always well," Freely smiled in the meaningless way she had learned to do at Haven Hall.

"Simone dear, this is Mr. Montague." She held the girl's hand toward a large florid-faced gentleman, "Miss de St. Pierre." She rolled the words out trippingly.

Freely gave a little gasp. It was the first time she had heard the name actually connected with her, then she bowed to Mr. Montague.

Mr. Montague held out his hand. "I must felicitate you, Miss de St. Pierre."

"Oh?" Freely wrinkled her brows.

"Ah yes, dear. You see Mr. Montague knows your little secret. I had to tell him." Mrs. Haven rapped Freely's hand with her fan, a gesture that though playful in appearance always had its implication. "You see, Mr. Montague is the architect I have employed to build a new wing onto this house for you and Philip. He has brought some lovely plans to show us."

Mr. Montague was already bending over his portfolio.

Freely sat down because her legs felt as if they would no longer support her. "But—but," she began, "Philip never told me you—you—"

"Philip doesn't know a thing about it, my child. It's to be my wedding present to him."

"Oh!" Freely exclaimed, her hand creeping up to her throat. She rose quickly from her chair. "Mrs. Haven, please excuse me, I—I'm not feeling very well."

She turned and ran across the lawn back to the house.

Mrs. Haven looked at Mr. Montague. "Really, I must apologize, Mr. Montague, but you know how a young girl is at such a time—just a little overwrought. She'll be quite all right after they're married."

"Think nothing of it, Mrs. Haven," he assured her. "I have three daughters of my own."

"We shall have to go over the plans ourselves," Mrs. Haven continued. "But I think I can safely make the decisions for Miss de St. Pierre."

"When is the wedding to be, Mrs. Haven?"

"It isn't actually planned yet, but I rather think in September. The garden is at its best then. The dahlias, you know, are especially handsome."

"And you wish to have the work started immediately after that?"

"Yes, immediately. You see they will be going on an extended wedding trip to Europe, six months at least, and I would like to have the work completed by their return."

"I'm sure that can be arranged," Mr. Montague said as he took a sketch out of his portfolio.

Philip, coming from the house, saw his mother in the garden with a stranger. Having no wish to interrupt her in the midst of one of her activities, whatever it was, he withdrew. Not seeing Freely with her, he had no desire to present himself.

22.

><<

THE day before the garden party was the first gray day in a long succession of bright hot days and it came with a sense of relief and rest. A soft mist hung over the distant hills and a blissful cessation seemed to come to the world of nature, as if "Halt!" had been cried to everything that had been growing, reaching, striving.

Freely, between her French and music lessons, watched from the windows the gardeners as they mowed and clipped the lawns, gave final touches to the already flawless flower beds, and got all in readiness for the party. In the kitchen, similar preparations were going on as Annah, the cook, made rows of tarts, cakes, and cookies; and in the pantry Sara brought the best china down from the shelves to wash and set in readiness. Freely thought with an ache of longing of the preparations in the house on the hill that had preceded any gathering of friends. Everyone would be helping in Susannah's kitchen, while the laughter and small talk that went before the party would be as enjoyable as the party itself. She longed to go out to the kitchen and stir up a cake or cut out a pan of cookies, but she knew she was in disgrace enough already with Mrs. Haven for having left Mr. Montague so precipitately and she dared not ask for any favor.

At luncheon, no one would have known that Freely was in disgrace, for Mrs. Haven was graciousness itself and she even suggested that Philip stay home that afternoon and spend some time with them both. He agreed to do so. Immediately after luncheon, when the dressmaker was announced, Mrs. Haven went upstairs, followed by Miss Carpenter, carrying the enormous box that held her latest creation. Freely put on the new dress and stood patiently while it was pinned and measured for the last time. A tuck was too much here, a frill had to be changed there. Each small change discovered another small change that had to be made before Mrs. Haven's critical eye could finally pronounce to Miss Carpenter that the dress was as nearly perfect as a dress could be.

"It does indeed suit the young lady," Miss Carpenter said proudly.

"Thank you," Freely murmured, stepping carefully out of the dress and into the one she had taken off which Miss Carpenter was holding for her.

"I hope you'll be very happy in it," Miss Carpenter said, then she took the dress over her arm and left the room.

Freely sat down wearily.

"Come, come, Simone," Mrs. Haven laughed, "you mustn't let a mere fitting tire you. You'll have a great deal more standing than that to do tomorrow."

Freely pushed her hands up through her hair to relieve the tension around her brows. "It's a lovely dress," she said, a little ashamed of herself that she had not voiced her appreciation sooner.

"I don't hesitate to think but that you'll be a lovely sight when you are in it," Mrs. Haven said in an effort to brighten the girl, for Freely's pallor had given her an uneasy feeling. It would never do to have the girl fall ill just when so many elaborate preparations had been made. "Run along now, dear. You'll find Philip downstairs waiting for you and you don't need to give another thought to the party until eleven o'clock tomorrow when my hairdresser is coming to do your hair."

Freely got up from her chair. "Isn't there anything I could do to help?"

"No, Simone. Sara has everything very well in hand. I'm going to rest for the afternoon, but you two young things can do whatever you like." Mrs. Haven held out her arms to Freely impulsively. Freely went toward her and kissed her in the same dutiful way that she had seen Philip do so often, but to her surprise Mrs. Haven clung to her. "I always wanted to have a daughter," she said. Then she looked at Freely as if she were taking pleasure in her.

Freely was perplexed. Mrs. Haven had always kept her at such a distance that it was bewildering to know how to accept her sudden show of affection. Freely smiled a brief, shy smile, then she turned and left the room. Long after she had gone Mrs. Haven felt as if she were still in the room. The girl was so quiet, she mused, so modest, pleased with so little and making few demands, but her presence made a strange impress on one. Mrs. Haven brushed her hand before her eyes. The girl was improving, there was no doubt about it.

Philip was waiting impatiently downstairs. He slipped his arm around Freely, then he looked searchingly into her face. "You look tired, darling. Was it an ordeal?"

She nodded. "Standing and turning, turning and standing, keeping shoulders back and head high so the fall of the skirt will be as it should. Oh, Philip, can a dress ever be worth so much fussing?"

"Mother says you look ravishing in it."

"That's good." Then Freely wondered what Benedict would have to say about a dress that did that to one.

"You know, you are slowly winning Mother's heart. I knew you would, if she saw enough of you."

"Do you think she likes me just a little?"

"Much more than a little."

They went out of the house and walked down to the river. Freely put her hand in Philip's. The gardens were like a stage ready set for a performance. The gray brooding quality of the day had not altered and since early morning there had been no change of light. It gave the day a timeless feeling, as if it were hung in space. There were no shadows to lie long on green grass or flowing water, and by their shifting mark the passage of hours. No birds were flying and the year was past the heyday of their songs. Only a cricket chirped from the grasses now and again to break the stillness with the first creaking bow of night's strident symphony.

The river moved silently through the gray day, a shudder of ripples disturbing it as Philip swung the canoe onto its surface. The ripples broke against the landing stage, making a slight sound. There was an eagerness to the sound, as if the movement of the canoe were welcome, breaking the tension of silence the day had imposed.

Freely lay back on a pile of cushions in the canoe. Philip, sitting in the stern, kept his eyes on her as he paddled slowly over a course he had known for years.

"Everything is so quiet," Freely said, her voice almost a whisper as if the day had laid its spell of stillness on her.

"Hawkins says there's going to be a storm tonight."

"Hawkins would have liked my grandfather. He was wise about the weather, too."

"He says being with horses so much makes one wise."

"I'm sure of that," Freely agreed. "Much, much wiser than with people. Animals are silent. They make you listen," Freely sighed. "People fill the air with talk and most of the time it's just noise."

Philip laughed at her, lifting his paddle and letting it drip water into her hand that lay palm up on the side of the canoe. "Oh, come now, darling, we have to talk a bit. I must tell you how much I love you!"

"Yes," she breathed happily, a smile coming over her face, "but the real things we never have to say to each other." The smile faded from her face and she closed her eyes again.

He rested his paddle across the canoe and they drifted downstream. After a few moments he spoke to her, softly so his words would not waken her if she slept. "Are you tired, Freely?"

Without opening her eyes her lips parted enough for the words to come through, "Terribly tired." She sighed again as if a weight were pressing on her.

"I'm sorry, darling. I'm afraid Mother's been asking too much of you."

The canoe drifted down the current, Philip touching the water with his paddle from time to time just enough to guide it.

Freely spoke quietly into the listening silence, her eyes closed, her lips barely opening. "I feel as if I've been climbing a long, long hill—almost against my will, yet knowing I must keep on because of my longing to reach the light at the top of the hill."

"What is the light, Freely, that it can draw you so?"

She opened her eyes and looked at him for a long time before she spoke. "You," she said, then she moved her head on the pillows. "No, not you entirely, Philip dear, but our life together." She smiled at him, wanting him to know all the rest that she could not say. Her eyelids fluttered over her eyes again.

"Grandfather used to say," she went on in a voice that seemed to be coming out of a dream, "that life was like that —a going up hill all the time, that you couldn't go back, that you had to keep on climbing; but though the hill was long, heaven crowned its summit." She smiled like a person smiling in sleep.

The canoe drifted on, the water breaking gently away from it.

"I'm such a long way from the top still," she said slowly, "and I feel as if I didn't have any more strength to go on."

He looked at her, wishing he were any place but in the stern of a canoe. "Oh, Freely darling——" he began.

The longing in his words reached to her and compelled her to open her eyes. Out of her reverie and from the depth of her weariness, her glance met his. Clear amber eyes met the gaze of earnest gray eyes, met and lingered while much was said that was independent of words. Freely smiled then, as if strength were coming to her. She drew herself up out of the pillows and leaned against the back rest to watch the course they were taking. Philip began to paddle energetically.

"How was Susannah when you saw her yesterday?"

Freely shook her head. "I didn't see her. I got almost there and then I found that I just couldn't go. I didn't know what I would say to her. How I would tell her what had happened to Freely Simon."

"But you'll always be Freely Simon to her—to me!" Philip said stoutly.

"How can I be, Philip, if I'm someone else to your mother?"

Then she told him about the dell and how she had looked down from its clearing across the waving trees to the land below her, while behind her reached the forest with all its strength and secrecy. "It's different, the dell," she commented. "It's like something waiting to begin its life again."

He leaned toward her excitedly so that the canoe rocked unsteadily. "Freely, Freely," he said, "wouldn't that be the very place to build our home? Of course, it's Simon land but if we could buy from Susannah those ten acres that have been cut over we could start our own life there!"

"Oh, Philip," she breathed, but the possibility of such happiness took all words from her and she found she could say no more than his name over and over again, "Philip. Philip."

His face was all eagerness and his eyes were shining as he leaned toward her, unfolding the plan that had been taking shape in his mind ever since he had known he loved Freely but never found utterance until this moment.

"We'll build our home in the clearing itself, halfway between Simonton and Millville, and, Freely, why shouldn't it be the beginning of a whole new community? There'll be people living on the hill again and the life that Millville drained from Simonton will flow back to it. Perhaps someday it will all be Simonton—the hilltop and the river village— and Mark Simon's dream will have come true! Freely, Freely, why don't you say something? Isn't it a marvelous plan?"

Freely was smiling in a mysterious way, not looking at Philip but across the river; not seeing Philip and his eager dream so much as his mother and her carefully prepared plan as she discussed with Mr. Montague the wing that was to be added to Haven Hall. With an effort she directed her eyes to Philip, while the mysteriousness of her smile changed to mischievousness. "Susannah will give you that piece of land for a wedding present," she said, her eyes twinkling. "I'm quite sure that she will if you build a house on it for us to live in."

"Darn this canoe!" Philip exclaimed. "I want to take you in my arms and hug you for that." He turned in midstream and started paddling back to the landing stage.

"You'll be able to do that anywhere after tomorrow," she reminded him, "for I shall be properly introduced as your fiancée." It was hard for her to make her words sound serious when her thoughts were dancing like the ripples on the river.

"Darn tomorrow," he said, paddling hard.

After they had beached the canoe and were walking leisurely back through the garden, Philip remembered that he had something in his pocket for Freely. He placed in her hand a small box. She opened it and saw a skillfully cut diamond ring, flashing fire even in the dull grayness of the day.

"It's beautiful," she said. "It must have been very costly." She shut the box carefully.

"It's for you, Freely darling."

Her eyes widened. "I have a ring," she replied, holding out her left hand as if to remind him of the stone he had brought her from the West.

He shook his head. "Mother says it isn't good enough to wear at the party tomorrow. She says that people won't think I value you enough if I give you just a little semiprecious stone."

"It means everything to me," Freely said firmly, looking at the stone. In its dull sheen it held within itself all that the diamond declared so resplendently. She pressed it to her lips, cherishing the secret that was for herself alone. She thought of the man who held back a wall of water so his comrades could get to safety. Then she felt that she was holding back a wall and the moonstone gave her the courage to be adamant. All along she had been doing what Mrs. Haven had wanted her to do, or what Philip had wanted her to do to please his mother. Suddenly, standing there in the garden with the little box in her hand, Freely knew that she had reached a point beyond which she would not go.

"I shall wear the ring you gave me, Philip," she said in a clear voice. "The other one may be beautiful but it has no meaning." She handed the box back to him and, almost without knowing what he did, Philip returned it to his pocket.

They walked toward the house. Freely noticed that the

wind had started to move, for the trees overhead were catching it in their branches and even the flowers were swaying.

"There'll be rain soon," she commented, breathing deeply, her country-bred nostrils catching the smell of it. "I do hope it won't dash the garden. Everything looks so lovely for the party."

"I wish tomorrow never had to come," Philip said heartily.

She slipped her hand in his. "So do I, darling. I wish the wind would blow it right out of the calendar."

At dinner that night Mrs. Haven was in an agitation of nervousness as rain lashed against the windows and wind beat around the house. Philip tried to persuade her to believe that the garden would recover and that it might be even more beautiful as the rain refreshed it after the long spell of dry weather they had had. But nothing would calm Mrs. Haven or assure her.

After dinner she gave Freely for the hundredth time instructions on how to receive guests and what she should say to each one; then she ran through a list of special people for each one of whom she had delegated to Freely some particular topic of conversation. Philip looked on, half bored, half amused, but more impatient than ever to have the day behind him so that he and Freely could begin to lay their real plans. He loved her for the way she had yielded to his mother's life but he was increasingly eager to see her back in her own life. She had stayed longer at Haven Hall than any of them had planned and only Susannah's constant assurance that all was well on the hill had made it possible.

Philip found himself thinking ahead with a new sense of freedom. Perhaps the day after tomorrow they would go to Simonton. He would talk with Susannah about the purchase of the land. They would plan their home. He wondered how long it would take to build. He was eager to carry Freely in his arms as his bride over the threshold in the country custom, but he did not want to wait too long for them to be married. He smiled to himself.

"Whatever are you smiling at, Philip?" Mrs. Haven asked irritably. "I haven't said anything in the least amusing."

"No, I'm sure you haven't."

"Simone and I are discussing very serious matters."

"Yes, of course you are." Philip picked up a book. He did not dare meet Freely's eyes. Their combined gaze might have been more than a challenge to his mother. The knowledge of something held secure between them would have made them both laugh aloud, and that would have been something his mother could not have understood. In the state of nerves she was already in, it would have agitated her even further.

Mrs. Haven said good night and went upstairs, calling back to Freely that she must go to bed soon to look fresh for the morning.

Freely turned to Philip. "None of it seems real. It's like a dream," she said.

"Would you like to keep on dreaming?"

"No, no," she shook her head emphatically, "it's the kind of dream I want to waken from."

"I'm afraid it won't be easy to sleep tonight with the wind and the rain racketing around as they are."

"The wind and the rain were my first lullaby," she reminded him, "and they've been one of my slumber songs for years."

She kissed him and started slowly up the stairs. He held her with his gaze until she turned the corner at the top. Almost he wished that she would waken from her dream. Almost . . .

23.

>>>>>>>>>>>>>>>>>>>>>>>><<<<<<<<<<<<<<<<<<<<<<<<<

THE rain ceased toward midnight but the wind increased. Freely had gone to bed early but her sleep had been a fitful one, checkered by dreams. She was in her room on the hill and she woke to the sudden realization that the door of the church had blown shut. Thinking she must open it in case any creature needed shelter, she sat up in bed; then she remembered where she was and sank back against the pillows.

A limb, crashing down from a tree, woke her again; but it was not a limb from one of the elms on the lawn at Haven Hall; it was from the oak that stood near Susannah's door and it was a limb that bore a squirrel's nest. The nest had come down and the curious stuff of which it was made lay scattered on the ground. Freely saw it all and then she saw that among the litter were three young and furless babies. She watched for the mother to come to them, but no gray squirrel with bright anxious eyes and twitching bushy tail appeared. Frightened into flight by the storm or injured by the fall of the limb, the mother had abandoned her young ones. They would need to be warmed by the stove and given some milk, Freely thought. They would need care, and why was she there but to give it to them.

Sitting on the edge of the bed, she fumbled for her shoes with her feet in the darkness. She came upon the dainty bedroom slippers with little curled ostrich feathers, which Mrs. Haven had given her. They, more than anything else, told her where she was. With an aching cry of frustration she flung herself face down on the pillows. She felt more helpless than the furless babies she had seen so vividly lying on the ground. In her loneliness she wept, but the tears gave her some relief and she fell asleep again.

The next time she awoke it was with a feeling that she had had all the sleep she would have that night; yet when she lit the lamp by her bed and looked at the clock she saw that it was not yet one o'clock. No dream with an anguishing need dragged at her thought then, but all the hill seemed to be calling to her. She wanted to answer the call, knowing she could not. She longed to see the church standing quiet and still while all else was in torment. She was hungry to hear Susannah's voice, to see the calm in her eyes, to feel her arms about her. But she would have to wait until morning. Perhaps she could persuade Mrs. Haven to let her go to Simonton before the party.

Freely drew the sheet up and forced herself to lie still; but the wind had fretted her and she could not lie still for long. She felt like a swimmer struggling for air against an overwhelming wave, and the air was Simonton and the wave was the life at Haven Hall. With a knifelike decisiveness that cut through all her misgivings, she knew that something in her —perhaps not her life but something equally as important— would die if she did not soon breathe the air of the hilltop. In the white light of her decision all feeling of fitness and propriety left her. The dignity that governed the new life fell away and she became her old self, responding to an urgent call without stopping to question it.

There was no doubt in her mind but that she must go to the hill on that wind-racked night. She must be there in case any creature lost or injured needed her. She must be there one last time while she was still Freely. By tomorrow she would have become someone else in the eyes of the world and perhaps the creatures would not trust this new person.

She dressed quickly, putting on the clothes that had been her best when she arrived at Haven Hall but which had so soon been discarded, and her sturdy shoes. She brushed her hair back and braided it, catching the braids together with a ribbon at the nape of her neck. She put out her lamp, opened and closed the door behind her, and crept quietly through the house. A dim light was burning in the lower hall and she could see her way to the wide front door. She stood for a moment on the threshold, looking behind her into the house, half wondering if she would ever see it again; for now that she was breaking away it was hard to imagine herself returning. She looked ahead of her, letting her eyes grow accustomed to the night.

The rain had eased off into a fine mist, but the wind was still high in the trees. Freely could see their leafy masses waving against the night sky; she could feel the surge of movement down their trunks as roots held fast in the earth against the force of the gale. The lawn was scattered with leaves and fallen branches. The flowers in the borders near the house had been flattened.

Freely drew the door shut behind her. With a deep breath and a sense of exultant daring like a swimmer plunging into cold water, she ran forward into the night, down the drive and out onto the road. She ran across the bridge with the river below her foaming and debris laden. Panting and breathless, she came down to a walk as she went through Millville, but even her walk was a rapid one as the wind hurried her on. The street lamps made a dim glare. Most of the houses were in darkness, but here and there a light burned behind drawn blinds. Perhaps someone was reading late or watching by a sickbed; perhaps someone had wanted the friendliness of light on such a night. Comforted by the cloak of invisibility given her by the night, she knew she would not be seen as she hurried through the quiet streets.

Up the long familiar hill she started while the wind breathed fresh fury. Noisy and tempestuous, it lashed around her. Trees creaked and groaned under its onslaughts. Fallen branches littered the road. Freely felt fear clutch at her, trying to force her to indecision. Her knees were weak and her feet cold, but she lowered her head and put the weight of her body against the wind. It was like an assailant of heroic force determined to keep her from her desire—that quiet which, even in the midst of tumult, belonged to the hill. To be filled with quiet, that was her need during this night of storm; but it had been her need during all the weeks at Haven Hall, and tonight was only the culmination.

Anguish and perplexity had been deepening for her during the days so that the quiet room within that was her mind was quiet no longer. Head bowed to take the wind's force, Freely could not see where she was going; she knew only that her feet were on the road. With a sudden gesture she lifted her head, standing still as panic ran through her. Not six feet before her a tree came crashing down to lie across the road. For hours it had withstood the storm, but it had been wrenched from its place by the last violent blast that had torn through the woods and gone howling on down through the valley.

Benedict had told her there was nothing ever to fear, and she had known and believed and put her trust in his words. There were times when she might have feared, but she had always been able to turn within, to listen, and to find courage. Tonight it was different. There was no quiet within to turn to, no behest that she knew she could trust. There was only bewilderment in her mind and all around her the raging of the storm. She shuddered again as another limb came crashing down in the woods to the left of the road. She wanted to run, but there was no place to run to. Back she could not go, and ahead the road was blocked. But fear would not be routed by running. There were some things from which there was no escape. Where was there to go, in this world of uprooted trees and crashing limbs, she asked herself; how was she to reach the hilltop that was the end of her desire.

She raised her head. On the right side of the road there were no limbs to fall for it was the cut-over area, the place that had once been secret and sacred, the place where she had been sure of finding God. She strained her eyes in the darkness and saw the white birch. Fascinated, she watched it bending to the fury of the wind, yielding to its tempestuous gusts. In momentary deference, the wide canopy of small leaves would bow gracefully; then, caught again by the arms of the wind, it would swirl high with an abandon of joy. It was going with the wind, not opposing it as some of the trees that had fallen had done. Well rooted, it could afford to be ardent, giving itself to the wind in its stride. With a secret of its own, it could exult with the wind yet remain essentially itself.

Freely could not take her eyes from the birch, for the birch had become herself or she had become the birch, it was hard to tell which. She could not fear for the birch; it was taking the storm with its innate bending power. Not fearing for the birch, she feared less for herself, and by degrees anguish eased from her mind. The birch was constant to itself; and because of the birch Freely knew she must have a like constancy if she would outride a night of storm. To hold to it might mean the sacrifice of everything, even—she caught her breath as the wind slapped against her—even of Philip; but she would have to take the risk. To be one's own self was primitive and ultimate. The birch was safe on this tempestuous night, safer than many a stouter tree in the forest, because the birch was doing what the conditions of its growth had equipped it to do.

Leaving the road that was blocked by the fallen tree, she approached the birch and put her arms around it. Philip had loved this tree too, she thought, as she felt its bark against her cheek. Peering into the darkness where her dell had been, she tried to picture what it would be like if a house stood there. A house would not be seen from the road unless a light were burning in it, but it would have a light in a window on such a night, Freely told herself, on any night. Someone coming up the hill might need shelter or guidance, or perhaps just the outreaching hand that a light in the dark could be. She hugged the white birch more closely and put her lips to the healed wound in the bark, the mark Philip had scotched to indicated to his woodsmen that the tree was to be spared.

Breasting the wind again, Freely resumed her way up the hill. She held her head higher, feeling more like her old self than she had in many weeks. If she maintained her own quiet, she told herself, she would have a sanctuary always within her and there would be no need to fear.

The stillness began to deepen. She could listen now, listen within herself. The stillness widened and she began to feel that she could listen outside herself. Gradually she became aware not of the wild rocking of the wind, the moaning in the trees, the crash of falling branches, but of the vast power that was behind the storm. An hour ago, when she had left Haven Hall, she had thought she could run away from the tumult within her and find peace on the hilltop; but she had not been able to run far and she had found peace within herself. That is as it should be, her grandfather would have said. She remembered a night of storm when she had stood by the kitchen window with him, watching it. She was a child then and her hand had felt small as it rested in his. She had not been afraid, though the sound of the storm increased and the house seemed to shake as it withstood the violence of the wind. Benedict had said then that they could not run away from the commotion, but that they could bring their own stillness to it.

She looked back at the birch for one more glimpse of it, then she thought of Freely Simon and she spoke aloud to the night. "Yes, I must be myself or I'll be no one, no one at all." A shiver ran over her, not of fear now but of pity at the loneliness of being no one at all.

In the windy restlessness of the night, something had become clear to her. She looked skyward, thanking the wind for all it had done. It had blown away the uncertainty that had dogged her, the haze of indecision, the mesmeric weariness that had been drawing her down deeper and deeper into a way of living that was not hers. Two things stood out in her mind: her love for Philip, her respect for herself. The two might be able to become one. They might not be able to become one. She did not know which it would be. And the night would not tell her. The darkness was impenetrable. A few rods before her was the limit of her vision.

When she came over the brow of the hill, it did not surprise her to see a lamp burning in the kitchen window. Susannah always did that on a stormy night. Freely felt a leaping of her heart. Susannah herself might even be sitting in the warm circle of lamplight, dreaming and drowsing by the kitchen fire; she often stayed up late, especially on a night when it might be hard for her to sleep.

Freely crossed the green quickly. She went toward the church just enough to be able to see that the door was ajar. Satisfied that it was, she went on to the house. She pushed open the door that had never known a bolt since it had first swung on its long iron hinges, and then she stood on the threshold of the kitchen. But she could not stand there long, though the sight of the peaceful kitchen with its shining stove, the quilting frame and a row of geraniums on the window sill was like the sight of land to a storm-tossed seaman. It was not the room itself, it was Susannah sitting in the lamplight that brought a cry of joy to Freely's lips. Running across the room, she dropped to her knees and buried her head in Susannah's lap.

Susannah had been dozing, but she nodded into wakefulness at the sight of the sandy head in her lap, at the clasp of the strong young arms about her waist.

"Freely!" she exclaimed, "Freely!" And yet the sight of the girl on such a night at such an hour did not seem to surprise her at all. "I was dreaming of you," she said. "I dreamed you had come home—" she took a little quick breath— "to stay."

Freely threw back her head. "I have," she said stoutly. She sat back on her heels while her eyes roamed the familiar room, coming back to rest on Susannah. There was safe anchorage here, she thought, in this room that had seen so much living, and the sound of the wind outside was like the sound of surf on a faraway shore.

In words that tumbled fast as water through an open sluice gate, Freely told Susannah of all that had happened to her since she had left the hill.

"But you might have said it in your letters and given me something to think about while you were away," Susannah rebuked her gently.

"No, no, Grandma," Freely shook her head, "it would not go into a letter. There were things that hurt my heart and puzzled my mind. I didn't want to tell you of them until we could talk about them together."

Freely spoke of Dombey and of her inability to help him in his time of need. "But I was so unsure of myslf, Grandma, and there was no one to tell me what to do. It frightened me. It was as if there were no one anywhere to whom I could pray. I couldn't do anything for Dombey but comfort him, and that wasn't enough for Mrs. Haven or Philip."

Susannah listened, but her gladness at having Freely with her again was no greater than her desire to hear what Freely's life had been for the past weeks.

"Grandma, you told me to come back when the way was clear to me," Freely said.

Susannah nodded, remembering what she had said on the day Freely drove away from Simonton.

"I've come back."

"Yes?" Susannah queried.

"I see my way. I saw it tonight as I came up the hill."

"And what is it?"

"It is to be myself." Freely spoke briefly and with finality, like a judge pronouncing a sentence within whose words a life was bound.

"That is all that any one of us can be," Susannah said quietly.

"Philip may not love me any more."

"And he may love you more than ever."

"Grandma, is life full of risks like this?"

"Yes, Freely, it is. Full of risks."

No words passed between them for a while. Freely's thoughts were far away and Susannah was seeking for words to say what was in her heart. Enjoying Philip almost as she might one of her sons and welcoming all that he brought to Freely's life, she realized that from the start she had been almost afraid of this first love of Freely's. She had known with the wisdom of her years and the sureness of her womanhood that Freely would not easily love again with the purity and intensity she felt for Philip. And yet, Susannah would not have had it otherwise; nor, she thought, would Benedict.

To assure herself almost more than Freely, Susannah said, "We all have gifts to give the world, Freely, and you have a gift of loving. Benedict knew. It was what he brought you up for all the years of your growing. Life will not deprive you of the way to use your gift."

"But Philip, Grandma, will he still love me if I am myself?"

"That was how you were when he first loved you."

They were still talking when the clock struck three. The wind that had been going down to quiet had become a light soughing in the oak by the door.

"And yet, dear heart," Susannah said, "it is not just this being true to ourselves that is so vital, for in marriage each one submerges a part of a life that a new structure may be built. It takes courage to break off from the old familiar ways and form a new unit, but in so doing the world moves forward."

Freely told Susannah of the house she and Philip had imagined building in the dell. "Halfway between Simonton and the river village it would be," she said. "But perhaps it's only a dream and if Philip comes here again, he may not even remember it."

"I shall deed all the land to you, Freely. It is yours by right since your uncles have no interest in it, but before doing that I'll be pleased to deed those ten acres to Philip. It will be my wedding present to him. But he shall have it—" Susannah's tone became serious— "on condition that he build a house there for you."

"I knew you'd say that," Freely smiled. "I'll tell Philip that just as soon as he comes here to see me—if he wants to see me again."

"Won't you see him in the morning?"

Freely looked surprised. "Where?"

"At his home. You are still Mrs. Haven's guest no matter what name she chooses to call you. The wind has gone down. If you knew your way here in the darkness you can find it back again. You must do what is expected of you."

"Even the garden party?"

Susannah nodded in the inexorable way she had when she felt firm about a matter.

Freely said impulsively, "But not that name. It isn't mine. I can't use it. I don't know why I ever let them put it onto me."

Susannah looked deep into Freely's eyes that had once been so free from troubling thoughts. "You may have a right to that name but it is not yours. It would not be honest to use it. You have your own name and it has been borne nobly by other Simon women who gave their all of love."

Freely returned Susannah's gaze, looking long into the eyes that were so calm, that spoke so persuasively of a life of quiet.

Susannah took a piece of paper from a pad that was beside the lamp. She wrote on it with a pencil, then she folded it and gave it to Freely. "This is for Philip," she said.

Freely got to her feet slowly, putting the paper in the pocket of her dress. "I shall go," she said, not so obediently as resolutely, "but I think that I shall be back tomorrow— after the garden party."

"Your room has always been ready, since the first day you went away."

Susannah stood in the doorway to watch her go, but night soon took her from view. The night had gentled as the storm fell away. There was freshness in the air and among the tattered clouds a faint appearing of stars. Susannah returned to the kitchen to lower the lamp and bank the fire. Freely had gone into the night as a soldier into battle, strong and fearless. Susannah felt happy now about the girl and she had no fear for her, for Freely had found herself. She was so young, Susannah thought, and all her life was before her. She was like the skylark in Wordsworth's poem, "true to the kindred points of Heaven and home" she could not help but be true to herself.

24.

FREELY knew that Philip breakfasted alone in the dining room at eight o'clock. She listened at her door to hear the sound of his footsteps going down the stairs, then she followed soon after him. He was already seated and had propped his newspaper up before him when she entered the room.

"Good morning, Philip," she said.

He put his paper down and smiled widely at her, as he had the day when he had first seen her—her head popping up over the edge of a pew, fox cubs clambering over her.

"Why, Freely, what a surprise! What a pleasure!" He rose from his chair and looked at her as if he had not seen her for a long time. "Are you going to have breakfast with me?"

"Yes, please, if I may." She slid into a chair near him.

Philip rang for Sara. When she appeared he said briefly, "Miss Freely is breakfasting with me this morning, Sara."

Sara, well trained as she was, neither spoke nor moved. The merest inclination of her head indicated that she had understood the words addressed to her. Freely looked at her and smiled, murmuring a good morning, but Sara's gaze was fixed on a middle distance somewhere above Freely's head.

Freely had put on the crisp gingham dress she had worn when she first came to Haven Hall. She had brushed her hair and braided it, looping the braids around her head in the old way. She showed no sign of her sleepless night, but her walk in the wind had brought color to her cheeks. There was a sparkle in her eyes and a suppressed merriment underlying her words and actions.

"Very good, Mr. Philip." Sara turned on her heels and left the room.

Freely had a healthy appetite and she was glad that being with Philip in the dining room gave her opportunity to have an ample breakfast. The dainty meal that arrived on her tray of a morning would never have carried her far today.

They spoke of the storm, of the freshness the rain had brought to the land, even though the wind had left a wake of devastation behind it.

"But nothing that the gardeners can't tidy up before afternoon," Philip commented.

They laughed and talked together as they had in the old days, the days when they had first met. Philip thought of the time when he and Freely would be breakfasting together every morning and he would go from their home to the woods or mill with a feeling of her love behind him, her love waiting for him. He reached into a pocket and brought out some sketches he had been making.

"It's the house, our house, Freely. I did them last night during the storm. It was hard to sleep."

She leaned over them eagerly. They were roughly drawn but the plan was clearly discernible. The house was to have the basic lines of a New England farmhouse, a two-story square. It would be like the houses that had been at Simonton, anchored by a large central chimney to accommodate many fireplaces, with a wide front door and evenly spaced windows like eyes to look over the countryside.

"Of course," he laughed, "it's hopelessly old-fashioned and it's almost a copy of Susannah's house on the hilltop, but it's hard to improve on that classic severity of the early builders. They put into a house all that it takes for living and that's all a house needs to have."

Freely sighed rapturously. "It's my dream, Philip," she said, looking at the rough sketches, turning them in her hands to see them from different angles, imagining how the house would look as it was approached from the road.

"I'm going up to Susannah tomorrow to see if she'll sell me a few acres."

Freely shook her head jubilantly. "You won't need to, Philip," she said. "Susannah has already given you the very acres you want. She told me she would. It was all just as I had thought."

"When did Susannah tell you that?"

"Last night, when I went to see her."

Philip stared. "Last night? But the storm—" Suddenly his eyes widened. "Freely, what have you done to yourself, you—you—"

"I've just gone back to being Freely again. That's all I can be."

Sara came into the room.

"Yes, Sara?" Philip asked.

"Will you please tell Miss Simone that Mrs. Haven will see her at ten o'clock?" Sara turned and left the room, her skirt rustling emphatically.

"Well, of all the—" Philip exclaimed. "Why couldn't she tell you herself?"

"Because she isn't noticing my existence," Freely said briefly. She shrugged her shoulders. There was nothing she could do about Sara and she had no intention of bothering her mind about the woman.

"I must tell Mother to speak to her," Philip said by way of apology. "Sara has been with us so long that she takes a good many liberties."

Freely brought from her pocket the piece of paper Susan-

nah had given her. She handed it to Philip. "This is Susannah's wedding present to you, Philip."

He took it eagerly. Then he read aloud the words Susannah
had written in her clear, careful hand, " 'All the land that has
been cut over on the westward slope of the hill I now give to
Philip Haven that a house may be built there for himself and
Freelove Simon to live in when they are made husband and
wife. In the event that no house is built, the land is to revert
in its entirety to Freelove Simon.' " Philip paused, then he
concluded, "Signed, Susannah Simon." He folded the paper
and put it in his pocket. "I shall never forget Susannah's
kindness," he said.

Freely had been gay all during their breakfast, but at that
moment her face became serious. "You may want to forget
after today," she announced gravely.

"Why?"

"Because, Philip, I can't go through with everything your
mother planned." She shook her head and added, "The change
in my name, the being someone I wasn't born to be."

Philip did not realize the import of what she was saying.
"It's just an expedient, that name, Freely. You have every
right to the surname and Simone is so easily twisted from
Simon. It pleases Mother to think of your French strain. It
makes you someone special." He smiled, thinking he was
humoring her.

But Freely was in no mood to be humored.

"An expedient?" she repeated, wrinkling her nose at the
word. "But that's what it has been all along—just this one
thing, just that—and how can I ever know where it will
end?"

"Don't take it so seriously, darling," he urged. "You've
made a good many concessions to Mother, but she can't ask
you for any more."

"Each one, Philip, has led me a step further away from

being myself—" she looked at him beseechingly— "and how could I ever be true to you if I were not true first to myself?"

"You're making much too much of this," he admonished, still looking at her playfully as he had the day he first came upon her in the church.

She looked at him earnestly. Her eyes were so startlingly clear that Philip had the odd sensation that he was looking into a mirror, but not one that returned a physical image.

"Can't you see, Philip, that I must be as I was when you first loved me? If I change to your mother's model I won't be the Freely you loved. Last night I woke up during the storm and I was frightened. I didn't know myself any more. I went up to the hill to find myself again."

"Did you?" he asked.

"Yes." she nodded. Reaching her hand across the table she laid it on his. "Say that you understand, Philip," she implored.

He took her hand in his and met her eyes with a steady glance. "I do understand, Freely, and I love you as my life."

"That is good," she said quietly.

He put his other hand across his eyes. "Oh Freely," he said, "if I should lose you I couldn't go on living."

The practical, sound sense of her nature came to the fore. "You're in no danger of losing me," she replied crisply, "but you have said good-by forever to someone who never existed, someone by the name of Simone de St. Pierre."

He took his hand from his eyes and stared at her. "But the garden party, Freely! The invitations that have all gone out! People will be expecting to meet you and what will they do?"

She smiled as if everything were entirely possible. "They can meet me, Freely Simon; but that other person won't be anywhere around."

A tide of misgiving carried Philip along with it. "But Mother, Freely, what will she think? What will she do?"

266

"She will smile at her guests and act as if nothing unusual had occurred. I have not lived in her shadow these weeks not to realize that she can meet any emergency in a gracious manner."

"But it will be so embarrassing, Freely dear," Philip said. "Couldn't you use the name she likes to call you just this once? You'll be changing your name so soon in any case."

"Ah," she flashed at him, "but that will be for my heart, it won't be for mere effect."

"Just this once?" he pleaded.

Her eyes lost their focus and a reverie came over her face. He had seen the expression before and he knew that her thoughts were far away. She did not speak for a full minute and then her words came slowly, each one like a pebble being dropped into a pool, each one sending out its own concurrent ripples. "Grandfather used to say that for happiness I should have nothing in my mind I would not share with God, nothing I wanted to hide from my fellows." The focus of her eyes sharpened and she looked at Philip. "If I stood before the world this afternoon as Simone de St. Pierre, God would not know me. I would be someone He had not made."

Philip's arguments withered before her words. He shook his head, conceding to her. He pushed his chair back from the table to stand beside her. She reached up to take his hands in hers and he leaned down to kiss her. "So be it," he said.

After he had gone, Freely went up to her room to await the proper time to present herself at Mrs. Haven's door. When she did, she was greeted by the polite formality, the distance and restraint that had marked their first meeting. Mrs. Haven's glance took in the gingham dress, the braided hair. "It would seem that you have something to explain to me," she said.

She listened quietly to what Freely had to say, but when Freely came to her conclusion and said she was sorry to cause any trouble, Mrs. Haven waved the words away as if contrition had no place at such a time.

"This is the first time in my life that my honesty has ever been questioned," she said sharply. "And by a mere child— a farm girl—a—"

"Please, Mrs. Haven," Freely interrupted. "I did not say anything about your honesty. I said that it would not be honest for me to appear as someone I am not."

"The implication was there all the same," Mrs. Haven remarked. She looked at Freely with dispassionate eyes. "Well, have you anything more to say?"

"No." Freely tried to smile.

"Then why do you stay?"

Freely left the room, holding her head high. She walked down the stairs and out the door. The gardeners were busy raking the lawn and staking up flowers. One of them touched his cap to Freely as she went by.

"We'll have everything tidied up in time for the party, miss," he said, "and you've got the sunshine today. That's something yesterday didn't have."

"No, there certainly was no sunshine yesterday," Freely replied. "But how beautiful everything looks today."

She went down to the river where she sat on the landing stage, watching the water flow by. It was still muddy from the storm and the current was swifter than usual. Saddened as she was by all that had happened, she still did not feel the anguish she had felt yesterday. There was a void within her, but Philip was still there. If she could keep steadfast he would always be there.

That afternoon, Freely wore the white dress Susannah had made for her graduation and she did her hair without help from the hairdresser. There was no receiving line and no engagement was announced. Philip and his mother mingled among the guests and Mrs. Haven, after everyone had arrived, made a gracious announcement that Miss de St. Pierre had been called back to France at the last moment because of an urgent need in her family. Freely helped the maids pass plates of cakes and cookies, glasses of punch, cups of tea. She knew none of the guests and none of them knew her so no comment was made. It was common knowledge in Millville that old Benedict Simon's granddaughter had been staying at Haven Hall that summer, but whoever wanted to think further merely assumed that she was working into some household capacity. The village on the hill was only a name to Mrs. Haven's fashionable friends and the Simon family was a legend of the countryside. A simple girl with unpretentious manners who kept herself in the background gave little occasion for talk. Had Miss Mattie Emerson been there it might have been different; but Miss Mattie had not been invited.

When the last guest had departed, Hawkins drove up with the carriage and waited while Freely's box was put in. Freely said good-by to Mrs. Haven and Philip as they stood on the front doorstep. Mrs. Haven took Freely's hand in hers, carefully guarding against any demonstration of affection Freely might make. Her hand felt cold in Freely's clasp and Freely had an overwhelming desire to warm it in some way. But she resisted the desire, merely shaking hands and saying her thank you for the past weeks. She turned to Philip, looking up into his face longingly; but even Philip seemed to have withdrawn into a world to which, Freely realized acutely, she would never have the key. He could not face her gaze. Dropping his eyes, he took her hand in his and put it to his lips. Freely turned and walked alone to the carriage, getting in the door Hawkins was holding open.

Her foot was on the step when she felt Philip's arms on her, turning her around, enfolding her as he held her against him.

She found her head resting on his shoulder while the curious rigidity that had marked her at her parting from Haven Hall began to ease a little.

"Freely darling," he breathed, "I can't let you go."

"You've got to," she said, "now." She lifted her head and smiled into where his face should be, but she could not see it for her eyes had filled with tears.

"I'll come to you tomorrow."

She shook her head, trying to free herself from his embrace. "No, no," she said. "Don't come until you are sure." Susannah had said that to her and when she had at last gone back to the hill she had been sure.

There was nothing more for her to say and she hoped that he would not speak again. The hold she had on her own emotions felt so slight. Comforted as she was by his love, she was chilled by the knowledge that Mrs. Haven was watching them. He did not want to let her go, but she broke away from him and got into the carriage. Hawkins shut the door and mounted the box. Philip stood motionless while the carriage went down the drive, his arm upraised to wave, but Freely never looked back. Sitting stiffly upright on the seat, she stared ahead of her.

Mrs. Haven was still standing on the doorstep when Philip returned to the house.

"That was an uncalled for demonstration to make before a servant," she said acidly, then turned and went up the steps into the house while Philip held the door open for her. "I always maintained that your background would show her up for what she is."

Philip did not reply soon and when he spoke it was with slow deliberation. "It has—" he said— "shown her up for what she is."

It was not until after dinner that evening that Mrs. Haven

told Philip about the visit of the architect. "I can't understand what possessed the girl," she said. "She's usually quite affable with strangers and she's always been appreciative of any little thing I've done for her, yet when we showed her the sketches of the new wing she acted in a most peculiar manner."

Philip was leaning forward in his chair. "Mother, do you mean to say you really thought Freely and I would live here at Haven Hall after we were married?"

"Of course I did. Where else would you live?"

Philip smiled grimly. "In our own house, Mother, the house I hope to help to build with my own hands."

"But, my dear boy—"

Philip leveled his eyes at her. "And you really thought we would go to Europe for six months?"

"Certainly," she said, defending herself but with an uncomfortable feeling that her defense was weakening. "It's quite the thing to do. Every young couple these days goes to Europe for the honeymoon."

"Not every couple," Philip laughed. "Do you know where we're going?"

She shook her head, dazed by Philip's self-assurance.

"We're going to Simonton!"

"But that," she exclaimed, "that isn't anyplace!"

"True, it isn't anyplace. It isn't even a dot on the map now, but it happens to be the place where our love was born and where, please God, it will grow."

"I was only trying to do what was right for you, Philip."

"Were you? You knew I loved Freely, and yet you never tried to understand her. Oh Mother, can't you see what she is? She grew up in an atmosphere of uncritical love, yet everything about her you would change. You have been trying to make her conform to some pattern of your own, but her pattern was made by God and, thank God, it can't be changed." He rose from his chair abruptly and started from the room.

"Where are you going, Philip?" she asked uneasily.

"I'm going to Simonton," he called back.

"At this hour?"

He did not answer for he did not hear her. He was out of the house and running as fast as he could to the stable for his horse.

25.

>>>>>>>>>>>>>>>>>>>>>>>>>><<<<<<<<<<<<<<<<<<<<<<<<<

FREELY resumed her life on the hill almost as if she had never left it. Now, in the mornings, lying abed in that brief interval between waking and getting up, it seemed like a dream that she had ever waited for anyone to bring her a breakfast tray. At six o'clock, with the sun streaming over the eastern hills and lighting up those in the west, she was downstairs, getting the fire in the stove for Susannah, going out to the barn to feed the horse and care for the cow and see to the hens. If there was still time before the smell of coffee and the sizzling of bacon served as breakfast bell, she would run across the dewy grass to the church to do some task there.

As in the old days, Sunday was a day Freely loved. Susannah read the lesson and Freely had her place at the organ. There were several voices to join in the singing, for the families that had come back to summer on the hill found the church part of their life. But it was not the playing of the organ or Susannah's reading that Freely liked best; it was the silence during the time of prayer. She listened then and what she heard she treasured, whether it came as wind in the trees, a singing of birds, or the thoughts in her own heart.

The August days moved on, full and rich, like apples ripening on a tree. The nights were heavy and warm, vibrating with the songs of a thousand insects. Flowers stood tall and strong colored and the vegetable garden was yielding great produce. Susannah began her yearly routine of pickling and preserving, for her thrifty spirit could not bear to see anything go to waste. Every morning when Dan Satturlee came up the hill he stopped at Simonton long enough to give his horse rest and water and himself a few minutes in the rocker in Susannah's kitchen. Sometimes it would be cookies she would have for him from a newly made batch, or doughnuts from the morning's baking, and always a tall glass of milk or a cup of hot coffee.

He never failed to have a letter from Philip for Freely. Freely would take it quickly and put it in her pocket, saving it for the moment when she could escape across the green to the church to read it. Dan Satturlee knew the small neat handwriting, the distinctive notepaper, and after Freely had left the room he would often indulge himself in a few minutes' gossip with Susannah.

"I saw Tom Slason the other day and he says they don't know what's got into Mr. Haven but he's working just like one of them now; none of that fancy driving around in his gig any more. Well, I could tell them a thing or two about your granddaughter but I always make it a practice just to carry the letters, not the talk, from house to house."

Susannah nodded her approval, wondering how clearly the difference was marked.

"They say he's planning to build a house just off the Simonton road."

"I believe he is," Susannah replied guardedly, wondering how much Philip's and Freely's plans had become public property.

"You wouldn't think he'd want to leave that fine estate of his for this scratchy hillside, would you now?"

Susannah bridled. "Benedict always said this land was some of the finest around here but that it took men to work it."

"Oh, I'm not saying anything against the land," Satturlee

said quickly. "Just seems a pity to leave a nice tidy place and start all over again."

"You're not reckoning with the pioneer spirit, Dan, that's still in man even when the land is subdued. Besides, Haven Hall is Mrs. Haven's home. Philip has a right to his own."

Dan winked. "I guess you have your own reasons for wanting to keep him near, haven't you now?"

"I always have had a soft place in my heart for boys, but don't you go drawing any conclusions, Dan Satturlee, and telling them along your route."

"No, ma'am," he raised his hands in horror, then he put his hand on his bag. "Land o' Goshen!" he exclaimed, "speaking of boys reminds me that I've got a letter from one of yours." He reached down into his bag and brought out the letter.

Susannah took it eagerly. "It's from young Mark," she said, seeing the California postmark and the writing that had changed little through the years.

"Aren't you going to read it?"

"In time," she said. Then she smiled at him, "I'll tell you tomorrow what it says."

He reached over and picked up his bag. "Well, I always have said there was no one like Susannah Simon for keeping a letter unread." He grunted and ambled forgivingly out to his buggy, getting in and settling back against the faded black seat. "That's all for today," he called out as he went creaking down the road.

Susannah went back to the kitchen and sat down in the rocker. She held Mark's letter in her hand and rocked back and forth with it, singing to herself, for a good few minutes before she opened it. She wanted to think about Mark, to see him, to have him in her kitchen—an eager, tempestuous boy, aping his brothers, trying to be like them, doing the work Benedict required of him but with his eyes on the world's horizons as hers had once been from the deck of a sailing ship. Thirty-four years ago he had walked out of the house in the deep snow and they had watched him go, waving to him until the dip of the hill took him from view.

She opened the letter and folded the pages back on her lap, then she read, savoring the words. A smile spread over her face and once a little sound escaped her. It was such a poignant sound that the cat in its circle of warm sleep behind the stove raised its head and blinked; then satisfied that all was well, it drew its paw across the back of its head and surrounded itself with sleep again.

When Freely returned, her own particular news speaking in the smile on her face, she saw Susannah in the rocker with the letter in her hands, and she saw that Susannah had been crying. Freely's heart gave a turn, then she realized that they had been tears of happiness.

"You've heard from one of my uncles?" Freely asked.

Susannah nodded. "They're coming home, they're starting to come home!" Joy had almost made her speechless, but taking up the letter she read from it to Freely. "It's Mark's son, the one who was married last year, the one whose baby Philip saw. Mark says he's a farmer through and through, but a New England farmer, that he wants to work on a small scale. He wants to be where winter is white and summer is green and there's the fairness of spring and the goldenness of autumn in between. He wants to come back to Simonton, to the close folding of the hills and the tight green valleys!"

Freely made a sound of delight, clapping her hands together.

"He wonders if he could come and live here, with us in this house, during the winter while they build a house of their own and he gets used to the country. He wonders if the Wheelmans would sell their acres and he could use their foundation. Oh!" Susannah put her hands to her face as if she must hide what she was feeling and showing. "The hill is going to live again. I won't have to give up the house, Freely, there'll be a man to do things. A farm is heavy on a woman but it rests well on a man's shoulders."

"You won't need me any more then, will you?" Freely asked.

Susannah looked up sharply. "I'll always need you, Freely, but you have your own life to live."

Freely dropped to the floor and put her arms around Susannah's knees as she used to when she was a little girl. "Listen to me, too," she said eagerly. "Philip has made all the plans for the house. He wants me to meet him down at the clearing this afternoon. He says they'll break ground for the foundation tomorrow."

Susannah smiled her approval. "Now, I am glad for your sake, for both your sakes."

"He says it's been hard for his mother."

"Poor lonely woman," Susannah murmured. "Sometimes I'd like nothing better than to sit with her and hold her hand in mine." She looked at Freely closely. "Freely, you must find the way for her to love you if you are to be her daughter too."

Freely nodded. "I've thought of that, oh Grandma, how I have thought of it, for I do so want her to love me. There must be a way somehow."

"Benedict used to say that even when there was no way apparent one would be opened," Susannah said slowly, "for every door has a hinge to swing open on."

At mention of Benedict, Freely asked quickly, "May we be married in Grandpa's church?"

"Why yes, dear heart." Then Susannah smiled. "Two new families starting life on the hill again! The church will have to have a real minister before long."

Freely was working in the garden when she heard the first ringing of an ax down in the clearing. She sat back on her heels and listened for a moment, pleased at what it meant.

Work was beginning on the land where their house would be and the sounds of such activity could reach to the hilltop. Halfway down the Simonton road as she would be, she would not be beyond hearing range of the hill. She finished her task, then brought the basket of tomatoes she had picked—lush and red and warm from the sun—into the kitchen. Susannah was upstairs resting and there was a feeling of midafternoon quiet pervading the house. Freely was thirsty. She could have pumped a drink at the kitchen sink, but she went outside to the well and lowered the bucket down into the cool water. From the same source Mark Simon had christened his hilltop and Benedict had christened her. She thought of young Mark's son soon to come back and start working the hill again and herself soon to start a life of her own. Shivering with excitement, she put the bucket back in its place and ran down the hill to the clearing.

Philip was there, working with his men, hacking at the brush that had grown up, hewing at stumps and logs that, worthless for lumber, had been left to rot. She watched for a moment, then she called his name.

He turned toward her quickly. "Freely!" he cried, an aching joy in the sound. He dropped his ax and came toward her.

She ran into his outstretched arms, then held up her face to be kissed.

"Oh, Freely darling," he said, "it's been so long since I've seen you." He held her away from him to devour her face with hungry eyes.

"Three weeks and three days," she reminded him, laughing, because now that it was behind them it seemed like nothing at all. "But I've had your letters, Philip, and they have brought you very near."

Arms linked, they went over to the wall and sat on it, under the shade of the white birch.

"I did come before, Freely," he told her. "I came the night you left Haven Hall. I rode up the hill on Prince but the moonlight was the only light in Simonton and I—I suddenly felt so unworthy. I turned around and rode back again. I wanted to have something to show you, to give you."

Freely looked earnestly at him, longing for confirmation and feeling that until she had it there was still some small part of herself she was holding in reserve. "You are sure now, Philip, about me? About our life?"

He nodded. "I came today and asked you to meet me here because I am sure. I had to come. There is only one way for us. We've known that all along."

"But your mother?"

He shook his head. "She does not willingly admit it, but she has said that I must go in the direction toward which my heart is set. I think you will win her in time, Freely, but—" he hesitated.

"But what?" she prompted.

"I know now that you will do it by being yourself and not by becoming her idea of what you should be." He breathed deeply as if he took in some strength from the hill and gave it out in joy. "So, here I stake my claim and here we build our home."

"And can we be married in the Simonton church?" she asked breathlessly.

"There couldn't possibly be any other place."

She told him about Mark's son and his family coming from the West to begin their life in Simonton.

"So," Philip smiled, "they have completed their plan. They were talking about it last June when I saw them."

"If we wait until October to be married they will be here."

"I wish we could be married tomorrow," he exclaimed, "but now there's no doubt any more I don't care how long we have to wait." Then he smiled quickly, "But let's not have it be any later than October."

"Sometimes I think we've always been married," Freely said dreamily, "since that first day we met. I can't remember when I didn't love you."

He pressed her hands in his.

"A golden Sunday in the autumn, that will be our wedding day," she said reflectively. "I shall have to take down those old green garlands in the church and put bright leaves in their place."

Soon they went back and watched the men at their work. Slowly it was yielding ground, this clearing where the house would stand.

"A good place for a home," Freely said, "where the fox came to quarry."

When Philip asked her what she meant she shook her head. It all seemed so long ago, that raw spring day when the fox had run through the wood with blood streaming from her wound and a second shot ripping through the quiet had made Freely share pain with the fox.

Tom Slason pushed his cap back. "We'll need more than a few sticks of dynamite to get those boulders out."

Philip nodded. "I'll see to that, Tom, in a day or two."

Tom looked at Freely. "There's a nice spring back away, miss, that will do you for a water supply."

"I know it well," Freely told him, "but I thought it had dried up."

Slason shook his head. "Not if you get below the surface. Water's there and will come bubbling out as pretty as you please."

It was late in the afternoon when Freely said good-by to Philip and walked back to Simonton. On the way, she went into the churchyard and sat for a while by her mother's stone. She felt enveloped in peace. She had so often brought her sorrows to her mother that now she was eager to share with her the joy that had come to her. It was happiness, yes, but it was not the wild ecstasy that had filled her being when she had first realized her love for Philip; it was so quiet, the feeling that possessed her, and with it was assurance like a promise that everything would be right.

After a while she went into the church and there she sat for another few moments as Benedict companioned her thoughts. She talked with him in her mind as she once had so freely when they had walked through the woods or worked together in the fields. He had his own feeling about quietness; to him it was the confidence of goodness at the heart of life. That gave one peace, he had said, filling heart, mind, and spirit as a tidal river fills its banks carrying the salty strength of the sea far inland.

"But I have so much of my life before me to live," she meditated, "can I always be sure of feeling the peace that I now feel?"

She could see the slow way that Benedict would shake his head at such a question, and the sweetness of the smile that would spread across his face, the sweetness mitigating the negative answer. "No, not always," he might say. "And yet, once one has seen the vision, one knows it is there; the darkest night, the longest road cannot deprive one of the vision."

After a while she went from the church and toward the house. She could see Susannah sitting at her quilting frame, a look of concentration on her face, and around her—almost as visible as the house—the peace of her well-ordered life.

These were the forces that had shaped her, Freely thought —Benedict's wisdom, Susannah's quiet—and it was what they had given her that she would carry into the future; that one who lay in the churchyard and the other who lay within a mountain in the far West had been unknown to her; they were like people in a story of whom one hears much but knows little.

Freely went into the house. Day by day things were becoming almost unbearably dear. This doorstep that she had crossed so often, so unthinkingly, soon she would be crossing it again as Philip's wife come home to visit for a little while. Everything around her was tinged with a delicious sadness. Things she had known all her life she would soon be parting with, and yet there was no sense of farewell for in some way they had become part of her. The house, the oak tree, the green grass—all were bathed in long warm shadows cast by late afternoon sunlight. A night would come through which she must pass and after which she would be different, but it was not yet, she told herself. For a little while more she could cherish this house, these things, this person as she always had. With a cry of delight she ran across the floor to greet Susannah and tell her of the afternoon with Philip.

26.

AUGUST moved into September as leisurely and inevitably as fruit mellowing on vines and trees. Freely and Susannah went about their chores in the mornings; in the afternoons they made preparations for Freely's new life, sewing, sorting linens, packing for removal certain things that were to belong to Freely. One rainy day they went up to the attic to go over its stores. Susannah turned the key in the lock of an old chest. Lifting the lid, Freely saw that a supply of household linens was neatly laid in it.

"They were the beginning of a little store I had been making for my daughter Freelove, your mother," Susannah explained. "It is only right that they should go to you."

Freely knelt down beside the chest and lifted the linen out until she had seen the full store. There were sheets and pillow covers, towels of various sizes, tablecloths, all the linen needful for a small household. Spun and woven by hand, it was soft and beautiful to touch and it wore well the patina of time in the slight change of color it had undergone. The stitches in the hems were fine and even, and every piece bore a delicately worked F and S. Running her fingers over the monogram, Freely realized that the initials were hers as well as her mother's and she was glad that they were, for the name had kept her within her own tradition.

"You must have been working on them for a long time," Freely said.

Susannah moved her head slowly. "Freelove was just a little girl when I began them and I was still working on them when she went away."

Kneeling on the floor by the chest, Freely looked up at Susannah with eyes full of wonder.

"You can't live on a farm or a hilltop," Susannah said quietly, "and not believe in the future."

In another chest were quilts Susannah had been working on during more recent years. Many of them were familiar to Freely for she had seen them stretched on the frame in the kitchen, and she recognized in them bits and pieces of dresses she had worn and loved and long outgrown.

"I remember when you were doing the Star of Bethlehem," Freely said as she unfolded one quilt after another. "Oh, Grandma," she exclaimed, "this must be your Dove in the Window that you wrote me about! And you've put into it pieces from my newest dresses."

Susannah's pleasure as Freely looked at the different quilts made her face radiant.

At the bottom of the chest Freely discovered the Friendship quilt. She stood up with it in her arms, shaking it from its folds so she might renew acquaintance with it all over again. It was the first quilt Susannah had done and she had made it during the early years of her life in Simonton when quilting bees held in the various farmhouses were one of the pastimes of the winter evenings. This quilt consisted of a series of blocks, each one made by a different person who wrote her name and then outlined the writing in colored thread. After the blocks had been assembled it had been quilted and enclosed in a border reminiscent of the life of the hill—a little church, a house, animals, trees, flowers. It had been the joy of Freely's life as a child to have the quilt put over her bed and to be able to read up and down and across it the names of the friends who had been the life of the hill when Susannah was a young wife.

"Is it for me?" Freely queried, stroking the quilt with careful fingers.

"They are all for you, Freely, to use and to enjoy."

It had given Susannah pleasure to work on the quilts when her friends were working on them too, and the kitchens of the old houses had been full of cheerful companionship; but as the years had gone on and life had left the hill, it had given her even deeper pleasure. There had been many hours alone, sometimes whole days alone, when she and Freely were the last people left on the hill. But the moving in and out of her needle had been company for her thoughts, and even though Freely had been at school and Dan Satturlee had not come by, she had not been alone. She had been with the boys in the West, or she had lingered in the past with Benedict. So she had sewn memories into the quilts, and hopes. Susannah could almost tell the places where her needle had gone more slowly as prayer had filled her with peace.

During the past weeks, and while she had been working on her Dove in the Window, she had prayed that the child who had been Benedict's companion and who had received the distillation of his life's long thinking might find a straight way in which to walk. Benedict had had so much to give, but a channel was always needed and his own children had not provided it. How it had happened no one could say, but Freely had become the channel through which the richness of his nature could flow. She was the evidence of his goodness and something of him had fused in her.

"Lead her in a plain path, O Lord, because of the enemies," Susannah had said in her heart as she bent over the quilt. There was always so much that could divert, absorb, distort. She longed for Freely to go forward, down the hill and into her life bearing her gift of quiet, and Susannah prayed that those toward whom Freely would be drawn would recognize the value of her gift.

She had been both happy and disturbed when Philip Haven had entered Freely's life; happy because in his own self he seemed to share much with Freely, and disturbed because all that had made his life was disparate from all that had gone into the making of Freely's. Whatever happened, Susannah was grateful that Philip had come into their lives. Freely had dwelt close to the hill, loving it so that she wanted never to leave it; but Philip's coming had shown her that the hill could not be her boundary. Philip might be the one to link Freely to the world, and in giving her love to him Freely would learn to share herself with others. It was then that the needle had gone slowly, Susannah remembered, as she saw her thoughts visible almost as stitches on the quilt.

"What are you thinking of, Grandma?" Freely asked as she commenced folding the quilts up again.

"More than I could put into words," Susannah said, "but not more than I can put into stitches."

Freely laughed. "You'll have to start making another quilt."

"I dare say I will," Susannah replied.

They carried the piles of linen and the several quilts downstairs, placing them in the spare room where Freely's collection was growing.

So the days went on, with fingers busy and talk flowing between two who had been finding it increasingly easy to share their thoughts, and gradually Freely readied herself for the new life. She went down the hill often to see how the work was going on, but when they started blasting the rocks to clear a space for the foundation of the house she remained on the hilltop. She did not like to hear the sudden shattering of quiet as a stick of dynamite split the rocks; she did not like to see the straining of the horses as they dragged the rocks away. She was glad that the birds had begun to migrate south for there were fewer ones to be alarmed by the noise. Listening to it up on the hill, something would thump within Freely, and she would be relieved by the stillness that followed. Though a rainy day delayed the work, she was secretly glad for one as no sound of blasting would rip through the gray serenity of the hill.

One afternoon, Freely and Susannah sat in the kitchen sewing. There had been several deep booms of the dynamite, followed by silence, but after one explosion the silence that followed lingered and deepened. Freely was not aware of it at first. After a time, when no more deep booms punctuated either their work or their conversation, Susannah looked up from her sewing.

"Seems they must be finished with the blasting," she said crisply.

"They couldn't be," Freely replied, shaking her head. "When I was there this morning Tom said that he thought they would not be finished for another two days. They're such big rocks, Grandma, and they're like trees with roots going far down into the earth." She smiled. "Grandpa would have liked our house foundation. It's going to be built upon a rock."

They went on with their work. Until the kitchen clock struck five, neither of them spoke, so absorbed were they in what they were doing. When the fifth stroke echoed into silence, Freely folded her sewing and laid it on the table.

"I'm going down to see what they're doing."

"Yes, Freely, go along, and I'll start getting the supper. Even sitting still can make us hungry."

Freely went out of the house and started down the hill. It was a soft late summer day, but there was a definite feeling of autumn in the air. She looked skyward. A haze had come over the sun. It might mean rain, she thought to herself; then she snapped off a stalk of roadside grass and bit it between her teeth. There was a stillness in the air, a waiting, an expectancy. No birds were singing. It may mean rain, she thought again, and it may just be the time between as one season waits on another.

She was surprised not to hear men's voices as she approached the clearing. Slason had moved his little hut on the scoot and set it up near the road. He liked to live on a job so he could take care of the horses and keep an eye on the work. Freely quickened her steps. Reaching the opening in the wall by the white birch, she called out.

"Philip!"

The echo of her own voice came back from the woodland.

"Tom! Tom Slason!" She called, but there was no answering voice.

She went quickly across the rough ground to the place where the foundation was being dug. For a moment, surprise and delight at the work that had been accomplished overcame her concern. The opening in the ground was yawning widely and granite rocks, instead of lying scattered, were being lined up into walls. The boulder she had loved to sit on had been shattered by the dynamite into jagged pieces and they were lying where they had fallen. No attempt had been made yet to drag them toward the walls.

Her pleasure at the progress of the work suddenly faded when she caught sight of Philip's coat hanging from a bush where he must have left it that morning when he arrived at the clearing. Picks and shovels were lying where they had been thrown down. The horses were not tethered in their accustomed place. Freely ran back to Slason's hut. The faithful coffeepot stood on the small stove, but the stove was cold. Tom must have been gone a long time for his stove to get as cold as that, Freely thought. A thumping sounded from the bunk and Freely saw Bess curled up on the grubby blanket, her tail going slowly.

"Oh Bess, where are they all? What has happened? What took them away?" Freely asked the dog, fondling the long ears and rubbing the smooth head.

Bess looked up at Freely with woeful hound-dog eyes and her tail went on thumping against the blanket.

If Tom were near, Freely thought, Bess would jump down and race from one place to another. Tom must be a long way away for Bess to be consoling herself with sleep.

Vaguely wondering what had called them from their work so precipitately, Freely walked back across the ground to the foundation. She picked up an ax and sunk it for safety into a stump; she picked up a shovel and leaned it against a rock. They had all gone in a great hurry. Why? Where? Quickly she turned and sniffed the air, but her keen nostrils took in no smell of wood smoke and she had heard no tolling of the bell in the Millville church that was the alarm for fire. A feeling of dread came over her, making her stand still. It was here that something had happened, she told herself. Perhaps one of the men had got hurt and they had taken him in to the doctor.

She sighed. She felt better now that she had found a reason for the abandonment of the place. She went over to the bush and picked up Philip's coat. He would be coming up to Simonton in the evening to tell her what had happened. She would have his coat for him there and, if it were late, it would not be damp as it would get if it remained here. She went on her way up the hill, telling Susannah as she sat down to supper why they had been so aware of the silence in the clearing.

"They all left the place for some reason or other," Freely said, "but we'll know soon. Philip will come up to tell us as soon as he can be spared."

"When I first came to the hill," Susannah remarked, "they were still clearing the fields with oxen. I suppose dynamite can be an unruly thing in the hands of a man; but I've known oxen not to do what they're always wanted to do."

They had finished their evening meal and Susannah was lighting the lamp, for the nights were beginning to close in early, when Freely saw the figure of a man coming over the hill and toward the house. He was walking quickly, but he seemed to slow up perceptibly as he approached Simonton. Freely wondered if he was tired from his walk up the hill. The thought crossed her mind that he was deliberately walking slowly because he did not want to reach the house. Then she recognized him as Tom Slason.

"It's Philip's foreman, Grandma. He must have come back with the horses."

Freely ran to the door. "Tom," she called, "what happened down in the clearing? I went there this afternoon and everyone had gone away."

Tom put his hand up to his head and pulled off his shabby hat. "I've a piece of news for you, miss," he began.

"Come in, please do," Freely urged. As the woodsman followed her into the kitchen, she said, "Grandma, here is Tom Slason with some news for us. Tom, do sit down."

He shook his head. "Thank you, miss. It won't take me long to say what I've to say and I've got to get back to my team." He paused.

Susannah came forward to stand beside Freely. She put her hand out to Tom in some instinctive gesture of entreaty, then she rested it on Freely's arm.

"I'm sorry, miss, but Mr. Haven's been hurt awful bad—" Slason dropped his head.

The kitchen was without sound except for the ticking of the clock.

"Philip?" Freely's voice came from a distance. "Philip has been hurt?"

Slason nodded.

"But what happened?"

Freely was shaking her head. No, no, this wasn't true. It was someone else Slason was talking about. Philip was her love, soon to be her husband. They had their life all planned. A house was being built for them. She had been getting the linen in order. Susannah had made quilts for their beds. Why, there was his coat. She was keeping it for him. He was coming up this evening. Of course, it wasn't true. That was what her heart said, but in her mind she could feel the cold words of question slowly forming. They would be shaped by her lips without volition from her. They would hang in the air as if they had no part with her. Tom Slason would hear them and in time he would answer; but whatever he said it would have nothing to do with her.

"What happened, Tom?"

Tom took a step nearer her. "We didn't want him to do it, miss, but he was wanting to get that biggest boulder leveled off. We lit the fuse but it didn't fire when it should and Mr. Haven went back to relight it—" Tom paused.

"Go on."

"We told him not to, miss, but he was kind of impatient-like. He wanted to get it done and—" Tom looked helplessly at Susannah, but Susannah had closed her eyes.

"And what, Tom?" Freely asked.

"Before he got to the boulder the fuse went off and he couldn't get clear in time. A shower of rocks went up in the air and when they came down—" Tom gulped.

"What happened?"

"A good-sized piece of rock came down on him. We got it off him, miss, and put him on the scoot and got him down to Dr. Vernon—"

"Yes?"

"He's there, miss. Doctor didn't dare move him any more."

"He's alive?"

"Yes, miss. He was when I left, but the doctor thought his back was broke."

Susannah stepped forward to be closer to Freely, but Freely turned to her, eyes wide with relief. "Anything broken can be mended," she sighed.

Susannah said nothing.

Freely looked at her earnestly. "Can't it, Grandma?" she asked.

Tom Slason turned and walked out of the room. They heard him shut the door behind him.

"Sit down, Freely darling," Susannah said. "Sit down."

Freely let herself be led to a chair. Like a plant bending under a strong hand, she yielded to the light pressure of Susannah's arm and sat down.

"But there must be something I can do for him," Freely said.

Susannah stood beside her, ready to comfort, ready to succor, but as yet there was no need. Freely was still so sure of Philip; she had not grasped what the others had.

Susannah looked away. "Let it fall gently, Lord, this blow," she breathed inwardly. One could accept anything if it came by degrees. It was only the first sudden impact that left one helpless.

"His coat," Freely said hoarsely, pointing to the peg on the wall where she had hung it when she came into the kitchen. "He may be cold without it. I must take it to him."

"Wait, dear heart," Susannah said softly. "I'll harness Ginger and we'll go down to Dr. Vernon's together. There may be something we can both do."

Susannah was crossing the kitchen when a knock sounded at the door.

Freely leapt from her chair. "It may be Philip," she cried, running past Susannah to be first at the door.

She opened it to Hawkins, standing with his hat in his hand, and beyond him in the darkness she could see the box-like outline of the brougham with its oil-side lamps making squares of light in the night.

"Miss Freely?"

"Come in, Hawkins."

He stepped over the door sill, acknowledging Susannah's presence with a grave inclination of his head. "Pardon me, ma'am, for calling so late but Mr. Philip's been hurt and Mrs. Haven sent me for Miss Freely to come and sit by him."

A joyous sound escaped Freely and she turned to Susannah. "Do you hear, Grandma, Mrs. Haven has sent for me! It's the open door Benedict said there would always be!" She turned and ran from the room, calling back over her shoulder, "I'll be ready in a minute, Hawkins. I must just get a coat and Philip will want his too."

She could not take the time to run upstairs so she threw Benedict's old cloak that hung on a peg in the kitchen around her shoulders and she took Philip's coat over her arm; then she went to the mirror to tidy her hair.

Susannah leaned toward Hawkins. "Can Mr. Philip recover?" she asked in a low voice.

Hawkins nodded. "Doctor Vernon says he has a fighting man's chance if he can be very quiet for the next few hours."

"Is he in pain?"

"Yes, I'm told so, ma'am, and he's been asking for Miss Freely."

Susannah smiled briefly. "And Mrs. Haven?"

"She told me to come for the young lady. She's there at the doctor's, too, but she's so upset and nervous that she doesn't dare go near Mr. Philip. She says Miss Freely can help them all."

Susannah smiled slowly this time, proudly.

Freely came out of the kitchen. She went up to Susannah and kissed her. "I'll be back in the morning, Grandma."

Susannah looked into her eyes that were clear and calm. "Freely," she said gently, "Philip's life may depend on the quiet you can bring to him tonight, and to them all."

Freely nodded.

Hawkins turned and went out to the brougham. Freely followed him. After the door had been shut, Freely looked out of the window, her face framed by the darkness all around her, a glow cast on one cheek by the small side lamp. She held up her hands and waved. Hawkins spoke to the horses and the brougham wheeled off into the warm September night.

Susannah stood in the doorway while the rumble of wheels and the striking of hoofs died away in the distance. So, only quiet could save Philip, she thought, and that was all Freely had to give him. The girl had gone forward into the night bearing in her hands her gift. Susannah went back to the kitchen. It was all good, as Benedict had always said. Life was good. She sat down in her rocker by the stove. It would not be the first night she had waited for Freely to come home.

27.

>>>>>>>>>>>>>>>>>>>>><<<<<<<<<<<<<<<<<<<<<

HAWKINS drove as fast as he could, but going
down hill and in the dark he had to rein the horses in to a walk
a good deal of the time. Freely sat upright on the seat. She
had locked her hands tightly together, for anxiety had begun
to creep around the edges of her mind. So sure was she of
Philip that, when Tom Slason called, she had not been able
to grasp the fact that anything serious had happened; so
pleased had she been that it was Mrs. Haven who had sent for
her, when Hawkins called, that all else had been ruled out of
her mind.

Now, in the darkness of the carriage as it swayed and
bumped over the road, she found herself putting the two together. Slason had been reticent because of the seriousness of
the injury. Mrs. Haven had sent for her because the need
was urgent, and the need was for Philip who was no less dear
to her as an only son than he was to Freely as a some-time husband. When the realization—coupled with Susannah's last
words "his life may depend on the quiet you can bring to him
tonight"—came over her, she began to reach back in her mind
to what Tom Slason had said. A wave of anguish rose before
her. No, no, she wanted to cry aloud against the fate that had
done this thing.

As she let the anguish overwhelm her, it brought its own
accompaniment of fear. Something icy and chill, like a search-

ing wind on a winter's night, crept over her, stealing every
vestige of warmth her being possessed. It was then she brought
her hands together, clenching them, locking them tightly,
trying to still the trembling that had seized her.

Philip's life? She found the question aching through her
mind, whistling, howling, and whining like wind through an
empty barn. How safe would it be in hands that were trembling as hers were then? Philip's life? The words sounded
lonely and incomplete. Freely's life one might as well say,
since love had united them.

She thought of her grandfather. There must have been
times when he had driven through the dark to sit beside a
friend in an hour of great need. But Grandpa would not
have gone in fear. Oh, no. The stout denial gave Freely a small
degree of strength. Grandpa had no use for fear. He had said
—Freely reached back in her mind for his words—he had said
that to dwell in fear was to dwell in a land where nothing
could be done, and that there was no such place for always
something could be done, no matter how insignificant or ir-
relevant. To fear was to doubt God, Grandpa had said, and
that doubt was the root of all the dismay and sorrow in the
world. Fear made thought turn inward upon oneself, and
what was needed was that thought turn outward to the work
that was waiting for one's hands.

There was work waiting for her to do.

Mrs. Haven had sent for her.

What was the work she was to do? They would tell her
when she got there. No. Susannah had already told her. It
was to help Philip to be quiet for a few hours. That would not
be difficult. They were at peace in each other's presence for
each had the heart's desire. Peace and quiet were indivisible.

Freely unlocked her hands and reached them out into the
darkness. There was nothing to lay hold on but the strength

that Grandpa had said was always near. Then she leaned against the padded back of the brougham and sighed. She felt at peace with herself and ready for whatever was ahead.

They were off the hill now and trotting down the main street of the town. Freely was aware of a curious, muffled sound to the roll of the wheels, the clop of the hoofs. Hawkins reined the horses to a stop in front of Dr. Vernon's. He got down and opened the door for Freely. When she put her foot on the pavement she looked up in surprise at the coachman.

"It's all straw—everywhere!" she exclaimed.

"Yes, Miss Freely," Hawkins said huskily. "That's so it will be quiet for Mr. Philip."

"Oh. . . ." her voice trailed oddly away. "Thank you, Hawkins, for fetching me so quickly." She turned and ran up the walk, up the steps, making no more sound than a breeze in light movement through a garden.

A nurse opened the door, nodded her head in brief but welcome recognition. In a low voice she asked Freely to follow her into the doctor's study. "Dr. Vernon will be here immediately," she said. "He wants to talk with you before you see either Mrs. Haven or her son."

Freely stood by the window. Dr. Vernon entered, closing the door behind him. She held out her hands to him for she had known him well through the years. His tall spare frame, massive white-crowned head, and deepset eyes gave out as much confidence as his words. He kissed her as he would a child, and she looked to him then little different from the child whom he had seen so often with her grandfather.

"Freely, my dear," he began, speaking without haste while making every word count, "something very serious happened to Philip Haven this afternoon. His back may be broken. It may not be. I have sent for a colleague of mine from Boston who knows more than I do and who will be able to determine the extent of the injury. Until he arrives, Philip must be kept absolutely quiet."

"I understand," Freely said.

"If it is a break, there is one chance in a thousand that the bones will go back into place of their own accord and the break will mend, but only if he is very still and completely relaxed. I cannot do for him what nature can." Dr. Vernon smiled at Freely. "You see, I am a doctor so I use the word nature. You are a parson's granddaughter; you may well use the word God."

Freely looked closely at Dr. Vernon. She said nothing, but the clarity in her eyes revealed her comprehension.

"He has been in great pain, but I believe the pain is lessening," Dr. Vernon continued. "I have given him all the morphine possible but there is a point beyond which I cannot go as the strain may be too great on his heart. It is when he wakes that I shall need you. Then, if he should become restless, want to shift his position, fretful—" the doctor shrugged his shoulders— "I cannot say."

Freely laid her hand on the doctor's arm. "I think he will be quiet," she said. "May I go to him now?"

"Presently. It is his mother who needs you now. He has been asking for her from time to time but she is in no state to see him."

"Has he asked for me?"

"Oh, indeed!" the doctor exclaimed, his eyes twinkling as he looked at her. "When the men first brought him he kept saying 'Where's Freely? Where's Freely?' And when I told him you were coming he relaxed as if he had been given an opiate."

"May I see Mrs. Haven?" Freely asked.

"Come with me."

They went together out of the study and across the hall into a sitting room. The doctor opened the door gently but he did not follow Freely into the room.

Freely stood for a moment on the threshold, for the woman sitting in a chair at the opposite end of the room was not the Mrs. Haven she had ever known. Then, uttering the small cry of joy with which she so often flew across the kitchen to greet Susannah, she ran across the room. She knelt on the floor in front of Mrs. Haven and threw her arms around her, crying out her delight at seeing her again. She reached up and put her arms around Mrs. Haven's neck, cupping the tear-streaked face in her strong young hands and kissing her. She looked deep into her eyes as she had looked into her grandfather's and Susannah's when there could be no words, only the bridge of thoughts. She took Mrs. Haven's shaking hands in hers, holding them close to her heart to warm them. She stroked the hands and held them against her cheeks; then she put them to her lips, covering them with kisses.

Mrs. Haven resisted, but it was no use. She drew her head up in the familiar, haughty gesture Freely had seen so often, but Freely's hands were quick and brought it down to her level. Mrs. Haven tried to free her hands, but the girl's clasp was strong. It was like a winter snowbank trying to resist a day of spring sunshine. The snowbank held its ground for a while, but bit by bit it relented until finally where snow had been was only the memory of winter and wet brown earth responding to the sun. Perceptibly Mrs. Haven's tension released under Freely's affection and the armor that had held her rigid for many years began to fall away. The fear that had immured her in grief and taken itself out in nervousness decreased as she shared it with the girl.

"Say that he isn't going to die, say it," she spoke hoarsely. "I may believe it from you."

Freely shook her head. "He isn't going to die," she said, and her words carried an authority that compelled Mrs. Haven to heed them.

They sat together, sometimes talking, sometimes in silence, but Freely kept her hands linked with Mrs. Haven's. She seemed able to sense the recurring of Mrs. Haven's fear, for when the older woman's hands tightened Freely would chafe them together, or put them up to her face. Looking straight into Mrs. Haven's eyes she would tell her a story of something that had happened on the hill, a reminiscence of her grandfather, or an experience she had had with an animal. Not wanting to listen, Mrs. Haven had been obliged to listen. She had even smiled and once she had laughed. When she was at ease again, Freely would ask her to tell a story about Philip when he was a little boy and Mrs. Haven would forget the urgency of the present with delight in the past.

Once Mrs. Haven let her hand rest for a long moment on Freely's sandy hair. "Such an odd name," she said. "Freely."

Freely smiled. It was the first time she had ever heard her own name come from Mrs. Haven's lips. "I always thought it was a name in the Bible," she explained, "and that was long after I could read and should have known better." She told her about the line, 'Freely, ye have received, Freely, give.' "I used to think that was God speaking to me."

"But you still do think it, don't you?"

"Oh, yes."

Mrs. Haven sighed. "That's good. Don't ever forget. Don't let anything make you forget. One goes such a far way when one forgets. It takes so long to come back."

"Are you tired?" Freely asked, anxiously studying the lined face.

"I think I am," Mrs. Haven sighed again. "It's as if I'd shed a weight." She smiled. "I don't seem to be worried about Philip any more."

There was a couch at one side of the room and Freely led Mrs. Haven to it, adjusting the pillows so she could lie down comfortably. She covered her with the cape that she had thrown over her shoulders before she left Simonton, the cape that Benedict had worn so often on his way between the house and the church.

Freely sat on the floor beside the couch, humming softly. "If you wake up and find I'm not here, you'll know I'll be back," she whispered.

Mrs. Haven nodded. Sleep was stealing over her, heavy and luxurious. She didn't want Freely to leave but it was a comfort to know that she would return. She had not known how tired she was, but she was losing her weariness as she felt herself dropping into a trough of dreamless ease. The muscles of her face relaxed. She looked almost young again, Freely thought, and quite handsome. It was the same high brow that Philip had. As Florence Haven shed her weariness in slumber she seemed to be shedding something else as well, for the artificiality of her life that had kept her and Freely apart was going from her like an article of clothing for which she no longer had any use.

The door of the room opened quietly and Dr. Vernon beckoned to Freely. She got up and tiptoed from the room.

"He will be waking soon," the doctor said meaningfully.

Freely followed him up the stairs to a bedroom. There in a high old-fashioned bed Philip was lying. A nurse stood beside him, her hand on his pulse. She stepped back as Freely drew near the bed.

"I'll be outside the door," she whispered.

Dr. Vernon nodded. "We'll be ready to answer your slightest call, but the next few hours belong to you."

Freely's eyes opened wide. He had given her a trust. He was making it a challenge. Her grandfather had always said that the test of a man was in his response to the challenges life gave him. Freely watched the doctor and the nurse until they had left the room and the door had closed behind them. But she was not alone. There had never been a time in all her life when she had been alone. Ah yes, she remembered, there had been—on the night of the storm when she had feared so greatly.

She stood by the bed and took Philip's hand in hers. He looked little different than he had when she had seen him that morning, but he had passed through such a night as she had never known—a night of pain, of suffering. Her pressure on his hand tightened as his eyelids fluttered, closed, then opened. He looked at her. Gray eyes meeting the gaze of serene amber eyes strove for recognition. A pucker came across the high brow and the gray eyes closed again as the effort to concentrate brought a twinge of pain.

"It's Freely," she said quietly. "Philip's Freely."

He opened his eyes again and recognition came with his glance. A smile curved the lips that had tightened earlier against pain and had not until then been released. He sighed, almost seeming to sink back farther against the pillows as if he were letting go.

He repeated her words, "Philip's Freely."

He wanted to know where he was and she told him, speaking slowly and softly and as if it were the most natural thing in the world for him to be in Dr. Vernon's spare room. He wanted to know what had happened to him and she told him, but knowing only the little Tom Slason had told her, she could easily temper the accident. "It will be better soon," she said. She had comforted many an animal with that simple assurance. Under its promise she had seen them almost visibly relax their tensions.

"Tell Slason to—" then he winced.

"I can't tell him until the morning, Philip," she said. "Why do we bother to think about it until then?"

He sighed as if an urgency had gone from him. He asked about his mother and she told him of the time they had spent together in Dr. Vernon's sitting room.

"She must be very happy, Philip, or she wouldn't have gone to sleep so easily. Happy for you and for me."

Philip moved his hand in hers.

Freely went on, her voice murmuring, her words long and slow. "We're richer now than we ever could have been if we hadn't known each other," she said. "I have your mother and you have my grandmother because we have each other."

"I knew," he said, catching his breath, "Mother would love you—once she got a chance—to know you."

All through the night they talked, their voices low, their conversation rambling and inconsequential. It did not matter what they said, Freely knew, so long as they kept their link with each other, so long as she could see the shadow of pain lying over him in a twitching of his lips, a furrowing of his brow, and she could do whatever was possible to lessen it before it made Philip restless. He knew he was not to move, but unless Freely had been beside him he knew he could not have stood the limitations of such stillness.

She had drawn a chair up beside his bed and all night she sat with her hand holding his, ready to do his bidding and happy that he was willing to do hers. Slowly, pervasively, the presence that was Freely became a part of Philip. He felt strength in the pressure of her hand on his; refreshment when she placed her cool palm on his hot forehead; the tangible evidence of her love when she laid her lips on his. There was peace in her presence, and a wholeness of which he knew he had need.

When the first streaks of light filtered into the room he turned his head on the pillow and a look of repose came over his face. Freely leaned near him. His breathing was coming naturally, a tinge of color had crept into his cheeks. She put

303

her hand on his brow. It felt as cool as her own. He had gone to sleep with his hand in hers, but she would not withdraw her hand for it still might be his hold on life. She looked out the window as the grayness of early dawn shifted into the light of beginning day, and she thought of her father holding back that wall of water so his comrades might flee to safety. She thought of the church at Simonton, catching the first rays of the rising sun, reflecting them from white walls and turreted tower. And she thought of her grandfather.

It was seven o'clock when the nurse pushed the door open quietly and came to stand by the bed. Freely withdrew her hand and watched while the nurse put her fingers to Philip's pulse.

"Almost normal," she commented. "How long has he been asleep?"

"Since just before dawn," Freely said.

"Dr. Matthews has arrived. You won't be needed for a little while."

Freely followed the nurse to the door where they met the two doctors. Even from the doorway Dr. Vernon could tell something of Philip's condition, and the look on Freely's face told him more.

"You've done your work well, little Freelove, I wish I had you always for a helper. Go down now and join Mrs. Haven. My housekeeper will give you some breakfast. I'll come down with the report of Dr. Matthews' examination as soon as I can."

"May I wait here, outside the door, in case you need me?" Freely asked.

"Yes, of course," the doctor answered, "if you're not too tired."

Freely smiled a little wanly. "I'm not going to think about being tired for a long, long time."

Half an hour later the two doctors came out of the room.

Dr. Vernon was smiling. Dr. Matthews went up to Freely and shook her hand. "May I wish you happiness," he said, "a lifetime of happiness."

Freely looked into his face, her expression half of joy, half of surprise. "Tell me about Philip," she said.

"It was not a break," Dr. Matthews replied. "The injuries are internal and they are serious, but they are nothing that time, care, and quiet will not cure. He must not be moved for five or six days. After that he can be taken to his home and his recovery will proceed normally."

"Thank you," Freely said. She turned to Dr. Vernon. "How long before he will be up?"

The doctor smiled. "You've got a plan, you two?"

Freely nodded.

"When is it for?"

"The first Sunday in October in the Simonton church."

Dr. Vernon turned to his colleague. Dr. Matthews turned to Freely and said, "Could you make it the last Sunday in October?"

Freely moved her head vigorously. "Oh, yes! Some of the trees will still be golden and the house may be finished by then." The import of what had been said by the doctors came over her and she clapped her hands to her mouth as if her joy might escape in too much sound for this household of quiet. "Does Philip know?" she asked.

"Yes, but we left him sleeping and it would be as well if he were not disturbed for a few hours."

"Does his mother know?"

Dr. Vernon shook his head. "We left it for you to tell her."

Freely turned quickly away from the doctors and went running down the carpeted stairs. She burst into the sitting room where Mrs. Haven was still lying on the couch.

At sight of the girl, Mrs. Haven sat up. She looked refreshed though somewhat disheveled, but she felt so thoroughly rested that she did not then care how she looked. The joy in Freely's face said more than any words. Freely clung to the door for a moment; then she let it shut behind her and with a small exultant cry she could not suppress she ran across the room.

"Your Philip will be all right soon," she said, as she put her arms around Mrs. Haven.

The older woman shook her head while a smile played over her face. "Ah," she replied slowly, "but he's your Philip now."